THE SICILIAN SORCERESS

MARY KNIGHT

This book is dedicated to my mom, who brings a constant stream of joy and love to the world. Thank you for nudging me on, having confidence in me, and supporting me throughout the book-writing process. Your incredible love kept my dream alive. I love you always across the universe.

TABLE OF CONTENTS

"Sicilians build things like they will live forever
and eat like they will die tomorrow."
—Plato

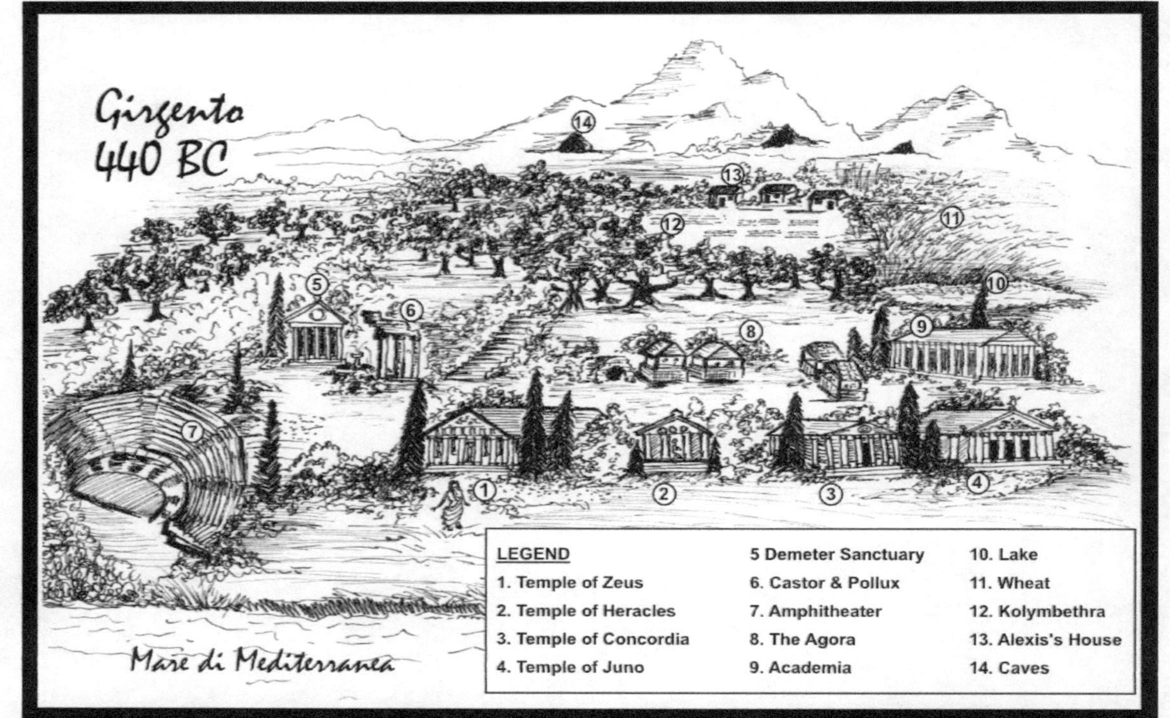

Girgento
440 BC
Mare di Mediterranea
LEGEND
1. Temple of Zeus
2. Temple of Heracles
3. Temple of Concordia
4. Temple of Juno
5 Demeter Sanctuary
6. Castor & Pollux
7. Amphitheater
8. The Agora
9. Academia
10. Lake
11. Wheat
12. Kolymbethra
13. Alexis's House
14. Caves

Isla di Sicilia
PALERMO
MESSANA
MARSALA
CALTAGICONE
MOUNT ETNA
SIRACUSA
GIRGENTO
GELA
Mare di Mediterranea
MARSALA
PALERMO
Utica
GIRGENTO
309 km
CARTHAGE

PART ONE

1

THE THEFT

July 2017

"Are you out of your mind, Stephen?" I blurted out before I had time to think.

"You," he practically growled while thrusting a pointed finger into my chest, "are the one who had the most to gain by stealing her. We all know of your affinity for Demeter. I contacted your former employer at the museum in Albany and they told me there was a question about a certain artifact from the Iroquois that came into your possession. Can you explain yourself?"

"There is nothing to explain! The chief gave me a small woven basket in recognition of my efforts to showcase the Iroquois's contribution to Upstate New York. How dare you investigate me like this!"

"Where is the paperwork to prove this? I can only assume you are pulling the same scheme," Stephen fired back. "I knew I should never have trusted these treasures with you."

The theft in point: an ancient statuette of the goddess Demeter, her head to be specific, circa 450 BC. She was part of a larger exhibit on loan from Sicily to tell the story of her ancient civilizations. Yes, I had unpacked it when it arrived in our museum and accounted for its presence on the inventory list. But steal it? Really! This accusation felt like an earthquake shaking my thin body—the kind that never seems to stop. My boss, Stephen, an uptight control freak, had a tendency to panic but at this moment was taking it too far. My job as a curator of ancient artifacts came with a vow to uphold the values of the museum and I took it seriously.

I clenched my teeth and drew in a breath to settle myself as I glanced around his sterile office. The battered old furniture looked like mismatched pieces from an architectural salvage and mirrored the dove-gray walls painted some twenty years past. A depressing place to work for a miserable, self-absorbed man.

The volcano in Stephen had erupted and now it was my turn to defend myself. If only I could control the beads of perspiration pooling on the armpits of my yellow linen dress that would now require dry cleaning. How could I convince him of my innocence and keep my cool?

"Maybe she just got misplaced," I offered. Typical hysterical Stephen.

"We have looked everywhere. She is not in her assigned space in storage. In fact, her box is empty," said Stephen, leaning forward in his chair, his dark beady eyes glaring at me beneath his round wire-rim glasses. His greasy, black, and probably dyed hair emphasized his nerdy look.

I was bewildered. Who would steal her, even have access to her? I wondered.

Contrary to the inner voice for calm, I accelerated the argument. "Your mismanagement is why Demeter is missing."

I usually shied away from conflict, preferring to take a

back seat, or better yet, walk away. But sometimes the words shot out, like darts, and this was one of them.

"How dare you . . ." he began, but I interrupted him before he could finish.

"How dare you! Bullying and falsely accusing me. I have never been treated so unfairly!" I yelled as I jumped up from my chair, my boot heel stomping the floor. It had all happened so fast. Did I really mean to confront my superior like this? My shoulders slouched as I hung my head, my body language displaying my shrinking courage and feeling of defeat even in my innocence.

Stephen, his drawn pale face now a bright red, pushed back his chair, which scraped the floor with a squeal, and stood up to meet my icy gaze.

"Alexis, you're fired!" he said with a flick of his wrist.

I almost giggled at the big blue vein beginning to pulsate on his neck. Then reality set in.

I have always had a fondness for the Greek myth of Demeter and Persephone, a mother and daughter separated by the underworld god Hades, until a pomegranate brought them back together, if only for six months out of the year. A negotiation of sorts was reached whereby Persephone was allowed to be with her mother on earth in the growing season but ordered to return to the underground with Hades for the shorter days. I loved how the myth's metaphor gave reason for the dark days of fall and winter, with nature going dormant, and the lighter days of spring and summer, when new growth emerged. The statues of her revealed a kind face and a wheat stalk in hand, her symbol of the harvest. Thinking about Demeter gave me pause to recall my own mother and to wish we could be reunited like the myth. I missed her. Demeter's lure had led me to Sicily and Greece as a pilgrimage of sorts to view statues of her, evidence of her presence in the ancient past. Nature, being the center of her existence, mirrored my own feelings as well, and I felt a kinship with her. She held qualities I strived for but often fell short on: confidence, strength, and persistence. No wonder Stephen suspected me.

"Alexis, did you hear me?" Stephen snapped me out of my stupor. He sat down, shaking his head, almost with regret for his actions.

"Stephen, I loved her but would never take her away from where she is meant to be," I quietly stated, now fighting for my job.

"The logbook says you were the last person in the room before she went missing," Stephen countered, his voice tense and abrupt.

"But anyone could have accessed the room without signing the logbook," I said, nervously pushing my long mahogany curls behind my ears.

"There are only six people authorized to enter the storage rooms and you are one of them." He just sat there, his jaw clenched and hostile eyes fixed on mine, almost hoping I'd confess. I didn't.

"One of the employees said they saw you leaving out the back door and you were tucking something into your bag."

It's true. I brought an Italian leather satchel to work every day. It carried my laptop, notebook, lunch, water, perhaps a book from home, and snacks. There's no way a life-size head of Demeter could fit into this bag.

"Who saw me? And when was this?" I queried.

"We wish them to remain anonymous. It was last Friday," he said, using a finger to push his glasses back onto the bridge of his tiny nose.

Friday. Now I remembered. I had borrowed a book from the research library on the care and handling of artifacts older than a thousand years. Even with all my advanced curator skills, I wanted to take extra good care of this exhibit.

"I borrowed a book from the library," I said. "You can look at the checkout card and date to verify." When anxiety set in, I had a habit of unconsciously rubbing the birthmark on my left arm and this was no exception.

"Hmm . . . Because you are our only suspect, and the serious nature of Demeter's disappearance, we've ordered a warrant to search your home," he said, the words spilling out of his mouth. It was more of a statement than an asking.

The icy announcement sent a chill throughout my body as my jaw dropped, and I could no longer hold back my tears. I couldn't help it. As I sobbed, Stephen handed me a box of tissues, not to console me but to shut me up.

"I'd like you to stay here, at the museum, while the police search your home," Stephen sneered.

I was hyperventilating now. This stunning turn of events from my happy morning to this. Where was my bravery, my fight? I was just sitting there, melting, agreeing to his demands.

"When will they be done?" I asked weakly. "I have nothing to hide, Stephen." Our trust had been broken. What did it matter anyway? I had been fired for something I didn't do.

"I'd like to call an attorney," I said. I didn't even have an attorney. "I'm going to the break room for privacy," I stated to Stephen as I left his office, wanting to slam the door behind me.

Maybe the guy who settled my parents' estate in New

York could refer me to someone here. With a sense of urgency, I picked up the phone.

My mind shifted to the past events leading up to the missing Demeter. A friend's invitation to visit Sicily two years earlier opened a door to the past that stirred my curiosity. I never realized the power that the remnants of monstrous Greek temples, their people and possessions could have over me. Each region laid claim to their antiquities and displayed them a variety of ways. In the town of Erice, ancient amphorae clustered in random and broken pieces along deserted alleyways. On one small island off the town of Trapani, called Mozia, small house-like structures, intending to be museums, showcased pottery and sculpture from the Carthaginians dating back to 600 BC. It amazed me that artifacts were in the open, left to a trusting public to admire. The treasure trove of small villages in ruins, scattered about the island and harboring relics from as far back as the Phoenicians, inspired me to inquire about bringing these mostly intact artifacts, on loan, to our reputable art museum. Back when he tolerated me, I had been successful in convincing Stephen of my idea. It took two years to accumulate the items and prepare them for their journey to the San Francisco Museum of Art.

Due to all my hard work and research, the exhibit items were now arriving week by week, and even though my boss, Stephen, was technically in charge, this was my baby. If everything went according to plan, our exhibit would be a real-life experience of what it was like to live in ancient Sicily, in the emerging city of Agrigento, circa 440 BC. Scott, our resident expert crafter of exhibits, would build mock temples and each guest given 3-D goggles to wear for a lifelike experience: holograms of oracles; the agora, or market and meeting place; recited lectures by Empedocles, the philosopher; and a visit to the gardens, Kolymbethra, where food was grown for the society. Another display would tell the story of the importance wheat played to Agrigento as a valuable trading tool and means of survival. Of course, ancient vessels, carvings of gods and goddesses, tools, and other remnants of an active trading culture would fill display cases. Our creative technology geeks had been working day and night to bring Agrigento to life and create the visuals.

The head statue of Demeter was on the list to be in this week's shipment, and the thought of seeing her in real life, even if she was a mythical goddess, made me giddy. A few rooms in the basement were reserved for the storage of these ancient works of art. Dark and temperature-controlled, the rooms often held items that never made it to the upper levels for public view. This made for a crowded workspace and allowed only two people at a time access to the artifacts.

That week, I think it was a Wednesday, my fellow curator, Frances, and I slipped on our gloves and began the task of unpacking the wooden crates, each one numbered for reference. I glanced at the inventory sheet and noted that crate three and box number four thirty-three contained the coveted head of Demeter.

"Here's the crate," Frances said, helping me on my quest.

"Hand me your crowbar, please," I requested.

After lifting off the top and sides of the crates, we identified crate number three and began to sift through the shredded paper, lifting out the artifacts box by box and placing them on a long wooden table. We would be working late, and the cool room prompted me to grab a sweater.

"Here she is!" I cried.

The box was larger than I'd expected—a three-by-five.

"Such a big box for a head?" Frances questioned.

"You take one end, and I'll take the other," I said as we moved her to our workspace.

Very gently, we undid the packing tape and folded over the cardboard ends. Demeter's well-padded head lay invisible, surrounded by fine wood excelsior. We carefully peeled the strands away until we came to the foam, the preferred protective agent for fragile items. With both hands, we lifted the foam away to finally reveal the object I'd desired—the head of Demeter. My body trembled with excitement and Frances, taking note, picked her up and aimed her toward me.

"Is this your goddess?" Frances asked.

"Give me a moment," I whispered.

I steadied myself and drew in a deep breath. She could have been one of a number of goddesses, but this particular statue came from Sicily around 450 BC and was identified on the paperwork as Demeter, the goddess of agriculture. Frances gently offered her to me. My heart raced as I tenderly cradled her head. Carved from terracotta and speckled from age, her spiraled curls wrapped around a delicate face that featured a slender nose. She had retained her glory for being over two thousand, five hundred years old. My fingers couldn't help outlining her narrow lips and hollow eyes as a sense of destiny washed over me. I wanted to hug her, tell her how much I admired her strength and purpose. I finally set her down on the workbench and studied her ethereal gaze, which gave her a certain sense of power and allure. No wonder she was my role model.

I scrolled through my cell phone contact list looking for someone to confide in and help me prove my innocence. No one from the museum, that was for sure. Someone was a betrayer, the real thief. I quickly returned to the present. This could wait. I needed a lawyer and now. My cousin, Rose, appeared on my screen. Perfect. She was smart and savvy and would get me through this. I quickly hit the call button, only to be sent to her voicemail.

"Rose," I said with urgency in my voice, "call me ASAP. Matter of life and death." I knew this would get to her.

Exactly two minutes later, my phone rang with Rose's voice on the other end.

"What's up, sis?" We always called each other "sis" because of our tight friendship, even though we were cousins.

"Rose, they are accusing me of stealing Demeter!" I blurted out.

"Who is accusing you and who is Demeter?" Rose obviously did not share my love of ancient history and I'm sure had no idea about Greek goddesses.

"It's a museum piece about to go on display. It went missing and they think I stole it. I didn't. Would never."

I was crying now, almost relieved as if I'd been in a confessional. "Can you help me? I need an attorney," I pleaded.

"I have an old college buddy in NorCal. I'll give him a ring and hook you up."

It was that fast. I had gone to the right person. Rose had all the connections and was quick on her feet. Nothing got past her.

"Really?" I said with relief.

"Anything for you, sis. Sit tight and I'll call him right now and get back to you." We hung up and I slouched in my chair, letting out a sigh of relief.

This would be over soon. I'd be cleared and that would be that.

The phone rang with an unidentified number. I quickly answered it and a deep voice said, "Alexis?"

"Yes," I answered.

"This is Burt Carmichael. I'm an old friend of Rose's. Anything for Rose. Can you describe what happened, in detail, please? Can I record your statements?"

"Of course," I said, and recalled my conversation with Stephen. When I finished, Burt asked me for the spelling of Stephen's first and last name, the museum's address, and my pertinent information as well.

"Call me when the search is over and let me know what they didn't find," Burt said with a sarcastic tone

Funny. I hung up, confident I'd made the right move calling Rose. I would send her a bouquet of flowers for her above-and-beyond help. The waiting was torture. I had been there two hours, scrolling my Facebook feed, browsing Instagram, anything to divert my attention from real life. At three o'clock, approximately three hours after our confrontation, Stephen strode into the room, his body stiff and his face stern.

"The police found nothing," he said, almost disappointed by this fact.

"Of course," I said, "because I didn't take her."

In an effort to take back his stance on firing me, because I was, after all, innocent before proven guilty, Stephen took a deep breath and said, "Alexis, you will remain on leave for a week while we do more investigating on this end and you can, perhaps, rethink your moves."

Rethink? What was there to rethink? My I-will-not-be-bullied self suddenly turned nonconfrontational. "Okay," was all I said. I gathered up my things and walked out the back door, angry and frustrated. Once in my car, the song "California" was playing. Ahh. Joni Mitchell—soothe my nerves. This was going to be a bizarre week.

A knot formed in my stomach as I arrived back to my Craftsman-style home in Oakland. How many of my neighbors had seen the police drive up and enter my house? It didn't really matter. Life in California was great, weather-wise, but there just wasn't the neighborly bond I'd experienced back home in Albany, New York. There, your neighbors were like your extended family, eager to lend a hand when needed. Here in Oakland, I barely knew who lived next door. People kept to themselves, so I did too.

My trembling hand grasped the door handle, turned it ever so gently, and pushed. I peered inside, half expecting someone to jump out at me, and immediately noticed where the police had searched. Drawers not closed, cupboards flung open, and boxes in my closets scattered across the floor. A glance at my watch showed not quite four o'clock, and I knew it would take me at least two hours to pull my house back together. I felt violated, like I had been in a fight and was licking my wounds. Why couldn't the police be more considerate of my property?

Instead of cleaning up, I chose to open the patio door and gather my thoughts outside in my quiet backyard. Signs of summer abounded. Scents of jasmine blossoms filled the air, vibrant red and pink geraniums surrounded me, and happy birds noshed away on the feeders. Plopping my feet up on the table in front of me, I closed my eyes in an attempt to quiet my mind. I didn't have anything to feel guilty about; I was innocent. But how to prove that would be another matter. Infuriated, I reviewed my options. My small inheritance would pay the mortgage on my cottage for the next several months, if the museum decided to fire me, but I would need an income soon. At age twenty-nine, I'd survived personal tragedy to make a new life and along with it, a name for myself. Just then, the phone rang.

"Hello?" I questioned, suspicious of almost anyone at this point.

"Alexis, it's Scott," a comfortable voice said on the other end of the line.

Scott. I breathed a sigh of relief. My coworker and inspiration.

2

FROM ALBANY
TO SAN FRANCISCO

I was never interested in ancient history when I was younger. Studying myths and Greek gods were for geeks. It all seemed so uncivilized. Constant warring. Power struggles. Too many names and places to remember or even care about. It was just too long ago.

In college, for my art history degree, I reluctantly took one required class on Greek culture and with the snap of a finger, reversed all my previous preconceived and unwarranted ideas. Suddenly the world of life and culture and foods of this period became my obsession. I took every class I could find: "Greek mythology"; "How ancient Greeks have influenced culture today"; "The Roman Empire built on Greek technology," et cetera. My world was opening up and I could not control my curiosity and appetite for more knowledge. After graduation, I booked a solo trip to Greece, Turkey, and Italy, specifically targeting temples, ruins, and archaeological museums. It was on this trip that I realized I wanted to pursue a career to curate these magnificent storytellers of time.

My first job was as an assistant to the curator of a

small museum in Albany, New York, my hometown. I grew up with a membership to the Albany Institute of History and Art, given to me every year by my grandmother. In high school, I became a volunteer docent, I knew the museum that well. I think learning about my community's history, art, and culture in such a personal way, with access to the behind-the-scenes activities, influenced me and accelerated my curiosity.

After an early graduation from New York University with a degree in art history, the museum granted me an internship and then offered me a job. The title of Assistant Curator of Local History gave me an opportunity to expand the exhibits, delving even deeper into the Hudson River valley's earliest inhabitants, the Iroquois Indians. I was always drawn to the Indian culture, and with my extensive research, curated enough artifacts from private collections and other museums to bring to life a visual exhibit of Iroquois and Mohican culture. Some of the tribe members that I interviewed for this project became friends. One even gave me a small woven basket given to him by his grandmother. He said I would take good care of it, and to pass it along to someone else one day as a gift to keep the Iroquois spirit alive. I told one of my associates about the basket and he was insistent I donate it to the museum, that it wasn't ethical for it to be in a private collection. My feelings were that if this is what my Iroquois friend wanted, then I would follow his wishes. To my dismay, he reported me to human resources. Nothing ever happened, but it was on my record as a discrepancy in ethics.

Because of the press our museum received on this exhibit and the many visitors who came from all over New York to view it, I was promoted to curator, despite my record. I summoned up the courage to query the Smithsonian about bringing one of their traveling exhibits through the Smithsonian Institution Traveling Exhibition Service, SITES, to our museum. A departure from "old" Albany. "Voices and Votes: Democracy in America" spoke to me on so many levels. Actually, it was my dad's influence, who so often rallied in support of the underdog, that inspired me to bring up this idea to our board and staff. All agreed unanimously, and I began working day and night to bring this event to fruition.

After an interview process from the Smithsonian, and approval from our budget department, we were deemed "qualified." I was on an upward swing in my career path and the job gave me a sense of fulfillment I'd never known. I loved working in my sweet hometown, surrounded by my friends and family, and my adoring dog, Lucas. Right after I began my job at the museum, a work associate, Giulia, found Lucas as a stray and delivered him to my doorstep, probably thinking a dog would be a man magnet. His curly tail and the way he loved to nuzzle my cheek melted my heart. We bonded immediately and he bloomed into the perfect company, always happy to be by my side. I thought the two of us would live in Albany forever and just settle in like most of my high school friends; eventually add a husband, then bushels of children.

And then the accident happened—the car crash that took both my parent's lives. Mom and Dad were Molly and Jeff, teachers at the local high school. Every morning they drove to school together. One of my high school girlfriends, Anna, was on her phone while driving and ran a red light, T-boning the car, killing both my parents instantly. The early morning bright sunlight could temporarily blind you and was used as an excuse for the accident, not the cell phone. I didn't buy it, creating resentment for my now ex-friend and deepening the trauma. My grandparents had both recently passed away and I was an only child, so I really didn't have any family connection in New York anymore.

So badly shaken by these events, and my anxiety at a peak, it was a relief when my therapist finally suggested a change of scenery, and I felt the lure of California, with its blue skies and mild winters. I would have an opportunity to start anew. Make new friends. Be brave and adventurous. I had a friend in San Francisco; someone who had crossed my path at the museum while he was on a research tour during my Iroquois Indian display. His name was Scott and he built exhibits for the San Francisco Museum of Art. We became pen pals, sharing ideas, museum gossip, and a love of history. With his encouragement and support, I set my intention to someday work with him there. I finally took a long weekend trip to explore San Francisco and visit the museum. See if the Bay Area would be a good fit.

California's charismatic culture drew me in like a long breath and was even more beautiful than I dreamed. My dad went to school at Berkeley, so I had an emotional connection to the place. He spoke fondly of his college days and how the liberal lifestyle suited him. I looked like a female version of him—oval face with amber eyes set far apart with heavy, dark eyebrows, and my distinguishing feature, a wide hawk nose that I usually hated. I wished Dad could be here with me, to show me around and tell me that everything would be okay. Yes, I would pursue a new life and see where the wind took me.

My five years at the museum in Albany qualified me for the open curator position at the San Francisco Museum of Art. Our director in Albany was swift to give me a glowing recommendation, and many interviews later, I was offered the job as one of six curators.

The role of curator for international works of art at a San Francisco museum was a dream come true. I loved my job and the anxiety lessened, even though thoughts of my parent's death still haunted me sometimes, causing panic attacks.

Frances, also a curator, and I became friends. Our team collaborations brought noteworthy periods of history to life. Last year, over two hundred and fifty thousand people viewed our collection of 1920s art deco French painters. The year before, we cultivated artwork recovered from shipwrecks in the eastern continents. Our exhibits were recognized as being some the finest in the world, and our staff dug deep to find things that told a story and provoked conversation.

Curators from all over the world consulted with us and begged for our secrets. Our "secret" happened to be a group of detail-oriented history fanatics who read all the latest journals, traveled the globe, and had expert negotiating skills. One of our perks, as a curator, was a round-trip ticket to a place on one of our top ten discovery lists for possible acquisitions. Every January, we met as a group and shared ideas on what would make an intellectually stimulating show and be of interest to the community. After identifying ten research projects, and ordering them by our first choices, one of us was gifted a trip to the top destination. I was the lucky recipient for a visit to Sicily a few years back. I had been successful in convincing Stephen to bring in artifacts from the Carthaginians who occupied the island for centuries. Sicily captivated me with its architectural ruins that popped up across the island. It wasn't like the mainland Italy I knew. The blend of Greek, Phoenician, Arab, Norman, Roman, British, and French cultures all left their mark over the centuries, molding Sicily into a conglomeration of the best of all worlds with a colorful past. What interested me most was the time period of Greek and Carthaginian occupation. Art and innovation flourished, but this bit of history seemed forgotten to the mainstream American. I wanted to educate the public about this fascinating time in the world. How was I to know that office politics would soon interfere with my dream job and at the same time, create another one?

3

FOUR MONTHS EARLIER

March 2017

"Deliver the gifts."

It was more of a command than a plea or asking, or even a request. I jerked my head up from the herb garden I'd been tending and looked around.

Again, almost in a whisper, just in case I didn't hear it the first time, a female voice said, "Deliver the gifts."

I jumped up and felt the tingle of goosebumps flood my skin. Was I hearing things? Ghosts? Was this my mom contacting me from the dead? In an effort to restart whatever I had just experienced, I closed my eyes tight and opened them wide. The whisper again. Now frightened but curious, I asked, "Who are you?" There was no response this time. Someone was telling me what I needed to do. But where, when, and what were these "gifts"? And how was I supposed to deliver them and to whom?

My mind confused, I pushed the demand aside to concentrate on more important matters. Like what I would make for dinner and where I would take Lucas for his daily romp. Where was Lucas? Suddenly it came rushing back to me. I couldn't shake the fact that my beloved dog of only eight years old had left me so suddenly. His death had created a deep hole in my heart, and it still wasn't real that my life did not revolve around him. My schedule was still on his time frame. Our lives were intertwined in every aspect. Sometimes I wanted to crawl into a hole and let the vultures eat me just so I could be with him again, wherever that was. I retreated even deeper into my loner lifestyle, not wanting to talk about him with friends; it only caused a waterfall of uncontrollable tears. I brought my thoughts back to the present and took a deep breath. When would this sadness end?

The next morning, I sat down with a steaming cup of my favorite Italian coffee to write my daily thoughts down in a leather journal. Intentions for the day, musings about love and my garden. As if possessed by someone else, my pen began writing fervently. An outpouring of recipe ideas using Greek ingredients hit the pages. Olives, olive oil, tomatoes, wild herbs. Maybe I needed to explore and expand my Mediterranean repertoire.

I went through these phases with my cooking. It was early spring and soon these ingredients would be at their peak. Puttanesca pasta with fresh tomatoes, olives, capers, and peperoncino came to mind. Fresh, creamy basil and parsley pesto. Garden carrot soup topped with mint, spices, and chopped almonds. I was getting hungry for dinner, and I hadn't even finished my morning coffee. I returned again to the message of delivering the gifts. Maybe I was just obsessing because of my intense involvement with the upcoming exhibit. I guessed time would tell, or I would wait for some sort of clue to help me fulfill this prophecy or demand or request. Was I the gift?

Somedays, I wasn't quite sure how I fit into this life. Work was intellectually stimulating but something was missing. What that was, I couldn't put my finger on. My life was full, as least as far as I knew what "full" meant. Is anyone really, truly, happy and satisfied with the life they are given? I harbored fears that I would never be enough. When these unsettling thoughts traversed my brain, I could sense a panic attack on its way. Rapid heartbeat, trembling, nausea, and a sense of detachment from the world. Randomly triggered by the accident in Albany, and so debilitating, virtually nothing could put a hold on my feelings. The attacks lasted about ten minutes. A cup of herbal tea usually sent them on their way after the allotted panic subsided. I would have to come to terms with the attacks or find a solution to reduce their intensity. Underneath, I had insecurities that set me apart, or at least I thought they did.

I felt a bit guilty, not wanting to be like everyone else. I knew I was different. I was a loner and had more men friends than women. I believed in love but wanted to make a positive change in the world more. My love was funneled into my garden, into Mother Nature. I loved creating a home for the birds and the bees and dreamed of becoming a beekeeper. Being born under a double Scorpio moon gave me strength, tenacity, and a certain fierceness that sometimes got me into trouble. I had a habit of opening my mouth and speaking my mind, almost to a fault. My life was more about being authentic than impressing others or being liked.

It was a Thursday in April and I had gotten into an argument with Stephen over some of the wording that described the artifacts from an upcoming exhibit from Sicily. It was silly, really, but I took it hard. At home that night, I opened a bottle of Valpolicella, poured myself a glass, and wandered around my garden. I began the perpetual routine of weeding, which usually released my stress. My mind dove into a meditative state, each weed releasing one anger and resentment after another. Finally, I settled in, unable to stop the grasp, tug, and pull movement the trance created. Each weed, their dangling roots lingering in my fingers, was so satisfying to eliminate, just like purging my negative thoughts. I could see the progress being made, let out a sigh, and took a break. What if time could stop and I could experience a simpler lifestyle? Deal more with plants than the people who frustrated me. Without thinking, I picked up my cell phone and autodialed Scott.

My feelings for him were growing stronger, even though I didn't want a serious relationship. I knew he didn't either. Nevertheless, he had a certain charismatic quality and air of self-confidence that drew me in. This was what attracted me to him; not necessarily his physical looks. Scott's ruddy complexion and square face gave him a boyish look. I wondered why he didn't have a significant other at age forty-one.

"Hello," a husky voice on the other end answered.

"Oh, hi Scott." I quickly composed myself from thoughts of kissing him.

I was distracted. Why had I called him? Was it the wine talking?

"What are you doing?" I asked. What a dumb question!

"I just got out of the shower. I've been digging in the dirt, like I do most days after work."

Oh my God. He's naked! I tried to visualize his tall, lean, muscular body, sculpted by natural exercise. I saw him toweling himself off, and my own body flushed with heat.

As an excuse for the call, I said, "I have a gardening question for you." I didn't, but asked, "Can you teach me how to use herbs for confidence and power?"

"Why in the world do you need that?"

"I am feeling unsure of my position with Stephen and think it would help me in other areas of my life as well," I answered, not revealing the status of my panic attacks.

"You must be careful what you wish for, Alexis," he advised, his voice losing some of its sexiness.

"Can we meet to talk about it?" I asked.

I felt hesitation in his voice. I knew he was attracted to me but resisted giving me any outward signals. I, on the other hand, am a flirt. An aggressive flirt at that. I had gotten myself into trouble on that street too. Flirting with the wrong man. What did I hope to achieve? Destroy and conquer? Feel like I had won? It had something to do with my lack of self-confidence—a kind of reversal action. It was bad. I kept thinking that I needed to tame this evil habit. Maybe I just wanted to feel that I was attractive to men.

"Alexis, Alexis, are you there?" Scott's voice echoed.

"Yes, I'm here." My recovery statement after my daydream.

"Meet me at Antonio's at seven, if that is all right for you," he said.

All right? Did he just make a date for us? "Of course! Should I bring the book you gave me on herbs?" I asked.

"No. I will bring my notes and show you some of my 'recipes.'"

So, finally he was willing to share his secrets with me. Making tinctures—an infusion of various herbs for a specific outcome—from his garden was his passion and he kept most of this information to himself. I wondered if he sold them to friends and family, or just had fun creating them, like a mad scientist. I would love to see his "laboratory." Was one shelf lined with bottles of brown liquids and drying herbs? What did his house look like? Was he scared of where this "relationship" might lead? I sure wasn't! I wanted to learn from him but also wanted to share more than just herbs with him. He was older. Maybe that was his reason for keeping a distance. I didn't care. Older men were always attractive to me.

I quickly showered and changed into something casual. Tight jeans, merlot-colored cashmere sweater to highlight my long mahogany hair, and tall brown leather boots. This was my going-out outfit. It showcased my tall and lanky features. I felt comfortable and sassy. I grabbed the notebook I collected information in and ran out the front door.

I approached our meeting place, Antonio's, which resided in a gentrified neighborhood of up-and-coming small bars and bistros in Oakland, and found a parking spot around the corner. Just before turning off my ignition, my oil light flashed. Darn. I'd have to call Dave's Auto Shop for an appointment. Just what I didn't need right now —to carve out time for maintenance on my car. I grabbed my purse and notebook and strode swiftly toward the door. Scott was already there at the bar, sipping a neat whiskey. I sidled up next to him, gave him a smile and a peck on the cheek, noticing a lingering of aftershave. He gave me a wry grin that acknowledged the kiss.

The bartender looked at me and asked, "What'll it be, miss? You seem like a red wine gal. Am I right? Been doing this so long I've become intuitive." He laughed.

"You are right! I'll have a glass of the Chianti." Italian wines were my new favorite. After visiting Italy several times, I began to love the earthy varietals, especially the homegrown grapes, distilled right on my friend's Tuscan farms. They were often less expensive than the California wines.

"Good choice," he said.

"Joe, this is my friend from the museum, Alexis," Scott said as an introduction.

"Pleasure to meet you, Alexis. Did you know Scott is our resident produce manager?" Joe said with a chuckle.

I raised my eyebrows at Scott who also laughed and said to me, "I'll tell you later." He was ready to shift the conversation.

"So, you want to learn my trade secrets?" asked Scott, leaning in.

He wore faded blue jeans and a dark-olive plaid shirt that matched his close-set eyes. We'd never been this close to each other. Our eyes met in an almost stare-down and I began to feel my heart beat a little faster.

Scott interrupted the gaze. "I'm sorry for staring, but your eyes have a golden glow, a mysteriousness about them," he commented, stroking his short goatee.

Heat flushed throughout my body and the expression on my face revealed flattery as well as embarrassment.

"Don't get me wrong," he said, acknowledging my blush. "It's a compliment. The amber center and ring of darker brown remind me of a cat's eye marble. Really stunning."

These comments made me stop in my tracks. Was he flirting with me? With all this attention, I didn't even know if I was capable of returning the flirt tonight. I just wanted to get to know him on a deeper level.

Stumbling on my words, I said, "I want to learn how to make tinctures. From my research on Agrigento, the ancients were adept at using herbs to make potions and medicinal remedies. It would be interesting to recreate some of them. What kind of potions have you made with your herbs?" I hoped I was not being too nosey.

Scott pushed a longish curl of dirty-blond hair, graying at the temples, out of his face and studied me just as Joe placed my glass of Chianti down. I raised my glass and said, "Saluti," in an attempt to diminish the seriousness of my conversation.

"I can start you out with something simple," Scott said. "I'll teach you how to make a mixture of valerian, verbena, and lavender to help you sleep better."

How did he know I was an insomniac? Had I said something at work or was he just a mind reader?

"How did you . . . know?" I asked meekly. "Is it that obvious?"

He just sat there grinning at me. I could tell he was enjoying this game.

"So, what else do you know about me?" I questioned.

"We'll have to save that for another meeting," he joked.

Was this just a "meeting" now? I felt like a popped balloon. But I'd take what I could get from this man who was becoming more charismatic by the minute. I wanted to kiss him, in front of everybody, but knew better. Scott tended on the shy side and was finally showing me his alter ego.

"So, sleep drugs it is," I quipped. "When do we start?" The wine was talking now, warming my heart, pushing words out of my mouth in a slow, sexy manner. "Are you free this weekend to show me the ropes? Maybe we can grab a bite to eat afterward," I asked. "What can I bring? A small bottle?"

"No, I have everything we need."

You bet he did! The music caught my attention, and I

pursed my lips as I felt the tone growing in my throat. "Wooooo hoooo, 'Witchy Woman.'" He laughed and nodded his head in agreement as he began singing along to this old Eagles tune. Our foreheads touched playfully and now I was laughing too.

"Have you ever seen the Eagles live?" he asked.

"No," I answered. "But my parents saw them many times and played their music incessantly. It's ingrained into my head!"

"I'm an old rock and roller," said Scott. "Give me the Stones, Beatles, Crosby, Stills and Nash, anything out of the seventies and eighties. The music was so true to itself. It told a story of the times."

I just sat there nodding my head in agreement. Who was this Renaissance Man that finally came alive in my presence, allowing me to see another side of his carefully guarded nature? My heart was beating hard. I felt so comfortable with him, as if we were old friends and had known each other forever.

"So, what's your favorite band?" he asked me.

"I like oldies too, but what really rocks my soul is Motown. I can hardly stop dancing when I hear the Temptations, Aretha, the Supremes, Marvin Gaye," I answered as I wiggled my hips in my seat.

"I'll bet you are a good dancer," he interrupted. "That kind of music deserves to be danced to."

So, this was what it was like when you met the perfect guy? The "meeting" ended shortly thereafter, and I had a date with Scott on Saturday to see a demonstration of tincture-making. Before we parted, he slipped a baggie full of something into my purse. "A gift," he stated. I lifted it out and examined the contents. A pinchful of tiny seeds.

"Plant them the first day of the waxing moon and see what happens," he said.

"What are they?"

"A surprise," was all he said.

We said goodnight and he pulled me close, only to kiss my forehead. It was a sweet gesture. But I wanted more. I always wanted more.

4

MAGIC HAPPENS HERE

The next morning, I searched my calendar to figure out when the next waxing moon would occur. It showed one week from today. If I was to learn to become a better gardener, I would follow the directions of my mentor to a T. In the meantime, I had a date with Scott tomorrow.

Finding Scott's house was no easy task. I meandered into the hills of Marin County, down winding roads until I saw a sign for his address at the end of a long driveway. The redwood trees surrounding his home were so dense, I could barely see the single-story wooden home tucked in between them, like a cabin in the thick of a forest. I knocked on the dark-red door, anticipating this meeting with curiosity and a certain amount of intimidation. Scott was so knowledgeable; I was just me. My lack of self-confidence was a constant challenge. My heart wanted to go one way, but my head won out most times. I would put on a good face today and show him how eager I was to learn. He could probably already see through me, though, so who was I fooling? Just like at Antonio's, I resolved to be myself around him. The door swung open with that thought.

"Good morning, professor! I am ready for my lesson,"

I announced.

"Good morning, future herbalist," he countered.

This was going to be a great day. "Come on in and I'll give you a tour of my family."

Scott's home was small and scantily furnished: enlarged pictures of white-washed houses on a Greek island, a mosaic-decorated cathedral in Palermo, and food stalls in Turkey. The walls told his story of love for art and history, delivering the only decoration for this room but speaking volumes. Dark hardwood covered the floors, and the lamps looked like consignment-shop finds. Double patio doors led outside and brought illumination into the dark interior. I imagined the light changed with the angle of the sun each day.

Scott led me through the doors to a walkway past tall, dark-purple flowering buddleia, the scent of lilac hitting my nostrils like a woman who wears too much perfume. The walkway curved left, and the yard opened up for as far as I could see. His property must be sitting on an acre or more. To the right of the path resided orange, pomegranate, almond, and pear trees. On the left stood olive, lemon, fig, and pistachio trees, in all stages of their fruit- and nut-bearing lives. A wooden carved sign named each tree, including its genus and when it was planted. So many details. Yes, this grove, garden, and yard were his passion, and I could feel Mother Nature's energy loud and clear. Just past the trees, light emerged and in front of us lay raised beds, about two feet wide by six feet long. I counted ten in all. This looked like a full-time job! How did he maintain all of this? Scott remained quiet. I could tell he was in his element. He melted into this landscape and was absorbed by it. Everything was so precise, just like his work at the museum.

Softly, he spoke, almost like he didn't want to disturb

the plants. "I rotate all my vegetables and herbs twice a year, so I don't deplete the nutrients in the soil. My compost provides most of what the plants need. I rarely use fertilizers."

He was spilling out his secrets but really these were just gardening tips, not secrets. I listened attentively, then asked, "Where are your herbs?"

"Follow me. They're in the back where they get more sun."

Huddled together grew tall stalks of thickly leaved basil, the Genovese style. I gathered a handful gently between my fingers and stuck my nose into the middle, their pungent aroma like a mouthful of pesto.

"What do you do with all this basil?" I asked.

"I take it to Antonio to use in his dishes. He is the lucky recipient of a lot of my Mediterranean herbs and vegetables. We've worked out a trade. I eat for free, and he gets fresh produce. Some deal, eh?" he said.

I laughed. So that is what Joe the bartender had meant about Scott being the "produce manager." His garden was full of foods I'd never seen before, like fava beans. The long broad beans required special preparation before they could be eaten. Shelled twice, then the beans released. It seemed like a lot of work to me, but Scott loved the challenge. Now I knew why he rushed out of work every day and where he spent his weekends. I had interrupted his date with his garden today and felt honored.

"Let's make a tincture," Scott declared and guided me to another part of his yard where the lavender grew tall and free.

He handed me a basket, pulled out some clippers from a holder on his belt, and began snipping away. "Here. Hold these," he said after handing me a few long stalks of the aromatic purple flowers.

I obeyed and watched him stride to another part of his yard. A tall plant with lime-colored leaves and cornflower-blue flowers was his next pursuit.

"Blue vervain," he noted. This time, he cut only the leaves, again handing them to me. We moved on. "For our tincture, we'll need valerian. It's a root and I harvested it a few months ago. It's inside."

My basket full, we traversed the yard, along ruddy-colored pavers, but not back to his house. In front of us stood a small structure, like a gingerbread house.

"I built this as my studio," said Scott.

On either side of the front door, red geraniums spilled out of tall ceramic pots. A wood-carved sign on the door said, "La magia accade qui." Scott translated the Italian phrase to "Magic happens here." With curiosity, I entered. Inside, neatly organized shelves housed amber bottles filled with brown liquid. Cupboards lined one wall, and a simple desk that looked like it could be his grandfather's sat facing a back window. A tall bookshelf wedged itself next to the desk. In the middle of the room, a rectangular workbench with drawers dominated the space, one tall stool as its sidekick. A community of drying herbs, along with braids of garlic and shallots, hung from the ceiling, emitting an array of scents from sweet lavender to pungent garlic. So, this was his laboratory.

Scott opened a cupboard with labeled cardboard containers and pulled one down. The box said, "Valerian." Inside sat a one-inch rootstalk the color of ginger, long fingers splaying out from one of the ends. He took a knife from his pocket and cut off one of the knobs.

"Valerian. One of the best roots to calm nerves which also helps sleep. Take a whiff." He held the root up to my nose and I inhaled.

"Earthy. Dirty socks," I commented, scrunching up my

nose. It was not the most attractive of scents.

"That's why I add lavender to it." He laughed. "Lavender has soothing properties that complement the valerian. Let's get started."

He demonstrated the process step by step, scaling out proportions and noting that this tincture would not be ready for use immediately. It needed to steep for a few weeks, brewing all those relaxing qualities until they peaked in their potency. Scott pulled another tincture in a jar, again labeled "Valerian," off the shelf, and grabbed a funnel and small dropper bottle. As he poured the dark amber liquid into the bottle, he stated, "This is for you. One dropperful in a cup of warm water before bedtime. Try it tonight and let me know if your sleep is more restful."

I knew how my sleeping could be improved but didn't dare pose the solution to Scott. He took out a small label, wrote "Sleep Therapy" on it, stuck it on the bottle, and handed it to me. I accepted, put my hands together at my heart, and bowed my head in appreciation.

Scott's lesson on tinctures fascinated me and at the same time made me dizzy. This was a precise science. The ancient Greeks were much more sophisticated than I had imagined and used remedies for many ailments we would not even consider today. I would need to practice, listen, and be more observant of my garden. There was a scientific method to this art. Using science to create art. I had never thought of it that way before. Scott was teaching me to be more mindful, the opposite of my impatient personality. Growing things was a waiting game; I knew that from experiments in my own garden. A new driving passion was growing inside of me, and I wanted to know more, be a better gardener. Learn to use my herbs and produce in new ways. From this one visit, Scott had inspired me. Maybe it was his calm demeanor, the way he felt about his "family."

A week later I rose early, eager to tuck my little seeds into their new home. I amended a two-foot section of my raised bed to accommodate Scott's mystery seeds. I used a chopstick to draw a narrow gorge into the dirt and as I sprinkled them along the straight line, said a silent prayer to the universe to give these seeds nourishment and use the wisdom of the ancient gods. I gently covered them up, tapped down the soil, and anointed them with a sprinkling of water. The waiting game began.

Two weeks passed before I saw my first sprout. It looked ordinary enough, like anything else that had begun life in my garden. As the days went by, I kept close guard, especially on the seedlings. What would emerge? As soon as they had reached an inch or so high, I noticed them beginning to thin out. Something was eating them.

"Darn bugs," I said out loud, assuming they were the culprits.

The next afternoon, settled into my comfy lounge chair with a cool glass of freshly squeezed lemonade, I saw the perpetrator. A mourning dove gracefully landed in my garden bed and proceeded to tug at the seedlings. Was she looking for worms and pulled up the sprout by mistake? No, she was actively seeking this particular sprout. Then I recognized her—the dove who wasn't afraid of me. Usually when I approached the feeder, all the other birds scattered with screeches of "enemy, enemy," but not her. She bravely remained and I would thank her for understanding that I was the one, after all, feeding her. Her plump chest of pallid white feathers and ring around her neck distinguished her from the other doves. If this was what she wanted, then I could spare the seeds. Besides, I didn't even know what these surprise seeds would manifest into. They must have some nutrient she needed. Maybe she was about to give birth.

In a few days, the dove stopped feeding on the sprouts, instead gorging on the millet seeds I provided in long feeders. The garden was mine again. My seedlings continued their spindly growth as I watched for signs of identification. I knew the basic herbs, but I guessed this was something exotic. Why else would Scott have given them to me? Skinny, olive-green leaves emerged with minute sawtooth edges on a sturdy stalk and grew straight up, the leaves branching out on either side. I perused the shelf of books with all my gardening references and grabbed Medicinal Herbs, a book given to me by my friend Amanda who dabbled in formulas for her baby and dogs. Leafing through the pages, and looking for leaves that matched my garden's, I came across vervain, from the genus Verbena. I had heard of Verbena, but not vervain. The herb had been around a long time, with first known uses in ancient Egypt. I wondered if the people whose artifacts I brought in from ancient Sicily had used it as a medicinal. Scott had obviously cultivated these seeds in his garden, and I wondered what he did with the plants. They would eventually produce petite blue flowers and had the capacity to grow five feet tall, crowding out my small garden bed. Oh well, this was an experiment, and I could transplant them to create a border in another spot in my yard. Perhaps it would attract hummingbirds and add even more color to my already vibrant garden of magenta geraniums and deep purple salvia. Humbled, I felt like I could not do enough for my garden, for what it gave me in return could not be measured.

Scott gave me a head start in gardening, harvesting, and tincture-making but really wanted me to find myself in all this. He was weaning me off of him so I could develop my own techniques and formulas. Once my vervain had grown to a recognizable plant, I asked Scott if I had correctly identified the herb. He winked at me and suggested I research opportune harvesting times because it could change the potency of the final product. I had so much to learn.

5

THE POWER OF TINCTURES

July 2017

"Are you okay?" Scott said, his comforting voice over the phone sensing my anxiety.

"Do you know?" I asked.

"About the theft? Yes. Word travels fast. I thought you might want some company."

Scott had become a valued friend and mentor. Our relationship centered around our gardens and his lessons on creating herbal tinctures. He always seemed to know just what to do, how to make you feel like a million dollars. I gratefully accepted his offer.

I changed into my favorite comfy loungewear: a frayed pair of jeans and an oversized cream sweater. Tonight, I did not feel like I had to impress.

Half an hour later, a rap on the door signaled Scott's arrival. I wrapped my arms around him in a tight embrace. Through my sobs I explained to him what had happened—Stephen's accusation, my irrational response. He was like my big brother, and even though I vowed not to tell anyone at work about my work hiatus, I really needed someone close by to confide in. My weeping subsided and

I released my grip on his shoulders. "Wine?" I asked.

We retreated to the kitchen where Scott eyed the bottle of Chianti and poured us both a glass. I motioned with my finger to follow me into the living room to have a seat on my sofa.

"It's a serious accusation, Alexis. Have you noticed anyone watching you?" Scott asked.

"I don't think so. I feel as if I'm being framed by someone. Yes, I love Demeter, but to steal her? Never! The museum is my second home. I left everything I had ever known in New York and came here, basically all alone. I would never jeopardize all that I have worked so hard for." I exhaled and waited for a response. It was slow in coming.

"I've heard rumors. About you. Stephen is jealous. He thinks you will take his place but knows you don't have the confidence to fight back. I wonder if he set this up to get rid of you."

I felt like an earthquake had just shaken me off my seat. I could not believe what Scott was saying. Someone envious of my knowledge? It really was a passion, something I cared so deeply about that I put my entire heart and soul into. I had trusted Stephen, and now this. But it was only speculation on Scott's part.

Scott's revelation would normally have triggered a panic attack, but this was not happening. His calming presence seemed to have a power over me.

He reached into his jacket pocket and took out two brown bottles. I knew one was the valerian tincture for sleep, but what was the other bottle for? The valerian had given me crazy dreams. I was living in ancient Greece and couldn't get home. It was a recurring dream that I chalked up to the Sicily exhibit items from the museum. The wild dreams were exchanged for the opportunity to sleep through the night. I would survive.

Scott looked me directly in the eyes and showed me the second bottle. "I crafted this especially for you. I knew you would need it someday."

I held my breath as I waited for him to continue.

"Several years ago, I made a similar potion for myself that allowed me to experience life with more purpose and awareness. Sort of like the Greek lifestyle we are learning about with this exhibit. For you, I've created a special blend of herbs I have never combined together before," he confided.

A list of herbs and their characteristics followed as I listened but didn't hear. My mind was racing. He tapped into my psyche and intuitively knew what I needed to help me move forward in this life.

"Start with two drops in the morning and then add two more drops at night as needed."

Needed for what? All I knew right then was that this man sitting next to me cared enough to devise a unique blend of herbs for my benefit.

"I'm in!" I declared, not really knowing what I was getting myself into.

The conversation shifted to his garden and what he was harvesting now.

"Wait! I have something else in my car for you," he said.

In a flash he was back with a bag of freshly picked carrots. He knew how I loved the produce from his garden, especially the skinny French carrots with tender green tops. I thanked him profusely, telling him I'd make something special with them.

Scott finished his wine and got up to leave. "Please don't go so soon," I pleaded.

Tomorrow was Sunday, so work could not be an

excuse, and I really didn't want to be alone.

"I'm repairing the roof of my studio. It's been leaking and there's rain forecast for the afternoon. Sorry, but it will be an early morning."

I understood. Home projects always came first. Maybe he could make some evening time in the middle of the week. Report back to me about the missing Demeter and the possible suspects. I could be patient, at least for now.

The morning garden beckoned. Sounds of chirping birds filled the air as I pushed open the patio door. Inhaling deeply, I closed my eyes and imagined a different life. Had I made the right choices in my past? I wasn't good at handling change and often thought of all the what-ifs. Everything happens for a reason, I told myself. My garden was the one thing that could console me.

Suddenly I had an idea. Something to distract me. I practically ran over to my new vervain plant and said, "Today I will transform you into something beautiful."

Just last week I collected several eight-ounce amber bottles, 80 proof vodka, and smaller one-ounce bottles with droppers in preparation for my experiments. I was ready to tincture. This would be my creative outlet, the kind Scott had talked about. I would do it all myself and then give him one of the bottles to try. But wait. Didn't Scott ask me to research the harvest time of herbs? Something to do with their potency? My notes were in a special journal I titled "How to Make Magic" that sat on the third shelf of my studio bookcase. It was here I kept all my gardening resources—many of them unread—just in case I decided to take it seriously. I pulled the green book down and flipped through the pages. "Harvest after a full moon in the waning phase." Scott said that this was because the sap content is high and the moisture goes to the roots, making the leaves easier to dry. I wanted to create the best tincture possible, and to impress Scott. A quick look on the computer told me the day to harvest would be the seventeenth. Today was the sixteenth. I'd have to be patient for one more day.

The next morning, I made my ritual cup of coffee and planned my day. I'd check on the herbs and gather all the components necessary to prepare my tincture. I felt like I was morphing into Scott. My garden always had my attention but even more so now. After a morning workout to release some anxiety, it was time for recipe-making, meaning tincture time. The vervain was finally ready to harvest. I touched each stem, caressing the leaves, not ready to separate them from their friends. Following Scott's direction, I cut several stems about five inches from the ground so they could continue to grow new leaves. Besides, the stems didn't contain as much oil as the leaves did. I placed them into my harvesting basket and transported them to the kitchen where I carefully removed the leaves. I got out my scale and weighed out five grams. The formula Scott taught me was one part herb to five parts alcohol. I'd need twenty-five milliliters of liquid to extract the oils. Using a sharp knife, I coarsely chopped the herbs and fed them into the jar. I poured the vodka slowly on top, screwed the lid on tightly, and gently gave the whole thing a shake to make sure all the leaves were drinking. The brew went on a shelf in my kitchen cupboard where it was dark and cool. Six to eight weeks was the recommended waiting time before straining out the leaves and imbibing. I really didn't want to wait that long.

That night, I put two drops of the valerian into my

bedtime tea and hugged the mug to keep my hands warm. I tried not to think about my dilemma and what I was going to do, but the worry kept surfacing. It would be difficult to get another curator job if I had a label of "thief." Maybe I would go overseas and work for a company doing archaeological digs. They could use and appreciate my extensive knowledge. That would mean leaving again. Starting over— again. Leaving Scott. But I was a big girl and would do what was necessary to make a living. I was jumping the gun. I hadn't even been fired yet, but I could see it on the horizon. I grabbed the book I'd been reading at night, the one about the woman hiding Jews in World War II France. These women were so brave. They risked everything to help other innocent human beings. I wondered if I could be that courageous, the consequences being as severe as they were. One slipup and your life, and those of the people you were trying to save, was over. These women were my heroines and I felt drawn to them. They never doubted themselves but trusted their instincts to do what was deemed right. How I wished I could translate their fearlessness into my own skin.

I drifted off into a heavy sleep, dreaming again of Demeter. This night she was the one chasing me for taking her away from her home in Sicily. She caught up with me, and with a tear in her eye, waved a stalk of wheat in front of me. I didn't know what this signified and as she reached for me, I woke up.

I decided to go against what my body wanted in the way of more sleep and got out of bed to shake off the dream. The sun was just coming up—maybe I'd go for a long walk to clear my head. There must be a reason for my encounters with Demeter. I went over and over our "meetings" and still came up empty. It was as if she had returned from the deep past and chosen me for some sort of mission. Was I crazy to think this? I did believe in past lives. But to have a relationship with a true goddess? It must be the tinctures talking. I came home and brewed a double espresso.

Just as I sat down to sip the dark coffee, the phone rang. It was Burt, the attorney.

"Hi Alexis, got a minute?"

"Yes sure, Burt. Do you have any ideas to help me?" I asked.

The coffee had kicked in and my brain felt refreshed. I listened intently.

"There is no evidence to accuse you, Alexis. We could file a defamation of character but then you'd most likely be let go and it wouldn't be good for the museum's public relations. I know you care about the museum and don't want to hurt its reputation."

"What is your plan, then?"

"We could negotiate with them. Have them give you six months' pay and a letter of recommendation."

"Doesn't that make me look guilty? I did nothing!" I insisted.

The money did sound good, but it wouldn't last long, and my reputation would still be tarnished, the story incomplete about my involvement—or not—in the theft. I thought of those brave women who fought for their lives. I would fight too.

"I want my name cleared," I stated emphatically.

"The only thing we can do, then, is to file a lawsuit against the museum. Do you really want to go in that direction? It could be costly. I'm sure their legal team is excellent."

I wanted the magic cure. I wanted it all to go away. I closed my eyes and sighed deeply.

"Let me think about my options, Burt. Can I call you

later this week, please?"

"Certainly, Alexis. I'd advise you not to talk to anyone about this until we find a way to resolve the issue."

"Of course," I said cordially.

We hung up and I was left to my thoughts. I had broken the "don't tell" rule. I told Scott. He was such a private person, and I didn't see him as a gossip. I trusted him. I had to trust somebody.

The optimistic side of me hoped that after this week all would be fine. They would find the missing Demeter, I would be back to work, curating the artifacts as usual. The relationship between Stephen and me would be fragmented. I would always be looking over my shoulder to see if he was watching my every move. I doubt he'd even apologize. I missed my coworker, Frances. She must have been working overtime without me to help her this week. The exhibit was due to be on display in six weeks and there were hundreds of artifacts to tend to.

I thought of Scott in his workshop at the museum, building temple ruins and then painting and texturizing them to match the limestone they were originally created with. I'd have to ask him for an update. Before I was told to take the week off, I had planned to drop into his studio to get a glimpse of the emerging city. In our group meetings, we had chosen Agrigento, a prosperous community for only a brief time in history but rich in cultural activity. I was the only one who had visited Agrigento, on my quest to find items from Carthage a few years ago. My visit had been brief, not nearly long enough, and consisted of a quick temple tour and a meeting at the Museo Archeologico Regionale di Agrigento in the hills of the city. The site had left an impression on me, or more of a curiosity. It felt eerily haunted by the gods and goddesses that the citizens worshipped, their toppled temples a display of a tortured and ransacked society. It had been a brilliant and lively place at one time though, its proximity to the ocean a coveted location. I could visualize the day-to-day activities there, more than the other ruins that were crammed into my schedule for the week. Yes, I was only granted one week on this exploratory research project, not nearly long enough to review five different sites and meet with their caregivers. The other excavated sites were lonely and forgotten, their once vibrant energy evaporated into the universe. But Agrigento felt different. I half expected to turn a corner and see a man dressed in a short white robe, tied at the waist, entering a temple. What I did see was a large white wolf-like dog, slinking between the temples. I asked the tour guides if they saw him too and they just shook their heads, thinking I had imagined him. I did manage to get a photo to validate for myself he was real. I longed to return on my own to delve even deeper into this mysterious society but funds were low, and besides, it was not the easiest place to get to along desolate parts of the Sicilian highway.

My daydream ended and my coffee was gone. I sometimes lapsed into these visions of what it would be like to live in another time. Knowing it wasn't possible, at least while I was alive in this lifetime, I decided to make the best of what I had. Maybe I'd go on a vacation, back to Albany. Rekindle some old friendships. I suddenly remembered the tincture Scott had prepared for me. Some kind of mixture of herbs but I couldn't remember which ones. I picked it up off the kitchen counter and examined the bottle. The label read, "Forza." I knew from the little Italian I had studied that "forza" translated to "strength." This must be the fortitude I needed to get through this mess. With trepidation, I gave the dropper a squeeze to gather up the green-brown liquid and held it up to my open mouth. One … two. The bitter flavor cinched my tastebuds. It was like drinking an Amaro from Italy, only worse. I replaced the cap and put the Forza in my kitchen cupboard, next to the valerian. I hoped the effects were subtle.

I cooked when I needed therapy. The food talked to me, opened my right brain, gave me a chance to express myself. I never thought of myself as an artist until I started cooking and combining various recipes together. My mother and grandmother were both talented cooks and bakers, allowing me freedom in the kitchen to experiment, under their guidance. Grammy, in her faded yellow apron with wide straps, especially loved teaching me how to measure accurately, zest a lemon, or chop an onion. My mom, on the other hand, was grateful for help with dinner and breakfast. She was the true risk-taker in the kitchen, once even cooking a goose for Christmas dinner. It didn't go over well, but we all appreciated her effort and we eagerly tasted everything she cooked because it was usually fantastic, and it fulfilled her caretaker role. I inherited my passion for food from both of them and learned quickly that the intent was as important as the process.

My small cottage kitchen contained the bare essentials: a few cookbooks stacked together on the granite counter, mostly Italian; my grandmother's antique bean pot, now filled with wooden spoons and spatulas; wooden cutting boards; and a knife block. To add a little life, I had painted one wall a cheery sunflower yellow and decorated it with a watercolor of oranges and lemons. Three small ceramic birds sat on my windowsill, along with a photo of Lucas and one of me high up in the bleachers of the Colosseum in Rome. What my sparse kitchen lacked in embellishment, it made up for with happy memories.

I remembered the carrots Scott had gifted me the night before. To talk to my inner shrink today, I would make carrot soup. Simple enough. Sauté leeks on a low heat until very soft and translucent, add chopped carrots, chicken broth, and to give it a twist, some cardamom. Cook until the carrots are tender and then puree. Add salt and pepper to taste. This would take my mind off work for a while. As I chopped the vegetables and my mind drifted off, I listened to the birds serenade me, with an occasional coo of the mourning doves. Birds had an allure for me. I was in awe of them and envious of their ability to fly. I started having dreams of flying when I was very young, and they continued to this day. How anyone could contain a bird was beyond me. They were born with wings for a reason. I opened the French doors leading to my backyard to peek at them at their feeder and spotted the large pot of mint growing out of control. An idea popped into my head. I would make a mint topping to swirl into my carrot soup. Give it a fresh edge. Maybe add some pine nuts or almonds. The recipe had come together so easily. Was it the Forza speaking or was I finally beginning to relax after the weekend ordeal?

Scott might like some soup. It would be an excuse to connect with him, see the rest of his garden, and learn more garden secrets. I wouldn't bother him today, but maybe tomorrow. I sat down to write out the recipe I had just devised in case it was so divine, which I was sure it would be, I wanted to make it again. When I finished, another idea spilled out. Fresh tomatoes with black olives, parsley, and garlic, not in a salad but another soup. This soup would be cold to celebrate the peak summer flavors, perhaps with a drizzle of basil and pecorino pesto. I was craving this taste. Tomatoes from Scott? He always had too many, especially the San Marzanos, so perfect for cooking. If he would share his bounty with me, I'd keep him stocked in fresh soups.

I added a pinch of cardamom to the carrot soup and continued to let it simmer into a spicy, soft medley. The sweet aroma filled my kitchen as I chopped mint for the creamy swirl on top. I'd recently become familiar with some new Mediterranean spices like Aleppo and ras el hanout. The latter had a sweet and spicy component that transformed tagines, eggs, and almost anything into a warm, spicy flavor. Tonight, I mixed yogurt, mint, and ras al hanout together for the topping, and would sprinkle some roughly chopped almonds on top. I hadn't eaten much since the incident and now, suddenly, I was ravenous. The immersion blender made quick work of converting the carrot chunks into a creamy puree and with the addition of a little salt and pepper, the soup was ready. The mint topping transformed an already luscious soup into a masterpiece, and I felt a glow of accomplishment. This recipe came together so easily as if another part of my brain activated, like when you have those bursts of inventive thoughts. I wanted to hold onto this moment, to try something else to see if the magic was still here, inside me. Instead, I did the unexpected. I picked up the phone.

"Stephen, how are you?" I felt bold.

"Alexis, what do you want?" Stephen said with surprise in his voice. He was obviously not expecting my call.

"I want to come back to work. You have no evidence against me, and I miss my job. I want to make sure the exhibit is ready in time for the opening," I said with confidence.

Silence. "We are still meeting about your position. We will notify you when a decision has been made."

Stunned, I asked, "Who is making the decision? I did

nothing wrong."

"I have to go now, Alexis. I'll be in touch." And then he hung up.

So that was it. I was going to be fired or let go or put on leave. All the bravery I had gathered seemed to vanish into thin air as I slunk down into my patio chair, considering my next move.

My attention was averted by a dove that flew in and perched herself on one of my orange tree branches. She looked like the fat white dove that had helped herself to my vervain seedings. All the other doves in my yard were smaller, soft-gray birds. "Mama," I softly called. For some reason, she looked like a mama, ready to give birth, she was so large. I didn't know if Mama heard me or not, but she remained fixed on the branch, in a sort of trance for several minutes.

Most of the birds flitted from feeder to grass to tree and then began the cycle again. Not Mama. Her confidence had a calming effect on me. I walked over to the tree as the rest of the flock scattered. Unafraid, her soft body slightly twitched, almost unsure, then relaxed back into her lookout. Not wanting to disturb her anymore, I retreated from her sight and grabbed the delicate pruning shears to clip some chives and oregano.

The summertime rain the night before anointed the leaves, giving a fresh glow to all my inhabitants. This was my favorite time of year in my garden. New vibrant blooms emerged daily like a resurgence of energy after a hibernation. It wasn't like I was a great gardener by any means. I just let some plants grow wild and planted what I liked to look at. I guess that's why I admired Scott so much. He planned out every detail of his garden and made sure each plant had exactly what it needed to thrive. It was almost too perfect. I could learn from him, but I would never be that controlling. I loved how random things sprung up, probably from bird droppings, and I let them stay, curious to see what they would become. Making the tinctures was the closest I'd come to striving for perfection. Little did I know that sometimes perfection is what is needed for survival.

I continued my homebody activities that week, taking Scott's bitter tincture, now two times a day. I wasn't sure what effect it was having on me, if at all, but I was giving it a try. Friday had finally arrived and since it was the weekend, I'd give Scott a call to see if he wanted to come for dinner and try my new soups. Every day that week, I found myself in my kitchen, with a new vegetable dish on the menu. Scott had left some tomatoes he grew in a hothouse, along with a cabbage, on my porch when I was out for a run. His ingredients, plus a few of my own, inspired me and took my mind off work. Maybe I'd have a new career making soup!

Every afternoon, as part of my new unscheduled life, I watered my thirsty flowers and checked on my herbs and vegetables. The pungent basil was at its peak for pesto, and nearby a few green beans struggled on the vine. I was still figuring out the weather patterns here and some weeks the dampness caused mildew on the vegetable leaves, like it was doing now on my zucchini. I cut out the infection, like a surgeon, and put the spotted leaves in the greens bin to get it as far away as possible from the other plants. If I didn't catch it soon enough, all leafy greens would catch the mold and I'd have to give everyone a crew cut.

As if it belonged to her, the mama dove landed in my vervain and ruffled her feathers while rotating her bobbing head to preen herself. When she finished, her beak reached into the ground to peck at the fallen and dried leaves. I observed her behavior and thought about how different she was from the rest of her flock. An outsider, like me. At that moment, we both completely understood each other.

An almost full moon arose between the trees in the evening sky. A perfect night for dinner outside. The time had escaped me, and I'd forgotten to call Scott. Maybe he'd still be up for a spontaneous simple supper.

Just as I picked up the phone to call, it rang.

"Hey Alexis—care to try my home-cured olives? I revised my technique and need someone to judge them."

"I made carrot soup from your carrots. Why don't you swing by and we'll taste-test both our latest creations?" I said, relieved that I wasn't the one making the first move this time.

I hoped he would have news from the museum, perhaps a few photos of the staging progress.

"See you soon," he said and hung up.

My intuition was telling me that Scott had something more to show me than just his olives. It wasn't like him to call me out of the blue and be social. It was out of his character. My suspicious mind took over and I began fabricating all kinds of reasons for his visit. I had a habit of anticipating the worst and wished I could be more open-minded, not try to predict what would happen but be able to live in the moment.

I reheated the carrot soup, took the yogurt-mint topping out of the fridge and got out two soup bowls and two wine glasses. We would celebrate Friday even though Friday was just another day to me now. I chose a Rosso from my meager wine collection and opened it so it could breathe. A knock came on the door. Scott was here. Tonight, he looked especially attractive in a V-neck black T-shirt.

We embraced and I led him into the kitchen where the scent of the earthy soup filled the air.

"Smells divine," said Scott as he unscrewed the lid off

the olive jar.

I poured him a glass of wine and we toasted to Agrigento, a place we both had learned about in depth since working on the exhibit. I dug into the jar with my fingers and popped an olive into my mouth, their meaty flesh reminding me of the olives I'd eaten high in the hills of Mt. Etna.

"Geez, these are incredible! You grew these?" I exclaimed.

I flashbacked to my research trip two years ago and a meal at an agriturismo on the way up the famous volcano. The olives had made an impression, large and meaty with a smaller pit, a mini meal in itself. One of my souvenirs included a small bottle of the farm's extra virgin olive oil, that my stingy side reserved only for special occasions.

"It's a Castelvetrano olive from the western side of Sicily. This nursery outside Boston specializes in hard-to-find olive varieties and I got it as a sapling. I planted it where it gets full sun but not as much water as the other trees, replicating its origins as much as possible," Scott said.

This was yet another sign of Scott's dedication to his nature family. No wonder he didn't have time to be social.

"It's taken five years of pruning and maintenance before the tree decided it was time to produce. I've been studying how to cure olives, and this is my first attempt," he said, blushing. I resisted the temptation to plant a kiss on his lips.

"Alexander the Great would be proud!" I exclaimed.

I served him a bowl of the carrot soup, to rave reviews, of course, and we discussed what was growing in each of our respective gardens, as usual. Sometimes this trivial chitchat got to me. I wanted to know more about him, where he grew up, his family, his best friends. This side of him remained a closed door to me for some reason. Our formal conversation gave me the impression he had something he wanted to tell me. I poured us each a refill of wine and began.

"Scott, how are things at the museum? You haven't mentioned anything, but I know something is going on. Stephen wouldn't talk to me on Wednesday when I called. Tell me what you know."

Scott turned his head away, trying to avoid my directness.

"What I know won't help matters, Alexis. There are people in this world who want power at all costs. And then there are people like you and me who must learn to balance the outside power that is taken away from us with the power that lies within us. Does that make sense?"

Of course it made sense, but I didn't know why he was giving me this little mini lecture now. What did it all mean? I leaned my head on his shoulder in a sisterly kind of way and took a deep sigh.

"I wish I could protect you, Alexis, but you need to fend for yourself. You will be fine," Scott said, his eyes piercing mine.

I tried to feel reassured but inside my mangled nerves struggled.

"Do you ever wish you could go back in time to a life with less stress and more guidance from nature instead of these useless power controls we have to deal with here?" I asked.

"The past may seem like a simpler lifestyle but until you've been there, you won't realize that their realities were just as demanding as ours are here," Scott said.

I gave him a quizzical look, like I wasn't sure where he was going with this.

After a few minutes of silence, Scott said with a lighter

note in his voice, "What's your schedule like tomorrow? Let's play in your herb garden. I'll show you some of my tricks of the trade. Besides, it's a waxing moon, perfect for what I have planned."

Like my schedule was anything but overflowing.

"Sure," I said. "Should I have coffee ready?"

"That's my girl!" Scott said with a gleam in his eyes as he put an arm around my shoulder and gave me a squeeze.

My girl? What kind of girl was he envisioning? A girlfriend? He was turning into a valued friend, a best friend. I longed for something more with Scott, but he was taking his sweet time. Isn't that how it worked? Great friends becoming lovers? Every time I was near him now, I felt an electrical charge and I found it hard to control the rapid beats of my heart. I wondered if he felt the same. My last romance in Albany came on fast and furious before we had really gotten to know each other. I wanted that spark of emotion that continually sizzles on the surface, even in tough times. The emotional connection dissolved over time. He discovered my weaknesses and preyed upon them. At first, I went along with it, then realized I was turning into a different person. I cut it off on our second anniversary of dating. Painful, yes, but I had found a new life in San Francisco, was back to my old self and enjoying my freedom. Until now.

He didn't stay long and performed the obligatory kiss on the forehead before heading out the door. Scott had given me a lot to think about. I reached into the cupboard that held my tinctures and instead of two, took three drops of the Forza. What harm could it do? Maybe I'd have some crazy vision that changed my life, I sarcastically laughed to myself.

That night, my dreams were so vivid, they were frightening. Demeter was once again chasing me, but we were in an ancient market, maybe an agora. I was weaving in and out of the crowd, trying to find a place to hide. Suddenly I sprouted wings and was flying over the marketplace, then higher and higher into the sky. My wings, or arms, began to lose their power and I drifted down, only to land at the entrance to the Temple of Demeter. The dream ended abruptly, my eyes wide open and my body trembling with fear. It took me a minute to realize I was back in my bed in my own temple of a house. It must be my imagination getting the better of me, this whole mess with the missing Demeter. I couldn't figure out why she was chasing me though. In the last dream, she waved a stalk of wheat at me. There was something she wanted but that part of the puzzle alluded me. I knew what Demeter represented as the goddess of the harvest, but could that be related to my current harvest of the vervain? I was overanalyzing this. It was, after all, just a dream. I'd go for a run this morning and clear my head, happy to be in this present world. Scott was due to come over for coffee around 9 a.m. so I had plenty of time. Still rattled by my dream, I visualized the determined goddess as I ran through the park and onto a dirt pathway. I was the god Achilles, and she would never catch me!

Feeling lighter after my jog, I prepared coffee in two espresso pots, one for each of us. This was how I made my Italian version every morning, and just last month, bought a second pot in case I had company. The sound and smell of the percolated coffee reminded me of my youth and my parents' larger, old-fashioned chrome percolator they refused to get rid of. I guess that's where I get my sentimentality.

I glanced at the Forza sitting on my counter, mentally evaluating whether or not to imbibe. It didn't feel like a drug, no altering states or psychotic episodes, but it did seem to deliver a calm and more composed me than usual. My anxiety was dissipating, and I found more pleasure tending to my garden and watching the birds while learning their patterns. Maybe this time off was doing me good. I raised the dropper to my mouth and dosed two drops, not three like last night. I didn't want to go into some sort of crazy trance while Scott was here.

"Coffee smells great!" Scott had opened my front door and was peering into my kitchen.

I hugged him and delivered a European kiss, one on each cheek.

"Nice greeting. Thanks!" He was in a jolly mood, happy to "play" in my herb garden as stated the night before.

"White or black?" I asked, meaning with or without cream in his coffee.

"Black as the night sky," he quipped.

I emptied the espresso pot of dark roast into a large mug and handed it to him. Holding it between his hands, he raised the cup to his nose and inhaled deeply.

"Ahhh. Someone who knows how to make coffee."

The compliment stunned me, but I graciously accepted it as I poured my own cup, white.

Scott smiled at me as he sipped and said, "I've come to enlighten you about how to harvest the seeds from your new plants. I think you'll enjoy this next step in your herbal adventure."

Harvesting seeds. I hadn't thought about using what I already had. I usually just bought new seeds every year. Sometimes they sprouted and sometimes they didn't.

"You'll have much more control over the quality of your herbs and produce if you know where they originated from," he said convincingly.

This made total sense and Scott's passion was

contagious. He explained the process while we sat at the counter and savored our coffee.

"Ready, Persephone?" he asked.

I sat up straight and a chill ran down my spine. Persephone, daughter of Demeter, the woman who persecuted me in my dreams. Persephone, the goddess of spring. Persephone, the Queen of the Underworld. He was just teasing but this name hit too close to home.

"I dreamed of Demeter last night," I said quietly. As I retold my dream, his eyes moved toward mine and widened.

"How did you know it was the Temple of Demeter?" he questioned.

"I intuitively knew. It wasn't on the tour two years ago, so I've never seen it in person. Maybe from the research photos we've collected? Is Demeter's temple one that you are building for the exhibit?"

"No, I am building the Concordia and the Temple of Heracles. I'm not sure I've ever seen a picture of Demeter's palace," he joked.

The dream interpretation was evaporating so I switched subjects. "I'm ready, Heracles," I joked back.

He chuckled. "Touché!"

My meager garden continually transformed with Scott's guidance and with my renewed energy toward it. The blue vervain flowers made pretty bouquets as well as tinctures and teas. I was a sponge, soaking up all Scott would teach me. In me, he discovered a kindred spirit, someone who appreciated nurturing nature as much as he did. Our passions were growing together just like our gardens. This realization hit me just as he bent over to kiss me, a simple brush on the lips. I quivered.

"Let's show this vervain some love," he smiled. "I like to focus an intention for the seeds and the plants I am working with. Do you have one in mind before we start?"

I liked this spiritual side of him. My intention: to use the power and courage of the vervain to guide me through this demanding phase of my life. It couldn't hurt to try it. Scott nodded his head as we began. The seed harvest technique was simple enough. Gather the spent flowers and lay them out on a piece of parchment paper in a single layer. Give them a day to dry before gently shaking them to release their tiny black seeds. Store the seeds in a paper bag in a cool, dry place. I could do the same thing with basil, cilantro, chives, or anything with a flower that went to seed. I'd make room on a shelf in my garage for my new collection.

Scott pulled out a small bag from his pocket, labeled French Oak lettuce, my favorite.

"A gift to add to your flock."

How he harvested seeds from lettuce leaves was a mystery but I was sure that would be a future lesson.

"Let me show you my vervain tincture," I said, leading him back into the kitchen where it gained potency in a cupboard that it shared with chicken broth.

I lifted out the dark bottle and held it like a vintage bottle of wine.

"Where's the label?" he scoffed.

"I only have one tincture," I defended.

"You could design a label with your trademark on it," he suggested.

I hadn't thought of that, and the vision triggered a collage of ideas. Of course, extend the art one step further. Scott was never at a loss for anything creative. He must have had ten lives to learn all this stuff. Could he be the savant of my dreams that I thought didn't exist? The one I had only read about in fairy tales?

Scott and I puttered in the yard, plucking the random

weed and cutting stalks of lavender that had grown wild to bundle up and dry in my garage. If only every day could be like this. We brushed shoulders, bumping into each other on purpose, in a teasing sort of way. His lingering gave me the impression he wanted to stay and help me give my garden even more attention.

"Where did you learn your gardening skills? Has this always been a passion with you?" I asked, hoping to unlock his past.

He shrugged his shoulders. "I guess so. My grandfather always had a garden. I think it was his way of having his own hobby, a way to spend time alone when the mundane part of marriage got to him. A way to let out his frustrations. Not that my grandmother wasn't a great woman—she was—but their way of communicating was based more on silence.

"I'd hang out with him on weekends and lug the heavy bags of compost or dig the holes for future trees. He was my mentor, showing me how to space the seedlings and when to harvest at each vegetable's peak. I never asked him how he knew what to do. It was mostly instinctual as far as I could tell. It wasn't like he was reading volumes of books on gardening like we do today. I admired his style and I think he was keen on having the company. We rarely discussed anything personal. Our conversations consisted of 'Hand me the pruning shears' to moments of quiet, watching the birds gather at their feeder. There was always a project for me. He sure crammed a lot into a small space." He laughed.

I watched Scott as his expression became somber. "I saw how much pleasure his garden gave him, and I guess that transferred to me. As he grew older, I made it a point to help out as much as possible so he could still enjoy his get-away space. When he died, my grandmother sold the house and moved into an apartment. I often think of my grandfather when I have a decision to make, hoping in my own way his spirit is guiding me. He was like my best friend."

I could feel the sadness in Scott's voice as he looked to the sky, almost waiting for a sign as he held back tears.

"You took the lessons from your grandfather and built a beautiful home for your plants and trees. I'm sure a part of him is there, getting a kick out of watching you imitate him and proud that you want to carry on his tradition," I said, loving his sentimentality.

To share this story with me on such a deep, emotional level brought forth my own memories, those I chose to push aside.

6

A RETURN TO THE PAST

A week had passed, and Stephen still hadn't contacted me. My time off had been a lesson in letting go, but a bigger part of me was anxious to go back to work. This idyllic life of putzing in the garden couldn't go on forever. I wasn't scared of the outcome, just wanted to know, get it over with, especially if it was bad.

The Forza's bitter taste had lessened, and I was growing to like the flavor. Scott had said it was a mixture of herbs. It was impossible to identify them from the taste so I decided to see if my nostrils could detect a specific herb. I had a hunch vervain was in there. He was so adamant about me planting it. What else? A hint of sweetness. Lavender? Basil? If I knew all the ingredients, I could look up what other attributes they possessed. Yesterday Scott wanted me to make an intention for the seeds after harvesting them. Did he give this tincture an intention for me when he blended it? So many things swirled in my mind. The whole business of enhancing my gardening skills had grown into another level—that of power. It is what I asked Scott for shortly after the conversation with Stephen about the missing Demeter. Scott seemed casual enough about it, but in reality he was taking my request seriously. It was almost scary. Was he a sorcerer of some kind? Did he derive pleasure in assisting in other people's lives? Was it all for the better, or could it sometimes be for the worse? I had to quit prognosticating and look at Scott for what he was. A kind-hearted man who was a great listener and truly cared for my well-being. And, from the tingles that rippled through my body when he was near, I knew I was falling in love with him.

Blue coated the sky and the outdoors called. I sat on the patio in the wrought iron chair that matched the small circular wrought iron table decorated with a mosaic I had designed. A single dove tile placed in the middle drew your focus, while the surrounding tiles represented the kaleidoscope of colors of my garden. The table and chair came from an estate sale of my neighbor, and I redid the damaged top to reflect my love of the ancient tilework of fifteenth-century Italy, Spain, and Portugal. I would mosaic the walls of my house if I could, I loved it that much.

The hot coffee burned my tongue due to my daydreams. I opened my notebook to begin brainstorming ideas for future employment and let the warming sunshine relax my mind. I heard a flutter of a white dove who perched in the nearby maple tree where I could watch her. At first it was their cooing voices that made me fall in love with doves, then came the way they sashayed across my yard, like a waltz. They were a social bunch, gathering to feed. Once I counted fifteen of them beneath the roses. Every now and again, they'd peck at each other in a playful way. I wondered if doves mated for life, and if they did, who did this white dove belong to?

The wind shifted and the clouds rolled in, so typical of Northern Californian weather. I retreated inside to make a cup of mint tea and curled up in my white kaftan. It made me feel like a Greek goddess, one of the nicer ones who didn't chase me. I wanted to call Scott, but my eyes grew heavy and I surrendered, drifting off into a deep nap. My dreams came in rolling waves. First, I was the white dove, searching for my mate. The other doves were cooing but their voices formed words: "Deliver the gifts." Again, this message! I hadn't heard it in months but now it was back in my dream. I flew up into the sky and finally saw my mate. As I swooped down to be with him, he vanished. I had landed at the Temple of Demeter, again. Next, Scott was there, somewhere, telling me to take another potion, that I would need it. He sounded urgent. I began crying because I couldn't find my way home. I kept trying to wake up, but the sleep was so deep, I couldn't. When I finally forced my eyes open and got my bearings, I was trembling.

These themed dreams were beginning to unsettle me. I couldn't help but read something into them. Were my dreams giving me clues as to who the real thief at the museum was? That was it! I was calling Stephen first thing in the morning to demand a meeting with him. This nonsense had to stop. It was disrupting my life to the point I was now taking tinctures to control my anxiety. I felt like a drug addict and was ready to detoxify my relationship with Stephen. Next on my list was a phone call to Scott to find out what exactly was in the "potion" I was taking daily. I hoped he wouldn't say it was a secret because if he did, I was afraid I'd blow a gasket and let loose my Scorpio stinger. This isn't always pretty.

"Hello, Scott?" I asked, knowing full well it was Scott.

"Hello, Alexis! How are you this now gloomy Sunday afternoon?" he said cheerily.

He seemed happy about something.

"Scott, I need to know what herbs are in the Forza

tincture you made me. I'm having crazy, wild dreams and that is the only thing I can think of that would be causing them. Please tell me," I begged.

"Let me recall." He paused. "I know there were five herbs: vervain, lavender, clary—"

I heard a door slam, then a woman's foreign accent say, "Ciao, darling! I've missed you!"

There was a pause in our conversation as Scott reciprocated her greeting. I just sat on the other end of the phone, stunned. I thought Scott was a loner, like me, but obviously not. Perhaps he had a secret lover or girlfriend or what? After what seemed ages, he finally returned to the phone.

"So sorry. Can I call you later?" he asked.

No explanation, just a request to move my question into the future. I needed answers now, but it was no use. I'd be my normal pitiful self and acquiesce to his wishes. I hung up feeling dejected.

That night, I made beet soup, again from Scott's garden stash, and garnished it with feta cheese. When I couldn't be outside in my yard, I was usually cooking in my kitchen, both ways to banish my anxieties. The woman at Scott's house added yet another dimension to this mystery man. I respected his privacy, and our relationship was platonic, even though I dreamed of waking up with him and having coffee together in bed. He kissed me yesterday, which is usually a good sign that someone likes you, right? We never discussed past relationships, so I didn't know what other women he associated with. He was, after all, twelve years older than me so he'd had more time to collect female companions. Scott did have that alluring quality of hard to crack coupled with hard to resist. He knew how to use it too.

After dinner, I poured myself a glass of Chianti, turned

on the BBC, and succumbed to the waiting game. Wait for Scott to call and wait for Stephen to make up his mind. My life was a game to them both and I was caught in the middle. The program on TV, *Museum Secrets*, always intrigued me. I loved seeing what other museums were hiding underground and in one show, how cats were brought in to eat an infection of mice that were chewing into the boxes of preserved relics.

The phone rang and Scott's name appeared on the screen. I was so engrossed in the show, I decided to neglect it and talk to him tomorrow. At least he was acknowledging my concern. Now he was the one who would have to wait for me and wonder why I didn't pick up the phone. His message went to voicemail.

I went to bed and tried to sleep but insomnia took over. Maybe it was the nap that kidnapped me earlier and my body wasn't ready to rest yet. Almost half-heartedly, I decided to listen to Scott's message.

In a low and encouraging voice he said, "I'm sorry for the interruption, Alexis. I can explain about the tincture tomorrow. I think if you take four drops of the Forza tonight it will counteract your disturbing dreams. You can't overdose on it. I've taken five drops of a similar combination and felt more clarity and focus. I think you are worrying too much about where your life is headed. It's time for you to embrace your power and trust where you are." He was right.

I reluctantly opened the kitchen cupboard and took down the Forza bottle. Four bitter dropperfuls it would be, maybe for the last time if I had weird dreams again. The words "embrace your power" echoed in my head. This might be the intention he alluded to when he showed me how to harvest seeds. I repeated the words out loud, trying hard to believe in them.

A rustle in the backyard shook me back to reality so I grabbed a flashlight to investigate. Critters frequently visited me at night and spotting them was a game we played. One night a large raccoon looked up at me from the deep hole he was digging for grubs. Another night, a frightened baby opossum peered down at me from the top of the fence as if to say, "Save me, I'm scared." I felt sorry for him, but this was nature, and I didn't dare interfere. Tonight would be no different as I rotated the light along the back wall and up the pathway. Not a thing. They must have heard me coming and crawled under the fence to wait until the coast was clear again. A dove cooed in the distance, and all fell quiet. The clouds had cleared, revealing a night sky brilliant with stars.

I took a seat on my meditation rock. When I bought the house three years ago, a large granite rock sat smack dab in the middle of my yard, a sage bush huddled up next to it. I tried to move it to a more appropriate place, but it wouldn't budge. Coalescing, I made friends with them both and used the rock for my quiet place, to think, write, and meditate.

The rock's smooth surface felt cool against my body. I reached for a sage branch and lifted it to my nostrils, taking in a deep breath. For once this week, my mind settled. A full moon centered the sky, throwing shadows across my trees; it must have been around midnight.

I let my eyes close, feeling the rays of the moon bath on my face, and visualized a garden of intermingling plants and trees, all living in harmony, and me in the center of it all, like a princess in a Disney fantasy. It was as if a magnetic force drew me deeper and deeper into a trance, and all I could hear was the sound of my breath which had slowed to a faint heartbeat. I must have sat there for five minutes or more, feeling a sense of peace wash over me.

Euphoric is the best way to describe it as an energy slowly wrapped itself around me and then picked up the pace and spun like it was weaving me into a cocoon. This energy then lifted me off the ground and whispered, "Deliver the gifts."

What happened next would change me and my life forever.

PART TWO

7

MY ARRIVAL

Girgento, Sicily 440 BC

I opened my eyes to face a dripping limestone wall. A cool nighttime breeze swept past my body, leaving me littered with goosebumps. "Eek!" I cried as a snake slithered between my feet, headed for a crevice in the wall. I stood motionless, unable to move, the snake adding to my fright.

"This isn't funny, Demeter. Let me wake up now, please," I said in a quaky voice as I began to hyperventilate.

Was the potion causing this vivid dream? It seemed too real. A wave of nausea came over me and I bent over to throw up last night's dinner. I steadied myself, took a deep breath, and forcibly shook my head as if doing this would reverse my circumstances. With trembling hands, I hugged the side of the cave as I crept toward its entrance.

"Ouch!" My bare toes struck something hard and sharp. Looking down I could tell it wasn't just a rock but some kind of sculpture. With shaky hands, I bent down to pick it up, its weight heavier than it looked. I held it up to a sliver of light at the cave's entrance and viewed what looked like a terra-cotta head of a goddess, similar to the one I had unpacked at the museum.

"No, no … this isn't happening," I whimpered as the sculpture slid out of my hands and crashed to the floor.

I had to get out of here and fast. Find my way home. Carefully I slid down the side of the cavern, navigated my way around a pile of pottery shards, and attempted to get my bearings. I turned around and realized this was part of a larger structure, maybe a temple? Why did I take Scott's advice and take the extra drop of Forza? This was all his fault! Maybe I was hallucinating from an overdose and could walk it off. Then everything would be back to normal.

"Where am I?" I croaked, with no one to hear me.

As if in response to my question, a golden glow of a figurehead descended from the skies and then evaporated as quickly as it came. Squinting hard to decipher this image caused my vision to blur, and my knees went weak as I collapsed onto the hard earth. A sense of foreboding and overwhelming dread swept through my body, and I curled up in a ball, trying to make myself invisible.

"Whoever you are, go away! I'm tired of this game," my mind commanded. My depleted and weak body lay immobilized, unable to grasp my situation. It took every ounce of energy I could muster to stand up and face the moonlit darkness. I had to find a way out of here. A well-worn pathway to my right beckoned so I followed it, treading lightly, afraid of disturbing whoever or whatever else might be here. Prickly pear cactus, tall, billowy lavender, and cypress trees lined the way. I didn't know where I was going but trusted this path would eventually lead to my ride home from this dream. The tincture was playing with my mind, and I was having an expanded consciousness experience—I hoped.

Something tickled my nose and I reacted to an infusion

of damp air with a forceful sneeze. I jumped aside and stood still, wondering if someone had heard me. Catching my breath, I put one foot in front of the other and edged toward the noise of water running over rocks. A narrow river lay about twenty-five feet away. My instinct told me to follow the water flow to see where it would lead. I'd lost track of time and sat down on a flat rock, plunging my feet into the cool water hoping the chill would somehow wake me up. Instead, it did the opposite and a wave of dizziness fell over me. Paranoia set in and I began questioning myself and my previous desires. Yes, I had wished to live in a different time, but now I wasn't so sure; if, in fact, that was where I was. My eyes became heavy like I'd been drugged. I was exhausted, mentally and physically. I curled up in my white dress, nestled under a tree's protective branches, and fell into a deep sleep, wanting to awaken in my own cozy bed, in my sweet and safe cottage home, snuggling with my best friend Lucas. As I slept, my dreams were not of my old life but of the life to come. The message I'd heard back in San Francisco kept whispering in my ear, "Deliver the gifts." It was like a broken record, one of those obnoxious dreams where you just want it to stop so you can wake up, but you can't. Then someone was chasing me, and I tried to scream for help but no words came out. I woke up sobbing, confused, and not ready to tackle this challenge

"Get with it!" I scolded myself as I stood up and stretched to clear my mind.

The sun's pre-dawn light gave way to streaks of orange and gray-black clouds as daybreak approached. I had no choice but to explore my surroundings. Bravely, I navigated my way around a grove of dwarf palm trees to an opening. Before me lay a sparkling stretch of white sand beach, hugging a turquoise sea, for as far as I could see. I gasped, my breath leaving my body like a wave breaking the shore. A warm breeze swept over me, drying the sweat my anxiety had created. Wait! What was that in the distance? A ship with a large square sail skimmed along the water in a broad reach, about a quarter mile in front of me. I'd seen pictures of these ancient sailing vessels but this one was here in real life. Where was I? Panic and reality set in at the same time as I froze in the moment, trying to make sense of it all. My instincts told me I was somewhere in the Mediterranean. Amidst all this beauty in a near-pristine land, I was not yet ready to accept my new reality.

The silence broke as a tormented scream pierced my ears. I turned to face the panicked noise to see a pixie-like figure with yellow-blond curls, wearing a light-brown robe that was tied at the waist with a gold knotted belt. When she saw me she furrowed her eyebrows, looking for signs of recognition, and cautiously approached.

"It's not safe here," she whispered in a language that wasn't English, but somehow I understood what she was saying. As I gazed into her steely gray eyes, I saw fear beneath her extreme beauty. Her creamy porcelain face had understated features: small narrow nose, round chin, thin heart-shaped lips. A real live goddess in human form.

Without blinking an eye, my new language flowed. "What are you afraid of?" I quietly asked.

"The women from Carthage. They are trying to steal my stones and crystals to eliminate my power," she whispered. "I caught them in the temple and I'm sure they took some of my sacrificial agates. The gods will be furious!"

So, this woman was an oracle. She further explained that there were rogue tribes of women, kind of like gypsies, who stirred up trouble. Most of the community members weren't afraid of them, but trying to steal another person's power and connection with the gods was, in her book, a high crime.

"Can you make me a potion to keep them away and protect me," she asked.

Why was she asking me this question, and when did I become bilingual in a foreign language I couldn't even identify?

I looked to the heavens as if expecting them to answer me, but all I saw was a flock of seabirds crossing the sky. This world felt so vacant and new; a refreshing change from where I'd just come from with tall skyscrapers and crowded neighborhoods with little or no privacy. Here it felt so calm, and without all the distractions I could think more clearly. My mind flashed back to my conversations with Scott about herbs and how to extract just the right amount of potency necessary for the tincture. Sometimes he said to only let the herbs "marinate" for an hour, sometimes it was for days. But for what she wanted, how would I know? I'd recently perused a book on herbs, now fascinated by their powers, and came across a few that intrigued me. Roots were used for protection, power, and divination. The perfect trio might be vervain, lavender, and Angelica root. I could try it. Now, to find the ingredients. I had just arrived, was desperate to leave, yet at this moment, contemplating making an herbal tincture—or was it a potion?—for this woman who I didn't even know. This was so typical of me. A bit scattered and indecisive, qualities in my life I was working on in therapy. How did it come that I was now the therapist?

I snapped back into this new present, grasped the woman's hand, and asked her name.

"Iris," she replied with confidence.

"My name is Alexis," I countered.

Iris had a charismatic quality about her, but I couldn't put my finger on it. She confirmed that she was an oracle from Girgento, and to her I must have seemed to already be a part of this society. Girgento—could this be the Agrigento our museum was attempting to duplicate with the recent shipment of artifacts? If so, the language could be Greek. It depended upon what year I was experiencing this adventure. How could I ask Iris without seeming crazy? A visit to Girgento would give me clues.

"Would you take me there—to Girgento?" I asked.

"I will come back later to get you," Iris responded.

But why later?

"Bring me the potion by the full moon," she cried as she fled off up the berm and back to wherever she had appeared from. I was alone again and sat down to contemplate my situation.

Iris thought I was one of them. What I feared most was entering Girgento and being cast away as a stranger or traitor, maybe even a spy. I was wearing the long white kaftan my friend Robyn had given me. A gift from the farmers' market. I had loved it because it looked so Greek! Sleeves just past my elbows, a small V slit at the neckline, a border of olive branches at the hem and across the bodice, musty green herbs, and muted red flowers. The thin white fabric had two side pockets and the kaftan-style dress fit loosely enough to be comfortable. The perfect "costume" to be wearing when time traveling to what I now deduced was ancient Sicily. Would this be my new outfit for Girgento? I reminisced and thought of my beautiful friend Robyn, who had always been there for me, through thick and thin. Always with the perfect little gift or remembrance. I missed her. How would she respond to this situation? She was brave. I assumed she would go forth with an attitude of exploration and curiosity. She was no wimp.

Back to the root herbs. Where could I find them? Did I promise more than I could deliver? I held that thought, took a deep breath, and strategized my next move. I was sent here for a reason. Maybe they needed my help. If I could tap into my knowledge from the future, could I somehow make a difference in this society? I had always tried to be a bridge for people to connect, to share their gifts with others. I knew this was my strength. I would discover the reason, whatever it was; I was sure of that. Somebody, maybe Demeter, wanted me here. Did I really travel back in time? Perhaps to serve a purpose? Still, unnerved, and scared—who wouldn't be?—I decided to go forth to see what the day would manifest. This was a true lesson or test of living in the present.

I mentally prepared myself for this challenge, finally decisive and accepting this new life as an opportunity to learn and grow. What else could I do? And if I was stuck here the rest of my life? I guessed it would be left to the gods to decide.

As I stood there with the sun scorching my neck, a figure appeared in the distance and strode toward me with confidence. I was expected. Relief poured over me and I started breathing again.

"Alexis!" he called. I nodded hesitantly in agreement, still uncertain of my association with this stranger.

The first thing I noticed about him was a gap between his crooked teeth as he announced, "I am Mikolos."

My gaze traveled up to his black eyes framed by long, dark lashes. He looked no more than twenty-five, his thick black locks reminding me of an ancient Greek god. He stood about five feet, four inches tall, and though not large in stature, his commanding presence drew me in. I already felt like we were old friends. His tanned hand grasped mine ceremoniously.

"Welcome to Girgento. Iris sent me to show you the way. Jory is waiting for you."

Somehow, they knew about me. My focus was narrowing. I tried to second-guess my mission here but had to let it go. I hoped Mikolos's warm and friendly welcome was an omen for my introduction to Girgento. My loneliness subsided—momentarily. Had I known what my new role would entail, including torture and treason, I may have looked for the next boat sailing to Sparta.

"Alexis," Mikolos said gravely, "we are in desperate need of your help. With our rising population, our polis needs to produce more food. The excessive heat attracted beetle-like insects looking for water. They infested our garden plants and ate half of this year's crop, including the fruit on the trees. Even the water from our aqueduct did not help to restore them. The insects have left but Jory is old and can't manage the restoration by himself. The Counselors in Siracusa told us of your abilities to propagate seeds in shorter amounts of time. They said another experienced gardener was arriving from Athens to work their own gardens in Siracusa, and that for us all to remain united, you were willing to come live here to help us once again prosper."

My jaw dropped as I listened intently. I did not come from Siracusa, I came from San Francisco. They must have gotten me mixed up with someone else. But my name matched the person they were looking for. It had to be a coincidence. Did I dare deny my capabilities as a master of seed propagation? I had some experience but not to the extent of restoring food for an entire society, or polis as Mikolos called it. I had no choice but to go along with this charade. Fate or Demeter or whoever had delivered me here for a reason.

We walked quickly together, going back in the direction of the grotto although on a well-worn pathway, not along the river as I had traveled earlier this morning. In my delusion, I must have somehow bypassed the city in the quiet of the early morning hours. Glancing ahead, I could see civilization, the city awakening with the sound of carts dragging heavy stone, pounding hammers, the subdued chatter of workers.

For some reason, my fear was evaporating, maybe because I thought this would be temporary and I would soon be transported back to the life I was born into. But this is the time I had dreamed of reliving, after learning about the artifacts brought from Sicily for the museum exhibit. From my studies, I knew that Girgento flourished from 520–406 BC and then was practically destroyed by the Carthaginians. I was always disturbed to learn that such a beautiful, prosperous society could be pillaged to ruins, leaving only a few clues to her existence.

Mikolos uttered only a handful of indecipherable words during the rest of our journey, pointing here and there and waving to people he knew. He seemed friendly enough, but who was this Jory person he insisted I meet? We arrived at a vast expanse of open areas, interspersed with towering, emerging temples that seemed so out of proportion for the small inhabitants, many much shorter than myself. I stood at five feet six and most of the other women who passed by were maybe five feet two at the most. The men, thank goodness, were taller than me, I'd estimate around five feet nine, much shorter than the taller men I was accustomed to being around back in San Francisco. San Francisco. It seemed like another lifetime. Maybe it was.

We passed builders hefting heavy stones up ladders, and a man standing on a box pontificating philosophy with a small gathering of engaged followers. Swirls of parchment-colored dust hung in the air and triggered a series of sneezes, my nose not yet accustomed to this new kind of pollution. I had a hard time keeping up with Mikolos's pace, the rubble biting at my feet reminding me that I was barefoot. I almost felt like an actor on a film set. It was all so surreal. But it was real.

We continued our trek past the temples, all in various stages of completion, into what looked like a vibrant farmers' market with scattered booths to showcase the merchants' wares.

Scents of roasting pork and frying onion filled my nostrils and reminded me of my hunger.

"The agora," stated Mikolos.

The curiosity in me wanted to stop and people-watch to absorb the makings of this society I was about to join, but Mikolos was on a mission and herded me through until the crowds thinned out. At a brisk pace, we made a sharp right at a temple, then descended a few stairs carved out of sandstone. Turning again, more stairs and a pathway lined with cactus and wild asparagus ferns led to a final descent into what I can only describe as paradise.

In front of us a deep valley appeared, lined by rugged cliffs on either side, some of which had small caves carved into them. In an attempt to orient myself, I mentally tried to remember the cave I'd climbed out of during the night before embarking on my river expedition.

"Where are we?" I asked Mikolos, who hadn't said a word since pointing out the agora.

He seemed not to hear me and instead of responding, shouted out, "Jory, Alexis is here."

I still could not figure out how they knew my name. Behind a fig tree, a small man, almost gnomish, short and pudgy, stood up from a squat. Thick wrinkles barely made room for deep eye sockets holding dark, warm eyes. As he walked toward us, I noticed a scar on his left cheek and a missing eyebrow. He reached out to shake my hand but I could barely grasp it, his stubby fingers curled so far inward.

In a steady voice, he said, "Welcome to Kolymbethra. I wait for you since last full moon."

I swallowed hard at this information, trying to recollect my whereabouts on the last full moon cycle but it was impossible. This was all so new, and I was disoriented, like having jet lag. Kolymbethra was the ancient garden I was denied visiting because of time constraints on my travels here two years ago, in 2015. I didn't even know what year it was but here I was some two and a half thousand years in the past, talking to a man with obvious deformities and who expected me a month ago.

Mikolos turned to me and said, "Jory will get you settled and show you your room. If you need me, you can find me at the Concordia."

Suddenly I became skeptical. I hoped I wasn't being brought here as Jory's slave! With that, Mikolos was gone, and I was left alone with my partnered gardener.

In a calm tone, Jory addressed me in mutters. "Your skills good. Must get to work immediately. Garden challenging but Girgenti accepting and kind. I show you where to work. Follow me."

On a reassuring note, Jory seemed nice enough, even though his speech pattern needed piecing together. For now, I would not be his slave and would go with the flow until I figured out how to get home, back to Scott, the museum, my own garden.

Behind a grove of trees sat Jory's, or for the present time, our workshop, simple enough. Small ornaments decorated the frame around the door. Some were goddesses, others tiny animals and birds made of wood and stone. I wondered if these were some sort of protective idols, or maybe just his way of thanking Mother Nature. Inside the cramped space, a tiny table wedged itself against a wall, a wooden stool pushed underneath. Oddly enough, carved horse hooves acted as feet and were secured to the table with bronze pins. Black and red clay amphora and vases painted with flowers and leaves lined a shelf above the table. Tools used for gardening—a spade, a shovel, and some clippers—took their place near the door. On the far wall, a window with no glass, but instead wooden shutters, let in a cool breeze. The dirt floor solidified the gardening shed motif.

"What is in the amphora?" I asked, suspecting tinctures of some kind or perhaps seeds.

"Seeds for planting during first quarter moon. Barley Moon."

Did he think I knew about gardening by the moon cycles and even what kind of seeds were in the vases? Jory was not the most talkative person but now the words spilled out of his mouth in almost complete sentences.

"You have good reputation from the Siracusans. After accident, I no longer able to perform rigorous duties job requires. For gardens to heal, we work steady for a solid moon cycle. We divide duties and you make the seeds grow into beautiful food and herbs. I guide you in the principles of gardening at Kolymbethra, which are different from Siracusa's climate."

Jory stopped momentarily to take a breath. "It is our job to protect this sacred oasis, vital to keep Girgento alive and to provide food for people. I take pride in every aspect of her life and guard it with my soul. You will see the many treasures that abound, and fall in love with her too."

No words could come out of my mouth. It was obvious

that Jory loved his place in society, and this accident, whatever that was, had certainly curtailed his duties. I had some big shoes to fill and suddenly became uncertain of my abilities to live up to his expectations. Scott had taught me a lot, but really it was just the equivalent of a beginner course. Maybe I could fake it until I knew the ropes. My reputation was on the line. What would happen if I failed? Would they kill me? Send me back? I knew only one thing —the pressure was on.

"Previous caretakers of the garden built small houses for living space. They are only rooms but have windows and provide safe place for sleep. I show you their locations," Jory said.

I followed him out the door and down another pathway that veered left through a grove of fruit trees. A few simple wood and mud-brick huts butted up against the valley wall. I guessed these were the dwellings he had talked about.

"My home is first one here," he said. "You can stay in either of other two."

Not wanting to sleep so close to Jory and because three has always been my lucky number, I choose the third hut down. A stuffed cloth bed and a firepit were the only creature comforts inside the approximately twelve-by-twelve room. It seemed so bare and impersonal compared to what my eclectic Euro bedroom looked like back home. The pictures that hung on my Oakland wall reflected my deep love of travel: a view from the Musée d'Orsay, an old print of the Piazza San Marco in Venice, the Tower Guinigi in Lucca, Italy, a flock of sheep on a ranch in Australia, a rocky beach in southern Spain. This room now epitomized the escape from reality I had wished for—although maybe not to this extent—in a time so long ago, mostly ignored by history books. I still couldn't figure out what mysterious element had sent me here, to be a gardener of all things. At least I had my own room, for the time being, and would make the best of it.

Jory interrupted my thoughts with "Time to eat."

My stomach must have given him clues, growling every five minutes. We returned to his home, and I sat on a little chair next to a well-worn wood table, while he scooped a soft mixture, much like oatmeal, into a pot and placed it on a tripod stand over the firepit. Jory then grabbed a stick, stuck it into one of the olive-oil lamps to get a flame, and placed it under the pot on a mound of dried twigs and leaves to ignite them. Poof, instant heat. He picked up a spoon that rested on the side of the pit and carefully stirred the porridge to warm it up. I noticed a variety of vessels on a shelf that looked exactly like the recovered artifacts sitting at the museum awaiting public display. A hydria vase: wide belly with narrow neck and base and three handles, used to collect, carry, and pour water; an amphora with reduced curves, a narrow neck and bottom, for wine; and a taller amphora, for the storage of grain. All decorated beautifully in black, with etchings depicting Greek life and myths.

I watched Jory's every move as he poured wine from the amphora into a kalix or shallow cup with two handles, and then added water from the hydria. He repeated this motion again with a second kalix for himself. Some societies at this time did not allow women to drink wine. I was grateful that Girgento was not one of them. Jory nodded to the cup and then up to me in a gesture to take it. The diluted wine, stored here in a cool environment, tasted refreshing. Not wanting to drink the entire cup as my thirst was requesting, I sipped slowly as Jory ladled the porridge into two clay bowls painted with depictions of dogs and pigs. He raised the cup to his lips and drank the thick liquid, slurping it so as not to burn his tongue. I followed suit. The gruel's thick texture resembled a chewy, watery risotto and the only taste was from the salt. We ate in silence, Jory surely worn out from our previous conversation. One thing was for sure, with just a brief glance of the garden, I knew I could do better in the cooking arena. Add a few green leaves to the porridge, as in some fresh herbs. We'd be eating gourmet meals in no time. It could be that he was allowed only a certain amount of food for himself, and the rest went to the rulers and community. I'd find out soon enough but would tread lightly on any suggestions until I gained Jory's trust.

The day seemed to last forever. So much had happened in such a short amount of time. I arrived in a cave and met Iris, an oracle. A man named Mikolos was expecting me and guided us to the thriving community of Girgento. I got my first glimpse of the city, although brief, and a walk-through of the agora before descending into an oasis where I would work side by side with Jory, who had somehow managed to be disabled and desperately needed my help with the garden. A giant garden, more like a farm. Fatigue was rapidly setting in.

Thankfully, Jory excused me after our meal, and I retreated to my new sparse lodging. A thin linen, stuffed with bits of wool and leaves, served as the bed. I pushed my hand down on the mattress to check its firmness and it sprang back lightly, demonstrating its comfort. Another wrinkled but soft linen sheet lay on top, something to crawl into when it cooled off. I opened the shutters to listen to the sounds of the tree leaves touching each other and to the birds chirping their evening song. There was no sleep valerian and no Forza tincture. Tonight, I was glad for that. It felt strange sleeping with no pillow, although I knew that cloth pillows were for the wealthy and the common citizen slept with a stone pillow. I had not yet earned the status of either but would work toward obtaining one, perhaps with a trade from a cloth-maker. With that, I fell into a deep and restful sleep, probably the best rest I'd had in years. There were no dreams of Demeter, no one was chasing me, and no Scott forcing a potion upon me.

I awoke at dawn, to a noise outside my door, disoriented and wondering where I was. Holding my breath as to not make a sound, I listened for signs of identification. Footsteps shuffled past and then disappeared. Jory was up early, I presumed, beginning his day in Kolymbethra. I rose, straightening the only garment I owned, brushed my long, wavy curls out of my face with my fingers, and opened my door. Vibrant pinks and purples streaked across the sky, announcing the new day. For some reason, I felt exhilarated and excited to experience this ancient history, something I'd dreamed of in passing. It was more of a wish when things didn't go as planned, a wanting to exit one life to enter another, thinking it could only be better than the one I had. I breathed in the morning air and summoned all my courage, knowing I would need it.

8

KOLYMBETHRA

Kolymbethra was often referred to as the Garden of Eden, and now I knew why. Tucked into a valley below the city of temples, this oasis delivered every possible ingredient you could need; a chef's dream. Fig, miniature pear, pomegranate, almond, and pistachio trees, to name a few, lined walkways, their weak and diluted fruit dripping from their branches. Deeper into the valley, artichokes grew wild, wedged into the cliffside, alongside untamed herbs such as mint, thyme, sage, and oregano. Capers hung, like deliberate decorations, on every possible towering rock. Garden beds fed by a streaming water source contained remnants of cucumbers, fava beans, lettuces, zucchini, onions, and peppers—ingredients known to me as Mediterranean and regarded as "healthy" to my culture of the future. The expansive gardens would need dedication to reseed and then bring them back to life to provide enough food for everyone. I could see that almost everything imaginable grew in this paradise landscape and, until recently, was unencumbered by pests, except the average critter that gratefully gnawed upon their roots and leaves.

On the far end of the garden, an artificial lake, the size

of a small neighborhood, was filled with freshwater fish for citizens to net at will; swans and birds floated on its surface, looking like a whimsical fairytale. It evoked memories of a lake in Albany my dad and I frequented to feed the ducks when I was a child. At first, I couldn't understand the value of a man-made lake because the ocean lay so close and abundant with a natural supply of seafood. It soon became clear that the sea creatures such as tuna and octopus carried high price tags accessible to those who could pay, mostly men of importance. The commoners relied upon this source of freshwater fish, which also held a hatchery, and treated it as a sort of benefit for society members. All were free to fish, swim, and enjoy the body of water fed from the nearby aqueduct.

I decided to revisit the entrance of Kolymbethra and walk the perimeter, something I hadn't yet done because my introduction yesterday was broken down into segments of necessity. I walked up the switchback with uneven stone stairs, to the polis, their Greek name for the city center, and then back down, as if entering the garden for the first time. Déjà vu struck me like a slap on the face. Scott's garden looked almost exactly like this. The trees lining the pathway, the emerging vegetable gardens, the herbs at the back. Scott did not have a pool of fish in his yard, thank God, so that part of the piece was missing, but the footprint was so similar. Scott had said that he had never been to Sicily or to Kolymbethra. How could his garden be modeled after this one? I retraced my memory of his backyard and yes, there were so many commonalities. It was eerie. What was it he said to me the one day he permitted me entrance into his mystery life? "My garden is a representation of me, who I am, where I've been, and where I'm going." But he said he had never been here. Had he looked at blueprints or was it just coincidence that his picture of nature matched this one? Now I was intrigued. This was a mystery that had to be solved. Perhaps I was the one to solve it. So many ideas raced through my mind, but Jory's voice brought me back to the present.

"Alexis! We get started."

My orientation to the workings of Kolymbethra was just at its infancy stage now, but what I was learning would serve me well as a curator—that is, if I ever returned to the twenty-first century.

Our tour began at the entrance to the aqueduct that fed the entire gardens and orchards. Jory turned me over to Galen, a man with dark blue eyes, taupe brown hair, and a thin build, unlike his other Greek counterparts. Galen knew the aqueducts inside and out, like a child who had a passion for Electra sets. As he led me through the tunnels, his energy rose, entertained by the engineering wonderment.

"The aqueducts were built and designed by the architect Phaeax, at the time of the Battle of Thermopylae in Greece," Galen said, "although the people from this island, the Sicani, actually began digging the earth well before then. A complex maze of underground tunnels twenty to thirty meters deep feeds spring water to the valley's gardens and lake, providing a constant source of hydration."

I was stunned at Galen's vocabulary and articulate speaking voice. It was as if he had given this tour many times before and memorized the words, but this was not something he did every day. I was seeing a much more sophisticated society than I could ever have imagined and hoped I could keep up.

"How long have you been maintaining the aqueducts, Galen?" I asked.

"I started working with my father when I was a child. He brought me here every day to help him check for leaks and to learn the mechanical intricacies. We have been able to divert water to where it is most needed depending on the lunar cycles. It is part engineering, part astronomy." I stood there, mouth open, craving more.

"It's essential to have fresh water for our citizens and this is one reason our polis continues to grow. We can grow food, bathe, and build houses and temples with an abundance of this natural resource, without bringing it in from long distances," he emphasized. "We are fortunate here in Girgento."

I asked if I could see the underbelly of this masterpiece which transformed an ordinary town into one that was becoming a destination and anchor for the entire island. Galen nodded and said he would show me the workings next week. The aqueducts were something I had read about but without being there, could not even remotely visually imagine. It was overwhelming and exhilarating at the same time. At this moment, I felt like I was on the set of a movie production and someone would yell, "Cut!" any minute.

Over a crest with a view of the wheat fields, we met up with Jory, who was unusually talkative today.

"Here is source of water." He pointed with arthritic fingers to where the channels had been dug and where the water led.

Jory drew his head down and talked to his feet in half words. "Controlled for different areas of gardens and fields," he continued. "We help with gardens, but slaves do cultivation and harvest of grain."

A large stretch of land reached across hundreds of acres dedicated to this valuable resource. The summer wheat had just been harvested and left the earth barren, ready to reseed. The Girgenti, I learned from Jory, harvested their grains once a year, in early summer. Several stone mills, turned by horses, ground the wheat into flour for breads and pastries. There it was again, the message from my dreams that I hadn't heard since arriving. "Deliver the gifts." My head throbbed as I gazed at the wheat, a surge of adrenaline attacking my body, like an electric shock. What was Demeter trying to tell me? It was obviously urgent.

Every day, I made my best effort to assimilate into my new society. I followed Jory around, mimicking his duties and eager to learn his ways. The vegetable gardens and fruit trees received our full attention as they were necessary to the food chain. Citizens of the community independently owned plots of land and they, along with slaves, tended to the grain fields. The wealthy possessed the lion's share of the fields but men from all walks of life had their own small lots to farm. Wheat and barley were trade commodities and helped even the poorest earn a meager living.

The garden's shade and cool breezes attracted an audience on warm, late spring days. Jory ignored them, his social skills practically nonexistent. Even though I was working, I secretly observed mannerisms to see how I could better fit in. The men talked loudly and laughed. The women said little or chatted among themselves in quiet voices. Back in San Francisco, I had read a book on Greek life that described women in Athens as sheltered, stay-at-home mothers who were not allowed to consume alcohol or interact with people outside of their homes. They were restricted from going to the agora and were rarely seen in public. The Spartan women, on the other hand, had the freedom to participate in agora activities, drink wine, and sell their wares publicly. Women's Lib was alive. The Girgenti Greeks, now Sicilians, must have come from the Sparta lineage as far as I could tell. I was welcomed as a woman gardeness, and was free to roam, something that would have been forbidden in Athens. I counted my blessings.

The visitors did not acknowledge me, but they did not gawk either. It was as if I were a part of them; no strange stares, no quizzes on where I came from or my credentials. I kind of liked this. The gardens were meant to be shared with everyone and I felt lucky to have this role as caretaker —it could be worse.

A cluster of weeds between the lettuces caught my attention. As I bent down to yank them out, I was suddenly bowled over by someone who must have been in a big hurry.

"Excuse me! Are you injured?" the man said as he lent me a hand.

I inspected my skinned knee and replied, "I'm all right. You must be in a hurry to get someplace."

"Yes, I have a meeting with Ignatius but wanted to check out a few things first," the man replied.

"And you are?" I asked furrowing my eyebrows.

"Ries."

I inspected him closer. Wavy black shoulder-length hair framed a chiseled face that highlighted his Roman nose and deep-set sable eyes. Handsome by my standards, for sure. He towered over me, his muscular body larger than the other men I'd seen on the island.

"I hold the position as the lead architect for the temple construction and building repairs," he boasted.

My flirtatious side kicked in—the attraction strong, even though I'd never seen this man before.

"I'm Alexis, the new gardener. Since you are in the building profession, can you tell me where I might find some large stones for our gardens? I intend to build more beds for herbs, and the stones would make attractive containers." I had started a conversation with Ries and hoped it would continue.

"I need to take care of some business, but what if we meet next week and you can describe your garden needs so I can find exactly what you want," Ries said.

"Lovely!" I exclaimed before I realized that this word probably didn't fit into everyday Greek vocabulary.

Ries furrowed his eyebrows, puzzled by my comment. I ignored him and said, "Thanks, Ries. I look forward to your advice and help."

Even though my words were Greek, I was speaking my English vocabulary and often wondered how exactly they translated. I giggled at the thought.

Although our meeting was brief, Ries promised to show me the temple construction and take me to his favorite part of the beach to watch the sea birds and collect shells for jewelry. It almost sounded like a romantic date, but in this culture, nature would be our chaperone, having a prominent role in almost every aspect of life. If all the members of Girgento were this outgoing and friendly, my adjustment wouldn't be so hard. I soon would find out that there were many who thrived on jealousy, just like the society of my future. I promised myself to hold it together and make the best of it as long as I was here.

Not that I was qualified for it at all, but part of my job consisted of being somewhat of a healer. Women and men alike came to the garden to request certain foods or herbs for illness and other health conditions. Jory gave me the role of interacting with them, probably because he wasn't exactly convivial. I struggled with this since Jory had just started showing me how to formulate herbals and I was not yet comfortable creating on my own. There were no books to study, only guidance from a disenchanted gardener. Iris had asked me to make her a tincture when I first arrived, and it was overdue. I would need to track Jory down and get to business. I found him removing weeds from the zucchini beds, oblivious to all but his plants.

"Jory," I queried, "how did you learn about herbs and their healing powers, and how long have you been making tinctures?" If he was going to turn this art over to me, I required some answers besides education.

Jory looked up at me and put his hand over his forehead to shield the sun. "My wife . . . Kora." He stumbled on his words, wanting to finish but halted in his thoughts. I gave him a moment and then he continued. "She and the herbs. They were connected. As a young girl, they spoke to each other."

So, Kora was the mastermind herbalist, not Jory. He was just doing his best after watching and working with her for so many years. Things were starting to fall into place.

"Everything alive with her," he choked.

"I'm so sorry, Jory," was all I could muster.

I changed the subject. "Iris has requested a tincture, but I need your guidance. Can we work on it tonight?"

He looked up at me and with a sigh and an exhale said, "Gather ingredients. Meet me at dusk."

I'd only tinkered with tinctures according to Scott's instructions. I wished he were here. He'd know exactly what to do. I needed his strong confidence.

I decided then and there to step into my new role,

knowing my limits were being tested and at the same time pretending I was capable—or else. Or else what? I didn't ask to be here as some kind of sorceress, even though that's what it looked like I was becoming. I could never fill Kora's shoes, but it was a matter of survival. I would work hard to learn my new craft, but would the lessons learned make me trustworthy? History tells us that being a good citizen does not guarantee you a life free from harm. And I was no exception.

Days evaporated into nights, the physical work causing my bones and muscles to ache, mostly in the evenings when I tried to relax. Tending to these gardens was much more structured than watching a few plants grow, like I did back home. Jory was more of a figurehead, helping when he could but mostly guiding and advising me. Where was Jory anyway? I hadn't seen him this morning and that worried me. I knocked on his door with no answer. Muffled sounds of coughing came from up the stairs, and I watched as Jory's wobbly legs gingerly made the descent into the gardens. His head was tilted downward and with shoulders hunched, gave the appearance of being much older than he actually was. I approached him with hesitation.

"Jory, what's wrong?" I asked.

"Not good," he mumbled as he looked up at me with dread in his eyes.

"Is it bad news?"

"Counsel wants us to double our crops," he said, beginning to shake.

I grabbed his shoulders to steady him. "We are doing the best we can."

"They don't think so."

"Who are "they?" I questioned.

"Ignatius, the military leader. Has influence over Alexander, the tyrant . . . We have six lunar cycles." He paused to look over his shoulder. "Something else. I tell only you this. Last night I checked the granary where we store wheat. It is empty. Maybe stolen." He looked down, then into my eyes. "Something not right. Maybe they steal our seeds too."

Stunned by both these revelations, I bent over to catch my breath. My world suddenly turned dark as my seemingly manageable life became threatened.

"We must figure out the thieves' motive. And the seeds. Who would want the seeds?" I questioned.

Jory shrugged and shuffled his feet in the dirt. When he finally spoke, he lifted his head, motioning toward the hills where the wheat was grown. "Someone greedy. Girgento wheat has high value. Worth money. Maybe traitor to Carthaginians sell it to Carthage. We must be on guard for our gardens too."

My head started swimming. Double trouble. So, a military leader could hold power over a tyrant because the tyrant needed the military's protection over Girgento. Blackmail, of sorts. Jory was advised that if we could not increase our yields, the military would take over and Jory and I could be exiled. The question that bothered me was why would the military want to take over the garden? What was in it for them? And now, wheat from the granary was missing. Jory suspected someone but didn't say who. He seemed to know a lot about the inner circle of Girgento and the different levels of power, but preferred to keep his knowledge to himself. No wonder he kept such a low profile. After what I had just learned, I now realized that my status was on the lower scale, community respect obviously not accounting for anything.

We didn't have enough seeds at this time to fulfill the request for a greater food yield and would have to harvest seeds from crops not yet ripe. The task seemed impossible. Earlier in the week, I thought about asking Jory for an apprentice to help us so I could continue to focus on my herbs and healing remedies. This request would have to wait. The two of us would be required to work day and night and cut back the time allotted to the herbals until we got caught up. I would talk to Iris to see if there was anything I could do to change the minds of the Counsel.

That night, my sleep came in waves. I'd wake up from a dream, only for it to repeat as I drifted off again. These dreams were more like visions. Each episode was dominated by Demeter, who looked just like the statue from the museum. As she spoke, the only words I could understand were "deliver the gifts" as she held out a thin package, urging me to take it. My hands reached out to grasp hers, so milky white, but I guessed touching was forbidden in the spirit world and the harder I stretched out to her, the further she drifted backward. I started to speak but woke up with a bolt. Just then I had an idea. An idea that could be a game changer, but it would take some experimenting. I had to get to work.

9

SECRET PLACES

Unbeknownst to me upon my arrival, the pockets of the robe I wore contained some seeds. You see, I wore this robe to pretend I was a goddess, planting seeds of wisdom and courage. Character traits I desperately wanted but even with all my reading and meditating found difficult to achieve. Maybe these seeds had a metaphorical meaning, and by consuming their offspring, I too would become wise and brave. Unfortunately, I never had the chance to see these seeds evolve as I was ripped away from my old life for this one. These were the seeds that Scott had given me, an undetermined name, a mystery seed that only he knew. Things were heating up in Girgento. Now might be the time to plant some of these seeds to see what manifested. If the results of the seeds could be formulated into something like the Forza, which could add strength and vitality to the gardens, we might have a chance of saving them. The moon was in its waxing phase, perfect for optimal growth. I retrieved ten of the seeds, found a spot between the oregano and mint, made tiny holes, and dropped them into their new home. I sprinkled a little dirt on top and I voiced the intention Scott had taught me. It now became a waiting game.

I guessed it was early June by the warming, long days and fruit forming on the fig trees. The stones I laid down to count each day numbered twenty-eight. I had only been here four weeks and it felt like four months; the job was so intense. With our increased workload, we continuously planted and tended to the gardens into the evening light. Jory, to satisfy my dedication to save our positions, gave me tincture lessons at night in his house, which doubled as a workshop. Between Scott's instructions and Jory's experience, I was becoming more adept in remedy-making. Jory took it one step further, teaching me about poultices, balms, and teas. I felt like I was in a hands-on immersion course.

One day, I asked Jory where he kept certain tincture ingredients, like valerian root, that were not on the shelf in his house. Without saying a word, he pushed the table aside, rolled back a red and blue woven rug, and looked up at me with raised eyebrows. A piece of wood with a latch revealed what appeared to be an opening to a hidden cellar. He lifted the heavy bronze fixture, tilting his head to make sure no one was listening. Steep stone stairs led down a narrow passageway and into a small cavern. Jory swept his hand toward the opening as an invitation to enter. He lit a lantern and handed it to me.

Cautiously I stepped downward. The chill of the stone cooled my body as I inhaled the musty air. Setting the lantern down carefully on the floor, I inspected the contents of this cave. Slim shelves held various-sized, unlabeled amphorae. I removed the lids, one by one, to discover olive oil, cured olives, salt-crusted capers, barley, wheat, honey, wine, dried herbs and roots, vegetables, seeds, and a few experimental tinctures. Jory had carved out a waist-high table on the opposing wall, presumably as a workstation. I imagined him alone here at night, concocting remedies his wife Kora had taught him in order to keep up with the demand she had created. All this while trying to tend to the gardens as well. All to keep his job. This is why he was so eager to teach me the trade. To fill his wife's shoes.

Deep in my thoughts, I glanced up with the light's flicker, and something on the wall caught my eye. I reached out and lifted it off its nail hanger for a closer look. Carved flowers, interspersed with green beads and tiny seashells, were woven onto a thin rope with a clasp on one end. Did the intricate work of art belong to Jory's wife? A lump formed in my throat realizing this as a memento of Kora's, perhaps made by Jory. I carefully replaced it and ascended the stairs.

"Why do you need to keep these ingredients a secret, Jory?" I asked.

"Needed for healing remedies. If in the open, thieves would steal them for food," he mumbled.

Now that Ignatius was breathing down our backs, this extra stash made perfect sense. I wondered how many extra seeds he had been hoarding and if we could we use them in this emergency. I decided not to ask. He would offer if the situation got dire.

"How long did it take you to dig the cellar?" I asked, still in awe.

"Over twelve lunar cycles. Did it at night. Sandstone not so hard to carve."

I imagined this humble man having a deep secret, to be shared with me only. It must have been exhaustive, digging out the cellar every evening after working in the gardens all day.

"Can I use this space for work if it gets too hot in your house?" I wanted permission to access this secret hiding place.

"Yes, but always leave a sign you have been here, so our secret is safe," he said cautiously.

"I can place a bay leaf under the jar of olives when I leave and then when you come down, you will remove it," I suggested. Bay leaves were bug repellants, so they served an auxiliary purpose.

"Good," was all he said.

Jory's immediate trust in me and his willingness to share something as secret as his cellar, made me a little nervous. How many people had I met, and in a short amount of time, trusted implicitly? Not many. I could only foresee that he felt comfortable around me and that I wasn't a threat to his job, unlike my situation at the museum.

I made it a habit to enter the hidden workshop every other day in an attempt to learn to identify the vases holding all the different foods and ingredients. They did not have the neatly written labels like in Scott's workshop. Jory knew where to find the products and that was all that mattered to him.

Olive oil, on the other hand, was too bulky to hide. These bottles were stored in an above-ground cave behind our houses. We seemed to be the warehouse for the precious oil, with the tyrants and oracles having the biggest demand and needing it to light their chambers and temples. Keeping track of the portioned bottles was also part of my job, but what wasn't?

10

MY NEW FRIENDS

The polis depended not only on our extensive vegetable and fruit gardens, but also on the wheat and farro fields for food. Essential to the diets across the Mediterranean, wheat was the primary sustenance and symbolized the continuation of life. Without it, people would starve and the economy would suffer. So vital to society, the wheat granaries were guarded by the military and seed collection was taken seriously.

The Sicilian and Egyptian soils were fertile and enjoyed a variety of microclimates, unlike the rocky landscape of other surrounding Mediterranean countries. The wheat grown here had a reputation for its prized flavor, its digestibility, and its tall sheaths. Producing a flour more yellow in color than other grains, Girgento's wheat excelled in doughs for savory baked goods and bread. A later harvest than other island wheats and a lower productivity served as an advantage, yielding higher prices.

Plots of wheat were owned by individuals. Some farmers had very small lots and others, like the aristocrats Ignatius and Alexander, had larger farms. The wheat was harvested once a year and sold in the markets, often to international merchants. Farmers relied on the crops as their sole source of income. It was a much tougher kind of farming and required tenacity along with many temple visits and gifts for the gods asking for their cooperation. With all of our efforts combined, Girgento was growing into a wealthy and powerful society, but would its power eventually become its fatal flaw?

I hadn't seen Ries since our first meeting, more than a month ago. One hot afternoon, I took it upon myself to investigate the nearby beaches and to go for a swim to cool off. Jory would have to be notified so he didn't think I vanished as quickly as I had appeared. He wanted to keep me happy as much as I wanted to find happiness here. I took a long drink from one of our wells and ascended the stairs leading to the main city to look for Ries. Dust covered my bare feet as I walked from temple to temple, passing the stares and whispers of the curious, most of whom I assumed were the more affluent women. They wore long white robes, tied with gold knotted belts, their dark hair braided and piled up on top of their heads. Working women were not always visible here, having their place in the agora or in the fields. The men's shorter robes, that showed off their bulging calves, were hard to ignore. A few groups huddled together for an afternoon chat, while others carried hydrias and amphoras to their homes or businesses. The air was ripe with hope and bustled with energy and excitement. It was all so surreal. My extroverted self wanted to make friends, to feel accepted for the time I was here, but for now, I was the stranger. The message "deliver the gifts" reverberated in my ear, a nagging reminder that this was a part of the puzzle I had been sent back in time, to this particular place, to solve. My mission was still unclear. This was a relatively new society that the Greeks from Gela, a nearby port village, had expanded to recently. It was almost too overwhelming. I thought of the stories I could bring back to the museum to make our Sicilian exhibit come even more alive. All of it fascinated me.

I spotted Ries talking with another man at the Temple of Concordia. He saw me too and we waved to each other like old friends. As I approached, hoping not to interfere with the conversation, he said, "Alexis! Come meet my friend and lead builder. Leandro, Alexis just arrived from Siracusa and is helping Jory run the gardens. Her skills come highly acclaimed."

Jory never said anything to him about me being "highly acclaimed." He must have gotten this information from someone else. Probably one of the leaders or tyrants who arranged to bring me here in the first place. Curiosity was eating at me. Up to this point, I had felt rather sheltered below in the garden, a sort of Persephone, finally coming up for air to the level of civilization.

Leandro's smile woke something inside of me. He seemed so familiar but I couldn't place my finger on it. He gave Ries the spotlight but I could tell that it was his vision building the temples, and making sure each one was accountable in its unique structure, to its maker, its god or goddess.

I finally spoke. "Good morning, Ries. How nice to see you again. It's a pleasure to meet you, Leandro. I have been so buried in my work that I haven't had the chance to explore the polis and your magnificent temples."

"The gods blessed Girgento with a plateau that aligns with the sunrise and sunset, providing the perfect temple placement. From the sea, all can view the colossal temples and the walls that surround our polis, providing protection from our enemies. Sailors marvel at the unobstructed landscape," said Ries.

I imagined this was Girgento's skyline for the city, its Doric temples boasting to all of their power and strength.

"Which gods are honored here?" I asked.

This time Leandro answered. "As you can see, where we stand, we are building the Concordia for the goddess of harmony, Harmonia. Behind us is Juno, wife of Zeus. In front of us sits Heracles, our oldest temple whose eves are decorated with lion's heads. Inside resides a magnificent bronze statue of Heracles sculpted by our own Timo. Zeus is next, and we are proud to say it is the largest temple in the Mediterranean. It took years to carve the giant telamon men who support the entablature of the temple with their elbows. Finally, near the entrance to your gardens of Kolymbethra, lies Dioscuri, or Castor and Pollux, and alongside, the small sanctuary temple of Demeter."

I felt as if I was called to attention at the word Demeter. Perhaps I could find clues as to my existence here in her sanctuary, if I was allowed in.

I returned my focus to the two men. "Are some of the columns created with marble?" I asked.

Ries figured it was his time to answer. "No. Marble isn't excavated here on the island and would be expensive to import. As we build the temples and heft each piece up to the next level, we use stucco to seal them together. The columns are then coated in the stucco, to replicate marble. This sturdy material protects them from the weather and gives them an elegant look."

"The vibrant blue and red trim near the top is a striking contrast to the white building. The gods must find joy in your artistic efforts," I said.

The lesson in temple architecture fascinated me, and I

secretly tucked all this information away to add extra depth to our museum exhibit back in San Francisco. Why was I thinking of this when my life was now here in Girgento? Would I ever get back? Refocus, I said to myself, inhaling deeply.

I hesitated to interrupt this educational conversation but said, "I'm heading to the ocean's cooler breezes and wondered if you had time to show me the beach you described last week? We wouldn't be gone long. I must get back to finish up work in the garden later today."

The smile on Ries's face told me the answer. "Sorry, Leandro. Can we finish up later?" Leandro had no other option but to nod his head.

There was so much I wanted to ask Ries but I would have to pace myself to avoid suspicion. One slipup and I might be labeled a witch, or worse. I didn't even know if they had someone like a witch in this era. I'd need to watch my words carefully.

The path we took to the beach was different from the one Mikolos and I had traveled a month ago.

"Thank you for coming with me," I said with a flirtatious smile.

"I needed a break too, so I am happy for the chance to get away for a while," Ries countered.

Ries seemed eager to talk. "Girgento has been good to me—a job and a lifestyle better than what I have had in the past. It is quickly becoming a thriving community and popular place to live and work, if only I can keep up with the demand for more temples." He laughed. "Are you enjoying the gardens?"

I tried to sound confident, hiding my true feelings. "It's challenging but I cannot imagine a more beautiful and peaceful place to spend my days. The planting season is coming up and there is a lot of preparation of the soil. Jory teaches me his tricks and is most interested in the effects of climate and how to get the most abundant harvest. He is really knowledgeable, and I try to keep up with him," I joked and then soberly said, "I am curious to know what happened to him, you know, why he has so many scars and deformities."

Ries responded, "Poor Jory. His wife was the herbalist for Girgento and was reputed to be one of the best in Sicily. When she died a few years ago, he became despondent and the garden suffered. There was no one to take over the herbal medicines. It's a very specialized talent to manage Kolymbethra, and its resources are vital to our survival. Our last leader, Perseus, was an unforgiving tyrant and punished him severely for his neglect, leaving him to die. One of our military men broke his ribs, smashed his hands, and bloodied his face. The intent was not to kill, but the man doing the beating did not agree. His friends and I hid him and helped him to heal. Thankfully, Perseus died a few months later. Our new tyrant leader, Alexander, is a reasonable man, and because there was no one else with Jory's knowledge to run the garden, he allowed him his job back. Jory restored Kolymbethra with a lot of hard work, but with the insect damage, our leaders insisted that we bring someone else in to help him in case Jory is unable to perform his duties."

I understood. This changed everything about Jory. No wonder he was so quiet and meek, like a little mouse, whispering here and there to only the plants. I would be kinder, more respectful; not that I wasn't already but there's always room for improvement.

"Thank you for sharing this information, Ries," I said.

Ries was so easy to talk to and didn't hesitate when I asked him about Jory. If he was this open, I could learn a lot. "How long have you lived in Girgento?" I queried.

Ries took a long breath and wrinkled his forehead. "About ten lunar years, I suppose. I came here as a young man after working with experts who built the temples in Athens. It is an honorable job to serve this community, and I hope I can make it worthy of the gods and goddesses."

Such profound statements from a man I barely knew. Ries had heart, devotion, kindness, all wrapped up in one neat package. I wanted to ask if he was spoken for, in a relationship. I didn't want to jeopardize our emerging friendship or make another woman jealous at this stage in the game. I was thinking of the old days, my days back in San Francisco, when this was a common question, a necessary one. Here it might be considered an intrusion. He knew I was single. Everyone knew I was single. The community was more like a small neighborhood where everyone knew everyone else's business, and I was the new girl on the block.

We sat down on the silky sand, the warm waveless water lapping at our feet, neither of us talking. Only a few fishermen occupied the shoreline, their long wooden poles stretched across the water, awaiting a nibble. The sun's angle indicated late afternoon and a light breeze began to blow, cooling the air. Seabirds circled the ocean, hoping to outsmart the fishermen and to be the first to catch their dinner.

I returned my focus to Ries. Not really knowing the proper etiquette of this time, I cautiously said, in a formal tone that shocked me, "What should I expect from the tyrant Alexander? I have not met him yet but know we prepare offerings for him to give to the oracles. Does he have a kind spirit?"

I did not want to get myself into a situation like Jory had. It was important to understand the demands and boundaries of this society as well as the repercussions.

Jory certainly wasn't going to tell me. I needed a confidant and wanted it to be Ries.

"Alexander is a sensible man, unlike some tyrants of the past. There is nothing to fear, Alexis. Girgento depends upon a strong economy and everyone here is doing their part. We are fortunate to have leadership that respects and values its people and understands their contributions. It's not like this in other parts of Sicily. For you to be here is a gift to us, and to you as well."

A gift. That word. Again. Someday this would become apparent to me, but for now I was satisfied to sit on the beach with Ries and watch the waves crash and retreat, like my life.

I began to feel I belonged here, hidden in the deep valley, alone with the plants and animals. It was a place of quiet and peace; a place where I could think, contemplate, and figure out my problems, undisturbed. For some reason, life seemed more focused here, in this lush paradise of fruit trees, streams, chirping birds, and ancient spirits who appeared to be channeling me. Rainfall, and the natural springs that flowed throughout the valley with help of the aqueducts, kept our gardens lush enough to provide food to the entire community and to traders that frequented the island. The responsibility to produce food here was enormous, and now the clock was ticking.

A raven darted in and out of my herb garden, chasing away the doves that sometimes nibbled on the herbs. This afternoon they seemed particularly interested in the tiny mystery seed seedlings I had recently planted. Suddenly I had a flashback to the one white dove who visited my Oakland garden and loved the vervain seeds Scott had given me. Since the doves were picky about which herbs they munched on, I wondered if the mystery seeds could be vervain or a hybrid version. The birds had just given me my first clue. Kolymbethra taught me many lessons but the ones I valued most were those I learned from observation, something most people don't take the time to do. It was really quite simple. Tune into nature and the teacher will appear. Each seed told a story of life, death, and resurrection, like the Eleusinian ritual in Greece. I believe in the spiritual realm, in our connection to nature, and in the continuation of life after death. By watching the miracles of my waxing and waning garden, like the moon cycles, life became more focused and intentional. I don't know if I would ever have experienced these revelations had I still lived in San Francisco.

A white flash darted between the fig trees, startling me out of my daydream. I stood up to identify my visitor. He remained still, as if he wanted me to discover him. "He" was a large, lanky white dog with pointed ears and a long snout. I approached him with care, not wanting to scare him away. I reached out my open palm in a gesture of respect to see if I could get closer. The gold eyes stared at me and accepted my invitation. I bent down and stroked his long, soft fur as he leaned into me, a whiff of musty sage emanating from his body.

"Who do you belong to?" I asked him. He wore no collar, and I knew from my studies that most family dogs wore collars, even in ancient times. I got up, patted my thigh as a "come along," and he followed me back to my cottage. The dog was thin, and I assumed he ate out of trash heaps. He might just be one of the many wild dogs that roamed throughout the polis. Perhaps he would like a bowl of farro with some dried meat mixed in? As I prepared his food, he made himself at home and stretched out next to me. The warmth of his energy reminded me of Lucas and the comfort of having a dog around. "Your name is Sparta," I said. He looked up at me and his body rocked softly as he panted a smile.

II

THE MYSTIC HERBALIST

Late August

Jory and I filled our days with plans for replenishing the future crops. Lessons included how to dry seeds from cucumbers, peppers, lettuces, and lentils. It was essential not to waste a single seed as the pressure was still on to bring forth expanded crops. The fruit and nut trees only needed a mild pruning, but the bushes, herbs, and vegetables required more attention.

It was nearing what I surmised was late August, according to the stones I had been counting daily. We evaluated our seeds and what to plant more of with our expanding society. We never dared plant all our seeds and held a small reserve in case of drought or fire or any other disaster, although this year, most of our limited seed stock would be used to get the gardens back to their abundant state. I now realized how critical seeds were to sustain a society. They contained everything essential for survival in such a small, compact, tiny seed. What would happen if the seeds didn't germinate? I decided then and there that we needed more of a backup plan. I would check other growers in the area to see if we could do a seed swap as a

124

way to biodiversify our crops. The pests hadn't returned but could be a problem if we didn't carefully integrate new varieties into our gardens. I was not an expert farmer, but living in the future did have its advantages of knowing some historical events about food shortages and their causes. Somehow these ideas were coming to me loud and clear. Demeter, are you out there?

The summer season was coming to a close, and it was critical to cut flower tops and herbs nearing the end of their cycle for future seeds, infusions, tinctures, ointments, and poultice ingredients. Timing was essential. Each herb, flower, and root played a medicinal role, and our job was to prepare each one for as many herbals as possible. Our workshop's shelves bulged with beeswax and olive oil for the ointments, wine for tinctures, cloth for poultices, and small vases to store the finished products. Now I wore two hats: gardener, and herbalist.

Come early September we were in full swing in preparation for requested medicinals. The herbs had reached peak potency and I felt like a pharmacist. Scott's lessons came back to me, so Jory didn't think I was totally ignorant in this technique, but Jory's experience was far more advanced than Scott's. He'd had years of perfecting his craft, thanks to Kora. I'm sure this is why they brought him back to work the gardens. He was a valuable asset to Girgento, and I was learning all his secrets, which is more than I can say for Scott.

Chamomile for restless babies, rosemary for purification, sage for protection. I had even formulated a shampoo with mint oil that I used myself and had become popular with the women. The list was long, and they were mostly single herb tinctures. Some days, when Jory was out in the garden, I experimented to combine various herb attributes. I would take these potions myself to understand how they tasted and whether dizziness, nausea, or heart palpitations occurred. Quickly, I learned how to increase or decrease the potency of specific herbs to balance the desired effect. It was almost like cooking, but I was playing with people's lives and it had to be right. Some of the combinations could be fatal and I approached them with respect and focus. I took my job seriously and the direct payment from our clients was motivation, unlike our garden work where funding came from the Counsel and was dependent upon yield. I felt like a real entrepreneur. Women began to trust me to create a certain type of remedy just for their needs: skin rashes, pregnancy nausea, digestive upsets, even sexual disorders.

After a few successful endeavors and compliments, I spent most evenings keeping up with the demand. So far, my reputation exceeded expectations and made it easier for me to slip into Girgenti life. I think this was because I hand-delivered each and every remedy to my clients and gave them directions for use. This way I got to know the people, and where and how they lived. I wondered if Kora had done this too. Even though business was booming, Kolymbethra was my priority. The additional income from procuring these tinctures allowed me a few luxuries not available upon my arrival. I finally had a real cloth pillow and a small table and chair for my home. I didn't have to wear the same robe I was dressed in upon arrival. Now I had an alternate outfit with a matching wrap for upcoming cooler weather and a pair of leather sandals whose straps wrapped up my ankles. Style had returned to my life!

I felt safe, fulfilled, and unbothered by trivial details like whose car got to park in the museum parking lot. Life was minimalistic, something I used to seek, although not to this degree. I would have liked to see more of Ries, but both our careers provided little time for outside interests.

People must date, I thought, or did they? I'm sure it wasn't called dating but more of a mutual meeting. Courtships evolved into marriage, but I was definitely not interested in that pathway. A simple affair would do.

I woke at dawn in an attempt to finish my daily tasks early so I could visit the agora. The plump lime-green figs had ripened to include a rounded pink bottom blush and needed to be picked before the birds ate them all. My basket full, I returned to the workshop and proceeded to pierce one end of the fruit with a long, sharp wood-fashioned needle and string them to dry. I popped a fig into my mouth and bit down, letting the pink perfumed liquid run down my throat. Pure sugar. These green figs had a sweeter flavor than the Mission or Turkey figs I was familiar with. One benefit of this job was tasting every single thing that we grew. I picked three basketfuls: one for my clients, one for Alexander, and one for Iris, the priestess, to give as offerings to the gods.

The fig symbolized peace and prosperity and a continuance of the mighty Girgento.

Iris and I became friends after our encounter on the first day of my arrival. Her desperate plea for a tincture for protection seemed an unusual way to meet. It had taken me a month to deliver it since all our work of planting, harvesting, and potion-making revolved around the moon's cycle. This was serious business that required careful attention to the seasonal flow, and a few misplaced days could waste an entire harvest's potency. Being born into a priestess family, and destined for this position, Iris had found her place in Girgento and done her job well. Women were so much more powerful in this time zone. We didn't even have women Catholic priests in 2017, yet these priestesses almost ruled the world. Men trusted them for their visions and respected them immensely. Iris depended upon me to create specific offerings, and my job became more stressful. Our lives were intertwined in this way, each of us looking out for the other.

This day, I took her a basket of the ripe figs as a gesture of friendship. She could eat them, share them, or present them to the deities. It was my offering of thanks to her. There she sat on a bench outside Dioscuri, the sanctuary dedicated to Castor and Pollux, her slender legs tucked up into her chin and her arms wrapped around as if she was giving herself a hug.

I greeted her. "Hello, Iris! I've brought you a gift."

"Welcome, Alexis, and thank you. Figs are my favorite fruit! How did you know? Is life sweet?" she asked.

This word "sweet" struck me like she was describing a chocolate chip cookie. "Yes," I replied. "Jory and I have a rhythm and work together well."

"I was really wondering if you have a special love interest," she inquired. "Isn't there a potion for that?" She giggled.

Love? Who could think of love under this pressure to produce?

"Unfortunately, this is a busy time for us in the garden and leaves me little time to myself. I met Ries for a walk along the beach, but I only get a glimpse of him now and again when I bring medicinals to our customers. What's he like?" I asked.

"The gods sent Ries here to help Girgento fulfill a mission to build grand temples to rival any in Greece. His expertise and commitment make him valuable and well-liked. He had a lady friend, but she left to go back to Greece to help her sister. It's been a few years and I think he might be looking for some company, outside of the temples."

"Really?" I said excitedly. I could use some male energy, outside of Jory, and there was a certain chemistry between us.

"I could arrange for you two to meet after work, if you'd like," Iris said. "I'll come to the gardens with the details."

"That sounds great, Iris. I could make dinner for him too," I said.

"You should get acquainted first," Iris suggested.

So, Iris would teach me the proper protocol. I agreed, we hugged, and I was onto my next mission—to drop off figs for Alexander, with whom I did not have a connection, yet.

The leaders, or Counsel, occupied a building called Athenia near the east entrance to the city. It was here they held meetings, discussed the economy and trade with other city states, along with the latest news of war and the ever-present threat of the Carthaginians they had recently fought off. Jory and I had heard nothing in relation to the conversation about yield a few months earlier. Even though this thought created a tightness in my chest, I made my way to the door of Athenia, basket in hand, when it flung open with a whoosh. In front of me stood the man himself, Alexander, the tyrant of Girgento. Tyrants could be brutal dictators who punished freely or rational leaders who used their power to guide society in a democratic fashion. Alexander was the latter, from what I'd been told, but now I'd see for myself.

"I bring you fresh figs from Kolymbethra."

Taken aback, he stood there and took inventory of me. We had never formally met but had seen each other from a distance. I could tell he was curious about me but was too busy to have a meet and greet. Taller than most men here, with a solid build and perfect posture, he commanded attention. His chin-length light hair complemented his turquoise eyes, and unlike most other men here, he sported an ear-to-ear beard, relegated to men of importance. He definitely fit the part of a ruler; his confident air set him apart as well as his dress—short robe with gold and red trim ribbon at the hem and neckline and a braided belt of gold fabric. I could have picked him out in a crowd if challenged. I'd heard that his wife was beautiful, and protective of her husband when it came to interactions with other women. I would tread carefully.

"I am sorry, I forgot to introduce myself. My name is Alexis, and I am tending the gardens with Jory. Please accept these figs as a gift from the garden," I said, returning the confidence.

He glanced down at me and put a hand on my shoulder in a gesture of friendship. "Thank you for your generosity, Alexis. I have heard great things about your talents and management of Kolymbethra."

Just as I was bathing in the compliments, a voice behind me said, "Alex, your services are needed."

It was a woman's voice, and it wasn't a request. It was a demand. So, this was the jealous wife and yes, she was gorgeous. Silky black hair wrapped up on her head with braided strands lining her heart-shaped face. On top of this masterpiece rested a wreath of laurel with tiny white flowers interspersed between the leaves. Pitch-black eyes and a delicate nose, not the typical wide-nostril type of Greek descent. She almost looked Egyptian. A long white thin robe almost matched his, with the same gold and red ribbon but with olive branch motifs on the sleeves. It was stunning and I couldn't help but stare at this petite woman who interrupted our conversation.

"This is Adela, my wife," Alexander finally asserted.

"I am Alexis, the gardener of Kolymbethra," I asserted, mustering up my best happy voice.

Adela looked at me and shrugged, and I hoped for a smile but only received pursed lips in a weak attempt of acknowledgment. So, we would not be best friends, but maybe she would grow to like me. I always wanted everyone to like me for some reason and I took offense when they didn't. I knew this was one of my weaknesses and it was a hard one to break. Alexander smiled at me, said goodbye, and the two of them were off, her arm latched firmly onto his. At least I made a positive impression on Alexander, and I would work on Adela's attitude. There just might be a tincture for that!

I drifted from plant to plant, checking each one for new buds and eaten leaves. The heat wilted the mint during the day and the damp night air resurrected it in the morning. The fishmonger's wife, Bryony, drank mint tea every day for her chronic restless stomach. Maybe I should plant more so she had a constant supply. This was my typical day. Knowing who needed what and making sure the herbs were at their potency peak. Some days I shopped at the agora for spices I didn't grow or that came from Carthage. What was it that the builder wanted? A new kind of peppercorn-infused drink that kept him cool while toiling on the new temples. Yes, the agora was a good idea, and I might just find something special for Ries. Ries. A handsome man; those warm, deep-brown eyes could melt my soul. This thought triggered memories of my friend Scott from the museum, even though they did not look alike. I'd describe Scott as tall, curly-headed, dirty blond with scars on his face where acne had plagued his youth. His ability to build a display wall to perfection, and practically blindfolded, was an asset to the museum. I loved his sarcastic sense of humor and calm energy. Scott's mysterious lifestyle intrigued me. He seemed intuitive, like the quote he came up with to introduce the exhibit: "Once you experience the pearl of Sicily, it will forever remain in your soul." It was almost as if he had been there in a past life and was channeling the experience.

I shook myself awake from my daydream, almost tripping on a rock, realizing once again, my life was here, in Girgento, two and a half thousand years behind what I knew so well. I was beginning to adapt but felt like I was at camp, being tested before I'd be released back to 2017. Was there even a way back? The portal had delivered me to an ancient Greek civilization in Sicily. Could I go back if it got too tough here? I was here for a reason, but my rational mind still could not figure it out.

I frequently took walks in the gardens on moonlit nights, which usually cured my chronic insomnia. Tonight, my new friend Sparta accompanied me, trotting along and stopping to sniff here and there. A deep breath recognized the must of the grapes alongside the sweet fragrance of pears just beginning to ripen. The grapes, now a deep purple, would be ready to harvest next month. I made a mental note to gather enough vessels to hold their juice.

The moon's shadow cast a deep yellow light in front of me along the path. I loved the tranquility this garden offered me. A true paradise, unlike any I'd ever seen or experienced before. It was rare to encounter other people after dark, but I often saw roaming dogs, foxes, or rabbits foraging for food. Tonight seemed eerily different and I couldn't figure out why I felt on edge.

A rustle in the bushes behind me confirmed my nervousness. I am not often paranoid but for some reason, I froze. Now if I were back in San Francisco, wandering around at night and heard someone, I would feel justified in my fear, but here, in this lovely oasis, what could be so scary? Sparta let out a low growl. I felt safe with him here. The noise was faint, but I detected bare feet and the sound of dirt squishing between toes. Most of the group was asleep. Who would be following me? In one brave movement, I spun around to confront my stalker. A sigh of relief washed over me.

"Jory!" My worries dissipated.

"Alexis, why do you wander the gardens in darkness?" he asked. "You are unlike other women. Are you mystic?"

Jory's intuitive nature had kicked in and he knew there was something different about me. But to suggest I was a mystic . . .

I didn't want to give myself away, and Jory's new awareness scared me a bit. Had I said something that caused him to question my character? We had formed a bond, a trust, in a short amount of time and he relied on me to get the hard work done. I would learn to reciprocate and do something to reassure him that I was genuine and only meant to be a positive contribution to Girgento.

Finally, I said, "Jory, this garden has taught me so much. You have taught me so much. I am grateful for the opportunity to be here in this paradise. The work is satisfying and gives me peace and a purpose. Maybe that's what you see in me." Jory's silence said he was thinking about my comments.

"In the past, I worked by myself or with another man.

Not used to being around woman who takes charge like you. You have natural affinity for plants. With you, garden is stronger than many years."

These few words acknowledging my work ethics were heartwarming but I still sensed his curiosity. I understood, and I was different. I came from another time. Maybe the Twilight Zone was real after all. I could tell he had wanted to have this conversation for some time but he hadn't been able to summon the courage to confront me. For me to remain credible here I needed an ally, and so far, Jory had filled that role. If he doubted me and told someone else, my career at the garden would end, and swiftly. All I could do at this point was to follow my instincts and watch my words carefully. My actions must be more powerful than anything else.

From this time forward, I was on my guard.

The moon signaled that it was time to plant. It must have been mid-September and even though fall was looming, the heat of the day still suggested summer. I chose the seeds that would grow above ground to plant first, pulling the earth's energy up into their frail bodies. The below-ground vegetables required planting when the moon was waxing, driving the energy downward to their roots.

My herbs and flowering plants had their own special place, in full sunshine, in between my house and the workshop. I often sat on a bench beside the garden, watching the birds nibble on the leaves and the bees pollinate them. Jory said that years ago, one of the builders created beehives, and the local honey, in high demand, could be traded for spices and beautiful cloth from afar. I wondered where these lost hives were and if I could resurrect them and begin producing honey again. How I wished I had a book or a computer to look up the proper technique, but my advice would have to come from the gods this time. Just one of my other ideas that would have to wait until the planting was finished and I had more time to dedicate to yet another hobby.

As I sowed the seeds, I remembered Scott's advice: "Your power has no limits. But to tap into it, you must have trust and accept your path." Power was the key word here and one I embraced with every passing day. I felt my power growing, and by power, I mean confidence and courage to survive here in a world so different from my own. I barely knew how I did it. Scott's caveat of having trust still baffled me. I thought I trusted, but did he mean myself? Others? I had accepted my new life but was this my path? What exactly was he talking about?

Despite it all, I was managing and actually felt a certain comfort here, completely different from my life in San Francisco where there were almost too many details to keep straight. Most of my days were spent in contemplation and interaction with the plants, trees, and herbs, not as a hobby but as a food bank and apothecary for our community. I felt more valued than I ever had before. The thought occurred to me time and again that I was brought here on a mission, but what that looked like was still a mystery. As much as I wanted to figure this out, my mind was occupied with playing the part and being fully in character in this play.

12

LEANDRO'S OFFER

I counted out one seed per inch for cucumbers, two inches apart for peppers, and twelve inches for artichokes. The Girgenti loved their artichokes, and I did too, so this year, I planted fifty more plants, which would yield about five hundred more artichokes. They could be preserved in olive oil, garlic, capers, mint, oregano, and spicy peppers for a nice lunch. I crouched over the seeds, pushing dirt just to cover them and gently tuck them into their new home. This small act brought a certain sense of comfort and reminded me of my childhood and the evening ritual of a bedtime story to lull them into a restful sleep. Planting the tiny herb seeds and marking them to tell them apart was a little more meticulous. By the time I finished, my shoulders ached, sunburn stung the back of my neck, and my fingernails were embedded with dirt. As painful as the required work was, the rewards were greater.

I squinted into the sun, wishing for my sunglasses, when I saw a figure approaching down the main pathway. Sparta didn't release his protection growl as usual, and instead ran to greet him. As he got closer, I recognized him as Leandro, Ries's builder friend.

"Hello, Alexis!" he called, giving Sparta a pet.

136

"Hello, Leandro! How nice of you to visit our garden on this sultry day."

Leandro's body size was smaller than the other men but much brawnier, a result of hefting heavy stones for the temples day after day. His eyes, like cats', sat close together; rings of brown outlined his soft green gaze, probably his best feature. Dark-blond curly hair hung straight at his broad shoulders. A bronze object with a Greek symbol dangled from his neck, giving him a bit of a hippie look.

"I came for olive oil and an ointment," he said, draping his bruised hand with torn fingernails in front of me. "A piece of loose sandstone fell off one of the buildings I was working on and as I ducked away, it smashed into my hand."

So, this wasn't a visit to chat but rather for business. "Of course, Leandro. I have some arnica and can mix it with some beeswax for a balm. Would you like to come to the workshop while I prepare it for you?" I asked.

Leandro and Sparta followed me into our workshop and watched while I pulled the arnica tincture off a shelf and lit a small fire to soften the beeswax.

"What do you do for pleasure?" I asked.

I had never asked anyone this question, but it was a normal part of life, to relax and have some fun; at least I thought so. The men seemed so focused on work, meetings, political gatherings. The opposite of the life I had recently left. I was curious.

"I take long walks in the hills and build cabinets to hold food staples for my friends."

I heard the words "build cabinets" and thought of our bulging shelves in this workshop. Maybe a trade could be involved. The extra space would shield my tinctures and ingredients from the light and heat. Leandro suddenly had something I wanted.

With hesitation in my voice, not knowing if I was overstepping my boundaries, I asked, "Could you build some cabinets for us? We really need a larger space to hold all the amphoras and vases filled with medicinals. You can see how little space we have."

"Maybe I could help you build another workspace," Leandro offered.

This generous suggestion caught me off guard.

In my shock, I wanted to say, "Are you kidding me?" but knew this was English slang. Instead, I nodded, smiled, and opened my eyes wide before saying, "That would be wonderful, Leandro! Think of how much more productive our work will become."

That was me, coming up with a practical comment when I really wanted to throw my arms around him in a giant hug.

"I'll see when I can get started. Maybe we should discuss this with Jory first." I agreed, not wanting Jory to think I was going behind his back. This was, after all, his garden in the first place.

The beeswax had melted during our conversation, so I carefully poured it into a shallow vase and stirred in the arnica, along with some olive oil, to make a smooth and soft paste. I sealed it with more beeswax and handed it to him.

"Wait here while I get your olive oil," I requested. The olive oil, along with the wine and other perishable items, was kept in one of the naturally cool caves built into the cliffside. I returned a few minutes later with the oil and said, "A gift. Down payment for cabinets and expansion of our shop."

In a businesslike manner, Leandro replied, "Thank you for your kindness, Alexis. Let me know when we can go over the plans with Jory." And he was on his way.

The talk of payment didn't happen. How could we afford to build an entirely new building? Supplies would need to be purchased, and what about Leandro's labor fee? Maybe this was a conversation for Alexander. We were helping the community and it was for the polis's benefit, not ours. Perhaps I could strike a deal.

13

THE AGORA

The scent of smoked fish drifted throughout the agora. It reminded me of the open-air markets in Italy and France. I vividly remembered stalls huddled next to each other, each offering a local specialty. Seafood paella sizzling in giant pans the size of small flying saucers, stuffed with shrimp and mussels and chunks of fleshy fish, all tinted with strings of orange from saffron and heaped upon a layer of crispy rice. A flashback of an oyster, just briny and slimy enough to slip down my throat at a fish market in Catania. I had a fondness for these gatherings, not only for the enticing food they showcased but for the social interaction as well.

Once a week in Girgento, merchants from surrounding cities participated in a special weekend market, the Agora Magna, and sold specialties from across the seas. I'd look around and see what had arrived from the Phoenician markets. Multiple small baskets of dried herbs and brightly colored spices competed for space on a wooden table, their combined bitter and sweet fragrances wafting through the air. A scrawny, gray-haired merchant used a long wooden spoon to reach the across the array of flavors to scoop up the desired seasoning. His wavering arm then filled up small envelopes of the spice, spilling leaves and powders into the other herbs as he handed them to his customers. I noticed cinnamon and ginger on the table, spices that were not grown locally. These could be used as healing components as well as in food preparations. I etched his location in my mind so I could return to his booth on my way home.

Across from the spice man, an elegant woman of exquisite beauty stood near bolts of pale linen fabric, the ends unfurled to reveal their flaxseed texture. Raven eyes outlined in black makeup darted toward me and lured me into her lair of beautiful cloth. Dark hair with streaks of gray coiled around her pointed head, which sat atop her posture-perfect figure. She modeled the latest style of dress, one that draped elegantly across her shoulders and was pinned with small ornamental clips and ribbons. I walked closer.

"This color would highlight your eyes," she said, holding up a piece of pale-green fabric to my face. "Can I show you the latest style?"

I stepped back and thought, where would I have the opportunity to be so glamorous? I was a gardener, my clothes often stained with dirt and mud and green from the herbs and vegetables I tended.

Much to my surprise, I answered, "Yes, please. My name is Alexis."

"I am Charissa. Come near to me."

The next thing I knew, Charissa was winding soft linen fabric like curls around my body, pinching the material here and there and fastening little tucks with pins. When she finished, she held a small hand mirror in front of me so I could take in my appearance. She was right! The color and her design made me feel like a princess and was quite captivating. But when would I wear this garment?

"How many coins?" I asked.

"Two," she answered, not wanting to make a conversation out of the sale.

The feminine side of my brain said, why not? So I asked her to help me undress and to fold the fabric so I could take it with me. This outfit hardly bore the label of an agora shopping outfit. She tied the square of linen with a string and wished me off, eager, no doubt, to entice the next shopper into her stall.

The agora held a high position in the community, providing a place not just for shopping but for gatherings, political debates, and speeches, much like Rome's Forum. There was something for everyone here, and unlike Athens, its rival in stature, women were accepted as active participants. I knew many ancient societies practically hid women away and forbid them outside activities, relegating them to the home or to entertain the upper crust of the time. Whatever force brought me here must have known that I might not have survived elsewhere.

The aromas intermingled, here in the heart of the market, and once again I was lured in by the scent of freshly baked breads, dark in color and dense in texture. A plump woman slid loaves of dough into a large wood-fired oven adjacent to the booth. I approached the stall, eager to taste this baker's breads, which were, I was sure, much better than what I had been trying to make. Some were small rolls shaped into twists, and others were topped with animal shapes and geometric designs. A burly man, with a sash tied around his forehead to hold his thick and wiry hair away from the food, reached out and offered me a slice of the brown loaf to taste. Inside, the bread was studded with black olives and pieces of rosemary, one of my favorite combinations.

How did he know?

"This bread gives strength," he said without any emotion in his voice.

I may have been paranoid, but it seemed like everyone here wanted to help me in some way. Then the voice came again, but not from the baker.

"Deliver the gifts." This time her voice was less demanding and sounded like she was right next to me. I spun around but no one was there.

"Trust your fate, Alexis," the voice continued.

Stunned, I again looked around only to find Iris in my shadow.

"Iris! You startled me," I said in a trembling voice. "Were you talking to me?"

"No, silly. I saw you here and wanted to say hello." Iris laughed.

"I must be hearing things," I admitted to her.

The baker stood patiently still during our conversation. I finally turned to him and said, "I'd like a piece of this bread," pointing to the loaf he had shared with me a few minutes ago.

He nodded and handed me a generous hunk, easily enough for two. I thanked him with a smile, gave him a coin, and turned to Iris.

"What good things are you finding here today?" I asked her.

"Oh, the usual."

"Which is what?" I asked curiously.

"A little bread, some cured olives, wheat for offerings, maybe some goat cheese."

"That sounds lovely. When's dinner?" I teased.

"Let's walk," she said, more of a statement than a question. "I've had some disturbing messages from the gods—a kind of forewarning."

Should I tell Iris about the voices I'd been hearing now

for months? Could these demands be related? I was beginning to think that Iris and I were linked in this life some way, perhaps for some purpose. I decided to remain silent for now. Trust was not my greatest virtue, having been betrayed by people I thought friends. I would not let down my guard now. If that time came, I would need to be certain.

"Maybe the gods want you to take action," I said unconvincingly.

"Could we talk about it sometime, Alexis?"

Why she trusted me was a mystery.

"Yes, Iris. I must continue if I'm to finish my shopping today," I said, more as an excuse to get out of this talk of "forewarning."

"Thank you, Alexis. I'll come see you soon."

We shared a hug, and she was off, as she always was, in a fleeting sweep and then disappearance.

The last time I was here, I bought dates and pistachios and used them to make sweet cakes for my best customers. They stored well and were the perfect afternoon snack that was quickly replacing the chocolate I used to crave but could no longer get. What else? Some saffron to bake with fish, a new cookware dish so I could make meals for more than just myself, a jar of honey. Honey. I had forgotten to ask Jory about the beehives. After next week's underground root vegetables were planted, I'd have time to explore making our own honey. Just as the thought crossed my mind, a bee emblem caught my eye and I kept it in my sight as I navigated through the many bodies doing the same thing I was.

"Umm, honey," I said to the man under the sign, my sweet tooth emerging. "Are you local or from afar?"

There were several honey-makers in the area, and I didn't want to appear ignorant.

"Hello, miss. I'd love to tell you about our local honey," the pudgy old man said. His crinkled face showed signs of age and red blotches from years of sun damage, a result of his occupation.

"I'd like that," I replied.

"My name is Philo. What is yours?"

I told him my name and the conversation accelerated from there. It's amazing how much people want to share with you when they have a passion for something.

"I am interested in beekeeping here in Girgento," I finally blurted out, "but would need some advice to get started. Would you consider teaching me your craft?" I held my breath in anticipation of his reply, making such a brave move with this stranger.

Philo said he was willing to train me, but I would have to travel to his town, Burgio, a short journey from Girgento, for the lessons.

"My children are builders, a job that provides a secure income for them. They aren't interested in buzzing insects. At my age, I would be happy to pass along the business to someone who appreciates the art of the bees."

I barely had time to work my daily duties and had no business adding another hobby. Despite this, I felt our short conversation was surely a sign from above and I eagerly snapped up the opportunity. We planned to meet in two weeks' time for my first class. Philo described where he lived, just outside of town. I hoped I could remember the way.

14

IRIS'S DREAM

That evening, I told Jory about Leandro's offer to help us expand our workspace and then about the beekeeper, Philo. It seemed I was taking charge of the gardens and Jory seemed relieved from any further responsibilities. For once he didn't have to make all the decisions and had someone younger with new ideas to move the garden forward. We would need to strategize a plan for Leandro's payment, but Jory was eager to get started. Leandro would build the extra needed room and cabinets under Jory's supervision, and he would decide where this building would be located. I agreed.

Taking time off for beekeeping might be a problem, but the planting would be finished soon and there were now two of us to work the garden. I would be allowed to go to Burgio at certain times during the olive harvests because, according to Jory, Alexander loaned his slaves to us for the strenuous activity of carefully removing the olives from their fragile branches. The harvesting steps had to be followed exactly, from sorting the olives, those for curing and those for oil, to the olive crush and then to the bottle. Olives and its oil were a necessity, not only as a food and preservative but also for our lanterns. Olive trees were practically worshipped, their fruit so precious. Jory was merely needed to oversee this process and maintain quality control.

The sky's sapphire canvas, along with the afternoon's warm breeze, lured me out of the garden and up into the city for a walk. Everyone else must have had the same idea, the city particularly active today and filled not just with workers but social circles alive with chatter. I decided to take time to check up on some of my clients I regularly made tinctures and infusions for. My first stop would be a visit to Iris to see if the potion I made for her confidence and power was helping or if I would need to make any adjustments to the potency. Her role in Girgento must have been demanding, to speak to all the gods, know which offerings and sacrifices to make, and to be of guidance to the leaders who all heavily leaned on her. She greeted me as usual with a warm hug and kiss on the cheek. For some reason I feared she didn't have many friends and that's why she clung to me like a sister. I liked her too but was skeptical of getting too close to a priestess, knowing she could use her power in a reverse way to negatively impact my stay.

"How are you feeling, Iris," I asked. "I've come to check on you." Iris loved the attention. She was off duty when she was with me, and I could see her body physically release its tension.

"I am good, Alexis," she replied. "Your magic potions work wonders!" She laughed.

Relief washed over me, knowing my new talents were helping people. "Do you think you could make me something that causes deep sleep?" Iris asked. "I've been having wild dreams of being chased and it is scaring me."

My jaw dropped as I remembered our conversation in the agora a few days ago. Demeter had chased me in several dreams too. Were our paths colliding? Bravely, I said, "Who was chasing you, Iris?" I hoped it wasn't Demeter.

"I couldn't see her face," Iris replied, anxiously grasping her necklace and rotating it back and forth, "but she was flying and wore a long white gown that trailed past her in the air."

My eyes flew wide open and I gasped. Iris and I had similar dreams. Could the tincture be causing them? Had I passed along Demeter's wrath to Iris? I wanted an escape, some sort of reason to not believe her or the coincidence. This was the first time since landing in the cave I felt uneasy in my new skin. Iris was intuitive. Could she tell how nervous I was? My face did not easily hide my feelings. My expressions spoke a thousand words.

"Alexis, are you all right?" Iris asked.

I looked her straight in the eyes. "I have had very similar dreams, but a while ago. It's just strange that we both had dreams of being chased by a woman. It was so vivid, I thought it was real." My birthmark began to itch, and I nervously rubbed my arm. Iris noticed this and leaned in to take a closer look.

"The mark," she mouthed as she moved her eyes up to lock mine.

"It's from birth, Iris."

"It's a sign from the gods," she said, almost in a trance.

"Is it bad?" I said, beginning to shake uncontrollably, now not so sure this life was for me.

Iris put her arm around me and rocked me like a child. "Don't worry, Alexis. Certain people are marked to make a change and you must be one of them."

Stunned by this statement, I felt a panic attack coming on with no warm herbal tea to squelch it. As I sat dazed and nauseated, Iris hummed something that sounded like a lullaby as she patiently waited for my recovery.

"Iris, I must tell you something in confidence," I whispered. "Could someone be trying to interfere with the wheat crop? I mean, halt production? Jory noticed the granary was empty."

Iris tilted her head as she pursed her lips, then said, "Girgento has thieves. The gods send me messages, but they don't name names. I will listen more carefully."

"Please say nothing," I begged.

"I trust you, Alexis. We are women of similar age and perhaps our lives are aligning in some strange way. You've always felt familiar to me, like we've known each other before."

Maybe she was right, and she said she trusted me. I had two people in my life who held this confidence in me. I was traveling through space and time to be here. It could be that she was someone I knew back in New York or even San Francisco. This thought made more sense now.

I finally spoke. "Yes, we do have a connection. I'll bring you something for your sleep within the next few days," I said, changing the subject. I had a lot to think about, and hoped by telling her about the wheat I wasn't jeopardizing the path set out for me by the gods.

Iris returned to her duties as an oracle and I to mine as an herbalist. I would find Leandro to see how his arnica ointment was working and to tell him the good news about our building-expansion idea. When I arrived at his workplace, I noticed Ries pointing his fingers as if showing a builder where he wanted one of the Doric columns placed. Ries was just the person I needed now. Someone to take my mind off the eerie conversation I'd just had with Iris.

Forgetting about Leandro for a minute, I headed toward Ries but not before he noticed me and did the same. I felt like a child admiring her teacher as I looked up at him. A hug would be welcomed but I knew that would not be appropriate at this stage in the game.

"Alexis!"

He was happy to see me. That was a good sign.

"Hi, Ries. I am so glad to see you!" I said as I tried to imitate his enthusiasm.

"What brings you up from the darkness?" he asked, referring to his comment about me being Persephone the last time we met.

"The day is glorious and I was in need of some people-viewing! It can get lonely in the gardens, even though I am surrounded by my family." I referred to my garden as my family, just as Scott had back in San Francisco. It gave me comfort and kept my connection with Scott alive.

I mustered up my courage to ask, "Would you like to have supper with me tomorrow evening?"

Where this bravery came from, I'll never know, but I was willing to take a chance.

"I have cucumbers, eggplant, onions, and some special spices I bought at the agora. I guarantee it will be delicious. You can be the first one to try a new fig cake I just made too." I looked at him for a swift yes, but he hesitated as my heart sank.

"I have a meeting with Alexander tomorrow but can come after. It might be around nightfall."

A broad smile crossed my face. "Perfect! I'll see you then. Come hungry!"

I wasn't ready to leave the city yet. The temples glowed in the late afternoon light, casting their shadows toward the promenade and providing shade for its strollers.

I stopped at the Temple of Heracles to take a closer look at the intricate details carved into its pillars. Life-size lions graced the top of the entrance columns, I guessed to announce the power of the mighty god.

To see this in real life humbled me and emotion rose in my throat, my eyes swelling with tears. For the Greeks, now Sicilian people, these magnificent works of art were part of everyday life, but to me, they represented the strength and endurance of a society. These attributes were embedded into the men and women who lived here, and perpetuated into future generations. How did our 2017 world become a haven of power for some, but for many, a world of lost hope?

I retreated to my valley, my paradise, and settled in for the evening. There were upcoming days to occupy my mind—my date tomorrow with Ries, a beekeeping lesson, and the festival of Thesmophoria next month. I didn't know much about this festival but did know it involved Demeter and her power and control over all our agricultural endeavors. The women of Girgento had started preparation for the festival to celebrate the harvest of wheat and barley, and the sowing of seeds for future fertility for the land as well as for the women of child-bearing age. Some of the wealthier women had asked me earlier in the month if they could hold the first day of their three-day ceremony in our garden. I was not invited because of my single status but nevertheless would oversee readying the area they requested, next to the grove of almond trees. Alexander's wife, Alena, also asked, really demanded, that I provide all the participants with wreaths of fresh herbs and flowers for their hair. Her attitude made me feel subservient and I still could not figure out why she didn't like me. It was her party, and she was married to the tyrant, so I adhered to her wishes. Sleep came quickly and there were no dreams of the goddess who haunted me.

Iris made an appearance at my door at daybreak. Sparta rose with me to greet our visitor. I rubbed my eyes to focus and noticed she'd been crying. She rushed toward me, and her trembling body embraced me like a child who had just had a nightmare.

"Iris, what's wrong?" I asked. She was visibly shaken and almost uncontrollable.

"Another nightmare. This time she caught me and was preparing me as a sacrifice."

I hugged her tightly. "Maybe you are thinking of the upcoming festival and worried that Alena will find fault with you." I shouldn't have said it, but I did. Alena rubbed me the wrong way, and I'm sure she put pressure on Iris to bend the truth to her and Alexander's advantage.

"She is never satisfied and always finding fault in me. Alexander likes me, but she is evil!" Iris wailed.

Iris needed consolation but I didn't want to slip into a situation where I could be implicated into gossip about Alena.

"Iris, it's okay. You are anticipating things that have not occurred. What happened to shake your confidence?" Iris looked at me and I could tell there was a secret inside her she was not ready to reveal.

"Nothing really, maybe a comment from Alena about how this year's wheat harvest must be the largest ever, so we could show our power to the hovering Carthaginians who constantly threaten to dissolve our society."

I was shocked that Alena had even insinuated that Iris might lie in order to protect Girgento. I could see where

Alena was coming from, a protection mode for her husband's future.

"Did she ask you to exaggerate the harvest yield?" I asked.

"Yes, but in a roundabout way. If the harvest records did not reflect a substantial increase in production, she would ask her husband to seek other oracles for Girgento. My credibility would be dissolved, and then where would I go? I would be an outcast and forced to flee into the hills with no one to believe me."

I was disappointed in this apparent blackmail. Alexander had no idea his wife was plotting behind his back, all to control his status and keep her in the height of society. Typical of women during this age, I thought. Some things never change. The thing that made me sad was that Iris was truly always wanting to help Girgento. Her connections with the gods and goddesses were real, and all she wished for was the best for everybody. She was not conniving or diabolical. How Alena could use Iris like this angered me, but I resisted the opportunity to implode like I would have in the past.

I'd have to create a strategy for both parties, a mutually beneficial agreement. This would take some contemplating. How much I wanted to get involved in the backstabbing part of this episode would have to wait. I had better fish to fry. Like preparing a dinner for Ries so delicious that he would fall under my spell. I'd much rather focus on a relationship that could possibly protect my career than worry about female catfights. I felt callous.

"Iris, why don't I prepare an infusion to relax you while you nap? I must begin my garden duties." I handed her a cup of chamomile tea and offered her my bed as I closed the door.

I replayed my conversations with Iris. Alena was

blackmailing her at the same time Ignatius was blackmailing us! There must be a connection. This was all about power. I had power too, but how would I use it? If it came down to it, I would do anything to protect myself, Jory, and Iris—and I mean anything.

In order to integrate into Girgento, I quickly learned that complacency was not an option. Right now, I was involved only so much as a gardeness and herbalist, and pretty much kept to myself. I didn't want to take sides. Girgento was an intimate society; even though there were about a hundred and twenty thousand people, there was no privacy, and at some point I would be forced to choose a side. I preferred the mediator status, but everyday life became a little more complicated with the friendships I was forming. I would hold off as long as possible, but sooner rather than later, I'd learn that my survival depended on certain relationships and others would need to be suppressed, possibly in ways never acceptable in my old life.

That night, Demeter appeared in my dreams holding a wheat stalk. Again, she tried to hand it to me, with a sense of urgency, but my arms were not long enough to take it from her. Her face appeared anxious, and for once I saw her eyes meet mine in desperation. My vision faded to darkness.

15

BEEKEEPING 101

I met Philo in Burgio, a small hilltop town about two kilometers outside Girgento. Beekeeping fascinated me but it seemed like too much work in San Francisco. My life back then had so many more components and time occupiers, like computers and going to bars and bistros. Who had time to watch a bunch of bees? Finding Philo was like an anticipated Christmas gift, all wrapped up in one neat package, just waiting for me to open it. I was eager to learn from a master; how often did this happen? The bees were kept in about fifty hives near a grove of olive trees and bushes of wild purple salvia. The island was ripe with an abundance of options for bees to pollinate. My mind was calculating the various kinds of honey options. Rosemary, lavender, sage ... The honey could be added to other herbs or used to flavor baked goods. The possibilities were endless.

Caught in this daydream, something I did often, Philo said to me, "Alexis, look! The queen is telling her workers to start the honey production."

I watched in fascination as the bees huddled together, each with its own job but working as a team to release the honey in the waxy shells lining the hives. We moved from hive to hive, each in rhythm with the next, mesmerized by their focused activity. Philo described all the steps the bees were taking as we watched them in action. No book to read, no notes to take, just observation as my lesson. This was the way I learned best, and it was all soaking in.

"I will work with you for one lunar cycle to teach you the bees' habits, and after that you will manage the hives yourself here in Burgio. When you are ready, we will move the hives to Girgento at nightfall so the forager bees will not be left behind."

"How will they reorient themselves once they have been moved?" I asked.

"We will block the hive for three days and leave plenty of room for ventilation. Before we release them into their new environment, we will place a branch of sage near the entrance. This marker will cause the bees to acknowledge its presence, navigate around it, and then recognize it as a place to return to. The upcoming cooler weather will make for an easier transport and more comfortable ride for the bees."

I laughed at this remark and began gathering up some honey to take home.

Jory and I had discussed the placement of the hives and decided upon a berm just behind our herb garden. The bees would be free to roam and then return to their hives, close enough for me to keep an eye on them. Philo would offer me his protective gear to wear when it came time to gather the honey. I made a small amount of money from my herbal business but not enough to start an entire new one. There would be no money exchanged between Philo and me. He was grateful to keep the bees alive and knew how important they were to the balance of nature. In return, he could have all the honey, olive oil, and herbs he wanted. It was a mutually beneficial relationship, although I thought I was getting the better end of the deal.

My first lesson ended, and I almost didn't want to go home. Philo was an old soul, a kind of father figure to me, and there was so much to learn from him—and not just about the bees. The bees told their own story and Philo interpreted them for me with humor and mystique. If he were alive during my old time period, he could have written a best-selling book. I would soon discover that adjacent to his kind soul, he had a darker side, like we all do, as well.

I would soon find out that with the bees comes the stinger.

16

SECRET LOVERS

Even though I didn't want to become part of the gossip circle surrounding Iris's issues with Alena, I did need to check on her. We were friends and she was literally the only woman I had a relationship with. I needed her as an ally, and she needed me, so for the time being, we would be confidants. She had requested a tincture for sleep, and this would be my excuse for the visit. Despite the drizzles of rain released from the sky, I threw on a hat and climbed up the stairs to the city. The weather didn't distract the people working but the energy was much subdued from yesterday's activity. Iris could usually be found at the Temple of Zeus, but I decided to start at the temple closest to the gardens and make my way down the street.

The Temple of Castor and Pollux stood practically at the entrance to Kolymbethra, its two columns designating it as a temple dedicated to the twins; a smaller sanctuary temple was attached to the larger structure and dedicated to Demeter and her daughter, Persephone. It was smaller than the other temples but with grand, circular pathways around it, leading to its doorway. I approached quietly, not wanting to disturb Iris if she was speaking with the gods. The temple seemed vacant, yet I heard her talking to someone. I was certain the gods didn't speak verbally. Didn't they communicate with some kind of silent signal or a vision?

The voices were more of a murmur, a moaning, and came from two people in an adjacent alcove. I couldn't imagine who Iris would be with. She never mentioned a love interest, but we hadn't really shared all our secrets, yet. It sounded like bodies pressed against the wall, and the sounds of passion grew louder. I felt like a voyeur, a busybody, but I had not asked for this. A final loud shove and high cry and it was over. I wanted to leave, but for some strange reason, wanted even more to know who her secret lover was. I hoped it wasn't Ries. She could not know I had been here, and my conscience got the better of me. I ran through the stone markers, violating the circle path and heading straight toward the stairs to Kolymbethra. Curiosity got the better of me and I hid behind a tree to watch for the man who was secretly having sex with Iris. It was a secret too. If she had a lover, why didn't she see him at night, in her own bed? Finally, a tall man with brown hair exited the doorway, straightened his robe, and looked both ways before quickly darting down a side path between the temples. I recognized him immediately. Iris was in a world of big trouble.

My mind swirled with this new information I had just witnessed. I didn't know if I should confront Iris or pretend nothing happened. If I confronted her, I'd be vulnerable to her possible manipulations, and if I didn't, and someone else found out, she could, and probably would, lose her life. I'd settle into my garden for a while and receive guidance from the plants, the only religion I knew. If there was another priestess here, I would go to her for consultation.

I needed someone to confide in. This was a secret too

hard to hold on to.

17

THE DINNER

I plucked some basil and mint leaves and concentrated on my dinner that evening with Ries. A version of caponata would be nice, followed by fish and then my special fig cakes, all washed down with a vase of red wine. How romantic. I'd need to cook the eggplant, capers, onion, pepper, and artichokes together and let the flavors marry before adding the herbs. The combination of basil and mint would add depth, sort of like a pesto.

I hadn't promised Ries fish but would surprise him and feed him like a king. In one end of our garden, a man-made pool, or lake, the size of six stadia or stadiums, held fish for everyone. A community fishing pond that provided a constant supply of protein for Girgento's citizens. I loved to eat fish, but killing them?

Sparta accompanied me as I mustered up courage for a fishing expedition. I grabbed a net the size of a tennis racket and marched bravely to the edge of the pool. This act would have to be swift. One swoop of the net into the water, a grab of the wiggly tail, and a whack on a nearby rock. And then it was over. The fish dangled from my fingers as I transported it back to my house to clean, gut, and descale. Sparta clung to my side, hoping I'd share. My prize was about a half a kilogram, easily large enough for two. He would be cooked whole and stuffed with onion, salt, pepper, and a few strands of my prized saffron.

Back home I loved to bake cookies, cakes, and pies. I'd share them with my neighbors and workmates. Here, I had learned to deconstruct the recipes I had in my head and adapt them using ingredients like olive oil, ground barley and wheat, and fruits for sweeteners. I mostly missed my butter. For the fig cakes, I cut up dried figs, then mixed them with ground almonds, along with fennel seeds, some wine and honey to bind them together, and a handful of chopped pistachios. A sprinkling of pomegranate seeds gave a dash of color elegance, like scattered rubies. This experimental recipe would become my signature and a gift to my best customers as a token of appreciation.

Ries arrived on time, just as the sun left the sky. His smile and penetrating eyes let me know he was just as happy to be here as I was to have him. I had fashioned a garland of laurel, rosemary, thyme, and sage flowers as a wreath for my wavy, mahogany locks, and placed a necklace of shells and colored rocks I had made around my neck. This was the most dressed up I'd been since my date with Scott that seemed like a lifetime ago. In Italy, they have this expression, "bella figura," meaning to make a good impression. This was my interpretation.

"Sparta, it's okay," I assured him in a quiet voice, in an attempt to stop his low, protective growl.

Ries reached out to him and calmly stroked his neck. Sparta slunk down then retreated to lie by my bed, keeping an eye on the situation.

"A gift for your generosity," he said, handing me a black hand-painted amphora decorated with leaves and flowers.

It was too beautiful to use, a work of art that would

finally decorate my barren home. I carefully placed it on a shelf, grasped his hand, and thanked him profusely, my heart beating a little faster. Ries had chosen this vase specifically for me and I was tempted to hold my hands to his face and kiss him in gratitude, but that would come later. I hoped.

We sat next to each other, the fire in front of us, and talked of life as we slowly ate the three courses I had prepared. Ries made faces as he ate the caponata, trying to decipher the ingredients.

"Umm," he said as olive oil dripped down his chin. With a swipe of his hand, it was gone, and he dug in for another spoonful. "Tastes unlike any caponata I've ever had. Nice blend of spices," he said.

"Just a little magic in my cooking is all," I said with the wink of an eye.

The flavors were subtle, each component complementing the other, making them difficult to detect. Besides the usual eggplant, peppers, onions, and capers, I had added raisins, olives, pine nuts, and a touch of must wine. When I told him my secrets, he asked for more. I had hit one of his soft spots—his love of food. Well, that was one thing we had in common.

One of the Girgenti lettuces was much like Romaine but with smaller heads and soft, tender leaves. Using my past knowledge of Thai cooking, I converted the idea of chicken lettuce wraps into something playful and easy to eat.

"This is how I like to eat the fish," I said as I spooned the fragrant fish onto the leaves and lifted it to my mouth. Ries followed suit, at first crinkling his forehead and looking perplexed.

"Ingenious! Are you a chef as well as a gardener?" He laughed and then after taking a bite said, "Saffron . . .

subtle but distinctive."

The leisurely dinner so far had lasted about two hours. The wine flowed freely as did my outpouring of thoughts to him. Certain things about him reminded me of Scott, like his self-confidence and ease of conversation. But he was different, maybe a bit more arrogant. Still, I couldn't stop the tingling of nerves that rippled through my body when I was around him.

He finally asked, "So, you promised me fig cakes?" And then he kissed me.

Ries did not go back to his own bed that night. I guessed the Greeks didn't waste time dating and they expressed their affection quickly. I was not shy and figured why not enjoy someone else's company in an era of free love, although ours must be secretive. Ries had sex appeal and I wondered how many other women enjoyed his body as well. I was not the jealous type and was only here for a short period, until the goddesses of time travel would allow me back. I would have no objection to this affair, as long as it didn't interfere with my or his work. It felt good to be with someone I could forget the day's cares with, especially since we really didn't know each other well. My private relationships would be kept secret and I hoped he felt the same way. We hadn't talked about this discretion, but it would be the first topic of discussion the next time we saw each other. Soon, I hoped.

<h1 style="text-align:center">18</h1>

ECLIPSES AND STINGERS

Iris was on my mind, and I wondered if her dreams were still aligning with mine. The recent addition of a wheat stalk to my visions of Demeter had me baffled. I checked the closest temple, Castor and Pollux, to see if she might be there, hoping not for a repeat of my last visit. Iris was kneeling at the altar, offering gifts to the gods and whispering inaudible prayers as candles flickered. I remained still but she felt my presence and turned around, motioning me to approach her.

"Am I interrupting you?" I asked.

"Sort of, but it can wait. I've been receiving guidance from Zeus, but with interruptions from Demeter."

Shivers ran down my spine. "What does Demeter say to you?" I queried.

"She keeps trying to give me a date. This number has been repeated over the years, but the message is stronger and stronger now."

I pushed further. "What kind of date? A number? A lunar cycle?"

"I get a vision of a dark moon blocking the sun," she whispered.

Perhaps this was a solar eclipse. "How often does that

happen?" I asked.

"Not since the greats last visited."

I had no idea what she was talking about, but it seemed like a long time ago.

"When will the sun go dark?" I asked.

"Soon. I will wait for more answers."

"What is this date in reference to?"

"I am not sure, but it seems urgent," Iris said.

"I need to tell you about a dream I had about Demeter," I began. "She came to me waving a stalk of wheat. Could there be a connection?" Iris scrunched her face in a puzzled look and sat quietly.

I continued. "This must be a foreboding—something to do with the missing wheat. What would happen if it was not discovered by the dark sun?"

"Disaster," was her one comment.

We looked at each other and realized that Demeter was working through both of us to send an urgent message.

I lowered my voice and said, "We must find out who is responsible. Who would want to hurt Girgento this way? Without the wheat, people will starve."

"I will do some investigating. I have inside sources," Iris said.

At that, we parted ways deep in thought, Iris returning to her altar and me back to Kolymbethra.

I was in our workshop, gathering tools for my daily caretaking activities, when a figure appeared in the doorway. I looked up to see the stunning Alena, every hair in place and her robe adorned with a large oval gold brooch, an obvious display of her wealth. I assumed she was here to discuss the festival details and probably add something else to the long list she expected me to do. As I fixated on the pin, she began speaking without a hello.

"Alexis, I have a friend with a husband whose eyes wander. This woman would like to bear children, but it seems he finds favor with a younger woman instead of his own wife. Can you make a potion to lure him back?"

This request set me back. I couldn't believe Alena was asking me for something to control, obviously, her own husband, not a friend's. I didn't know anything about aphrodisiacs. My herbals had uses in medicine and small injuries, not in manipulating people's lives. I wasn't sure what to say to her or even how to conjure up this specific tincture.

For some reason I answered, "I think I can help your friend. Give me a week's time to formulate it. I will bring it to you when it is ready."

Alena gave me a halfhearted smile, thanked me, and left swiftly. Why had I promised something I didn't have a recipe for? If I didn't come up with anything, she might think me a fake and make more trouble for me. A plan came to mind. I would make a flower tincture with red clover and chaste berry for fertility. And she would drink it, not Alexander. Alena would believe in the tincture, seduce her husband, and hopefully get pregnant in the process. Here I was interfering in people's lives, but it was for the better, right? I'd be helping both of them and maybe mend their strained marriage as a bonus. Inspired, I got right to work.

My beekeeping lessons carried on, weekly now, and I gained confidence, learning how to handle the hives to avoid being stung. Philo's enthusiasm made him the perfect mentor, sometimes his teachings so intense I was afraid I couldn't remember it all. It was as if he wanted to cram it all into my brain as quickly as possible.

"Alexis, it is time to extract the honey from the hives. Here are the important steps you need to follow," he said. "Step one, the bees must be out hunting pollen. This usually happens in the afternoon. Step two, put on your face net and gloves, just in case a lone bee is still in the hive. Step three, lift the covers off the hives one by one and carefully pour the honey into these small vases. If you see a few sharp, tiny black stingers in the hive, remove them and place them into this cloth."

I didn't know why he wanted to save the stingers but adhered to his instructions. Together we followed the procedures he outlined. When the honey was all collected, I removed my glove to inspect the hive for stingers. Three stingers sat randomly in the bottom of the first hive, and I used my fingernails to pick them up. The next hives were barren of stingers, but the last hive contained five. All the stingers were placed on the specified cloth, and Philo wrapped them up and put them in his pocket.

Then he said, "Let's taste the honey and see if we can tell which flavor the bees decided upon."

I stuck my finger in a vase, scooped up a large glob of glistening, thick golden syrup, hunched over, and quickly brought it up to my lips, the excess honey dripping to the ground. "Sage!" I exclaimed.

Philo did the same and after his taste, said, "Brava, Alexis! A master beekeeper you will be someday."

I replied, "If I am to be a master of my craft, I must know why you save the stingers."

Philo hesitated and finally said, "A very wise man, the one who taught me the trade, cautioned me to never let a stinger remain in the honey. You see, the stinger contains a poison which can make a person very sick."

"Yes," I said, "but the stingers were at the bottom of the hive, and I was careful not to let any of them enter the vase."

"You listened to me, Alexis. Good. Someone else might not have, and then the honey could be tainted. The stinger needs to inoculate the honey for at least a month to increase its potency. After that, it could be deadly. We harvest the honey immediately, so it is not a problem. But left too long ..." His voice drifted off.

I was taken aback by all this. I'd never heard of a stinger being used as a poison, but it made sense. Some people did die from bee stings. Would he destroy the stingers we collected, or was he saving them for something or someone? I tucked this information into the back of my mind, hoping I'd never need the stingers. But if times got desperate?

19

THE FESTIVAL OF THESMOPHORIA

October

The festival of Thesmophoria would begin in two days. I pruned the plants near the grove of almond trees where the celebrants were to gather, and wove herbs and flowers together for forty or more hair crowns for the women participants. I didn't quite understand why single women were not permitted, especially me, the person who brought health and sustenance to the community. Demeter and I were old friends, working together in harmony for successful crops and also for fertility. I thought of the tincture I created for Alena and wondered if she had used it or what effects it might have had on her unfaithful husband. She never acknowledged me in public nor reported back. I'm sure this wasn't the last of her requests from me, especially if the tincture proved successful.

At dawn, a processional of white-robed women carrying torches entered Kolymbethra, in single file, down the pathway into the garden. As they reached the last step, I placed a wreath on each woman's head, my only contribution to the ceremony. I watched as they gathered in a circle and began singing softly. The day before, two

170

matriarchs of our society brought basketfuls of sacred objects to be placed in another one of Demeter's more rustic temples—a cave— a short walk away. This chamber harbored an underground room that represented a womb, and sacrificial objects of dough cakes fashioned in male and female genitalia adorned the altar, indicating, as far as I could tell, tools necessary for fertility.

Piglets were burned and their charred remains added to fir pine cones. The piglets and pine cones, prolific as they were, exemplified things that reproduced in abundance. Finally, wheat seeds and mulch were sprinkled on top to ensure a hefty and strong crop. The entire sacred ritual, dedicated to the two goddesses Demeter and Persephone, would also bring more babies to Girgento, specifically male babies to continue a powerful military and strong workforce.

In order to not feel left out, I too made my own contribution to the ceremony. The night before the event, I slipped into the musty ceremonial cave and wound my way down the stone steps in the cavern that held the sacred sacrifices. A small amphora sat next to the altar with the seeds that would be mixed into the fertility ingredients. Still uncertain of the role I was to play in solving the mystery of the missing wheat, I had decided to cover all bases, both in the physical and the spiritual world. I reached into my pocket and pulled out the small bag of Forza seeds I'd been saving just for this event.

As if Demeter were watching, I gently stirred some of my seeds into the ceremonial seeds and whispered, "I honor you, Demeter, and your daughter, Persephone. These seeds will bring renewed life to Girgento and fertility to our crops and people."

I stood for a minute, taking it all in. Here I was, standing in a temple, speaking to a goddess I revered and admired. Her words scared me at first but now I found her presence comforting, as if she would protect me if anything happened. A kind of peace washed over me, with the hope I had fulfilled one of Demeter's missions. I took a deep breath and, making as little noise as possible, ascended the tiny stairs. A glance around told me my visit had gone unnoticed.

Thankfully, the participants only stayed for a short while in the garden before their next spiritual walk to visit the sanctuary temple of Demeter and Persephone. The ritual continued for three days, most of the activity at the temple. I only knew part of what happened, told to me by Iris one day. The rest of the function was kept a secret, only to be divulged if I were to marry. Not likely.

20

UNDER THREAT

With the future move of the hives and accompanying equipment and vases, I was eager to get our second building going. Our tiny workshop bulged with vases for my medicinals and drying herbs and flowers. Leandro was due for a meeting today and Jory and I would lay out the plans for construction. We decided on the perfect spot right next door to our original workshop and could now designate one workspace for me, my herbs and honey, and the other for Jory, his tools, woodworking area, and storage for drying vegetables and fruits. It was as if I was getting my dream home on a sweepstakes, but it was only a mud and sandstone building to house necessities for work. I had very little money but would give Leandro what I could each week. Jory really didn't have any more money than I did, at least I didn't think he did, but would contribute his fair share too. After the meeting, Jory asked me to walk with him through the gardens. He had something on his mind.

Jory and I were amicable but not necessarily chatty with each other. He opened up a whole other world of gardening to me, far more advanced than anything I could ever imagine. I learned mostly by observing and then by doing, not by speaking. As we walked through the sacred groves of olive trees, their now barren branches waving with the breeze, he finally spoke.

"Alexis, my body cannot take hard work much longer. I tire easily and have no one to care for me, to cook or help me. My cousin lives in Gela and wants me to live with him there. You understand how Kolymbethra works, but can you do it by yourself?"

Jory didn't sound convincing. His words were forced, almost rehearsed. The way he went into a trance as soon as he picked up a tool to prune with, you knew he was in another world. Why this sudden idea to retire and leave me alone? Then I remembered seeing a man talking with him while he was planting a new seedling tree. This had struck me as odd since Jory rarely talked with anyone outside of our garden. I didn't question him, but maybe I should have.

"Who did you meet with last week, Jory?" I finally asked.

Jory took a deep breath. "One of Alexander's military men. He wanted to make sure garden could be kept safe if Carthaginians attempt an attack again. We all know this garden is respected all over Sicily, and damage to it could bring ruin."

"Is that all he wanted, Jory? Are you sure he did not ask you to leave before they made you, for whatever reason?"

Jory bit his lip, like he was thinking of what to say. He was most likely under oath not to repeat a word of the conversation and was given a story to tell if questioned.

"Alexis, I can't lie to you." Jory's compromised speech suddenly became articulate. "Our garden is under threat but not from Carthaginians. I trust you will tell no one what I am about to tell you."

The conversation went from bad to worse, and I could not believe what I was hearing from Jory. The military thought if they took over the garden, with slaves doing the manual labor, they could collect more money to fund their army, and hire and recruit more men to protect Girgento. Ignatius would be in charge, and I would be allowed only to provide medicinal resources and have little control over the garden. It would be a disaster. The slaves did not understand the lunar cycles and when to plant or harvest. They had not been trained to properly prune a tree or harvest grapes and olives. I was the gardeness of Kolymbethra and didn't want to give up this hard-earned title.

"Can I talk to Alexander about this?" I pleaded.

There was just too much to lose, and I wasn't giving up without a fight. I knew Jory did not have the backbone or confidence to confront Alexander, but I did. Plus, wasn't Alena now pregnant, thanks to me and my fertility tincture? Couldn't she be of influence?

"I promised not to share this information with you. I could face the senate and be tried for betrayal."

"When did Ignatius say this transition would occur?" I asked.

"Not for three lunar cycles." Jory looked like he was about to cry.

I leaned in toward him, looked him straight in the eyes, and said, "I will not give up easily, even if there is a battle to be had. These gardens will remain here for thousands of years, to feed and teach future generations."

Confusion washed over Jory's face. He couldn't figure out if I was just making a blanket statement or if I was predicting the future. My outburst had given away a clue about me, something that no one else could know. My secret with myself. I would be more careful with my words and get to work. Our timeline of three months was short, but long enough to convince Alexander to reverse this catastrophic decision.

"Alexis!" Ries's voice echoed down the garden pathway.

I emerged from behind a tall salvia bush, my arms full of the purple blossoms. Late afternoon clouds blanketed the sky, making it seem later than it was.

"Are you looking for me or for Jory?" I asked, without even a hello. I wondered if he knew of Ignatius's scheme to take over the garden. He was one of the top men of Girgento and I wasn't sure how intertwined their confidences were.

Without hesitation he reached out and pulled me close to kiss my lips, then released me slowly.

"I take it you missed me," I said with a chuckle.

It had been more than a week since our night of intimacy. I had remained Persephone, underground, and he above.

"What do you have for a man who works too hard with little time for play?" he teased. "I think of you when I should be studying our plans for Concordia." His eyebrows raised up and down in a seductive manner. "Speaking of plans, there's a lecture tonight in the outdoor theater, given by Empedocles. His philosophy is worth listening to. Will you go with me?"

I had heard of the philosopher and scientist Empedocles, even seen him talking to groups of people in the agora. I wanted to exchange ideas with him of the medicinal kind but there were always too many people around. Listening to him speak would be of interest.

"I would love to join you and hear his views," I

replied.

"Okay, great. Meet me at the theater after dusk," Ries said, and I nodded my head.

He smiled and turned around to walk back up the steps to the above-ground world. I wondered what he had planned for us after the lecture.

Empedocles helped put Girgento on the map as their official celebrity. Philosopher, astronomer, physician, a little bit of everything brainy, he also was a contemporary of Socrates. Our society was proud that he was one of their own, born here and a contributing citizen. I was curious to hear about his latest discoveries and also to see the reaction of the audience. He was ahead of his time with his theory of the four elements of fire, water, earth, and air. To be honest, I had never heard of the man before living here, and now I was about to see him in person.

Ries was standing near the entrance and motioned me to follow him down the steps to a second-row seat.

He leaned over and said, "Do you have any of that fig cake left?"

I knew what he really meant and would welcome some company in my swiftly changing world. Empedocles entered the stage, wearing a purple robe and golden sandals, his standard attire. We leaned in to listen as Empedocles described how math and numbers could explain the universe, a theory introduced by Pythagoras and now embraced by him.

"Four elements govern our universe," he began.

The silent crowd sat motionless in their seats, taking in every word.

"Earth, air, fire, and water are material causes of existence," he continued.

I struggled to understand his scientific approach, but he did combine science with a sort of mythical theory as well.

I remembered learning about the four-element theory but had no idea that this man, in front of me now, was the creator of these ideas. He caught my attention enough to put him at the top of my list of people to meet to discuss herbal medicine and how it integrated with science. Our gardening had so much to do with the lunar cycles, and if I could understand the astronomical implications, perhaps we could grow stronger crops.

Sparta crouched behind a bush by my house waiting for me to come home. He was a one-person dog and suspicious of other people, especially men. When he heard Ries's voice, he growled softly. I reassured him with long pets and neck kisses, and he slunk back to his hiding place, in hopes Ries would leave soon so he could be the one to sleep cuddled up next to me. I didn't have the heart to tell him he'd be alone tonight. I opened the container of my fig cake and handed Ries a piece. I also poured us both a glass of wine, just like I would have done back home, although I wasn't sure if this was the custom here. Wouldn't hurt to try. Ries accepted both gladly and we sat down to tell each other the past week's adventures.

The temples took years to build, and the Concordia would be a masterpiece, he said. I wanted to tell him about Ignatius's plan, but could I trust him? We joked about Alena's pregnancy and how she finally got her way with her husband, although I secretly suspected Alexander was still seeing Iris. This fact I would never reveal to Ries. I pried gently about Ignatius and what kind of person he was. He too pried, asking me questions about how I learned to make tinctures and medicinals. How strong could I make a tincture? he asked, and I wondered why he was interested. Pain medicine, he answered, for his men on the front line. I didn't give away any of my formulas but teased him mercilessly about what I could and could not make. It was a game we were playing with each other, back and forth, until I finally decided to end it and initiate the kiss. His kisses made my body quiver, and the social connection with him made me feel safe and secure in these shaky times. Emotional therapy. Once again, Ries kept me warm at night, folding his strong arms around me like a pretzel. He was growing on me, physically and emotionally. It was a mutually beneficial relationship, and at the moment, I was grateful for it.

The seeds Scott had gifted me now reached a height of one long finger and serrated leaves were beginning to form. He called them "special" seeds, which I took to mean that they were not the vervain I grew back in California, although they did share the same characteristics. I thought of the Forza Scott formulated. The day he gave it to me, he had rattled off five different herbs, but I could only remember three of them: vervain, lavender, clary sage.

The evening before I traveled back in time, he promised to tell me the ingredients the next day. But that day never happened. I'd have to use my new knowledge and make several experiments to recreate the tincture. Would these seeds I just discovered, now growing profusely here in my garden, be a part of this herbal? Somehow, I didn't think so. These seeds were meant to be on their own, a single tincture. Only time would tell.

I was more determined than ever to save our gardens and felt time would soon evaporate. I now had a prominent role in this society, but could I use my influence to sway the decision to turn over the garden to the military? An idea popped into my head. Iris had a relationship with Alexander. Why couldn't I ask her to intervene, talk to him about all this, tell him how valuable Jory was, and how the gardens would suffer under inexperience? It would be a risk and could get both Jory and me into trouble, but I had vowed to Jory to do everything in my power to save our jobs. Now I was calling up that power in a big way.

"Iris," I called into the Temple of Heracles. She often was here in the middle of the day, validating my hunch.

"Alexis! Where have you been?" she cried.

I had been to visit her a week ago, but she had been preoccupied. "The garden keeps me busy, and now with the new hives coming in soon and the construction of another workshop, well, you know," I replied.

I wanted to approach the conversation about Ignatius with a delicate touch so carefully formulated my words.

"Are you friendly with Ignatius? What's he like?" I asked.

Iris looked surprised. "Why, are you interested in him?" Why did she always think I was interested in men in a relationship way?

"No," I replied sharply. "I need information about him and wondered if you could help me."

"He constantly brings offerings to the gods, especially Heracles, and asks me to have the gods give his military men protection. He is obsessed with power and money, and sometimes cruel," Iris said.

"What do you mean, cruel?" I asked.

This part about being cruel scared me and was what I needed to know about him. If I made trouble for him, would he punish me in some way?

Iris said, "By cruel, he often beats the men who are the weak ones. He says it is to make them stronger, but I think he just enjoys using his power in a negative way. He uses women but has no wife. Sometimes I see him arguing with a merchant about price, trying to get a better deal. His ego is swollen."

I took a deep breath and raised my eyebrows in comprehension. I was taking on a major figure in Girgenti and I was just the gardeness. I would need all the help I could get, and I hoped I'd found it in Iris.

"Can I confide in you, Iris?" I asked, finally realizing I could trust her. She looked at me in a quizzical fashion then shook her head up and down without speaking.

"Ignatius wants the military to be in charge of the garden in three lunar cycles. Carthaginian slaves would work it. He insists they need the money from the garden to hire more men and build a stronger army. I'm afraid they will destroy our beautiful Kolymbethra with their ignorance and lack of knowledge. They can't nurture her like Jory and I can. They want Jory to leave and for me to just make medicinals but have no part in the rest of the garden. I just can't let this happen! Can you do anything to help us?"

Iris looked perplexed and then nodded her head again. "I can see how he could be difficult. Perhaps I can have a word with Alexander, but I need some kind of strategy to be convincing."

Strategy was the key word here. Alexander was a smart man and could not be easily swayed without good cause. This is what made him such a strong but gentle leader. It was Alexander who brought me to Kolymbethra in the first place, to replace Jory should he no longer be able to do his job with all his disabilities. He believed in me, but would he side with the other power force, Ignatius?

Iris finally spoke. "Couldn't you make a tincture to weaken his power, or to make him lose his mind?"

"Iris," I said, "I want your help to deal with this honestly. A tincture will not change him." Or could it? I secretly thought to myself.

"I am beginning to think that Ignatius has something to do with the missing wheat. He is just too persistent in his obsession to take over the gardens."

"Meet me tomorrow morning while everyone is busy, and we can take a look about," Iris said. "Maybe try to locate the missing wheat. Not a word to anyone."

I agreed. We hugged like sisters and went our separate ways. If Iris couldn't help me, I'd go to Ries for advice. As I left, Alena entered the temple and walked straight toward Iris, in her usual haughty way, head held high and full of confidence. I could almost channel what was about to be discussed. I guessed Alena used Iris for many things, not just exaggerating harvest yields. Please, though, nothing so bad it would trigger a repeat performance of Iris's nightmares last month when she ended up on my doorstep.

21

THE INTRUDER

Leandro sat on a bench outside our workshop with something in his hands. I had just returned to my gardens after a discussion with Iris and was not in the mood to talk. His smile reversed my decision and I invited him in for a cup of tea. Before we had a chance to step into my house, Leandro looked to the distance and in a humble voice said, "Alexis, I found this in one of my drawers and wanted you to have it."

He handed me a wooden box carved with olive leaves. Another gift from a man. These men in Girgento were so thoughtful and the attention I received was heartwarming. The top of the box lifted off to reveal a small carved bird nestled inside. How did he know how much I loved birds? I picked it up, the size of my baby fingernail, and admired it up close, the intricate feather carving so lifelike.

"Leandro, this is such a special gift. How can you part with it?" I said, our eyes connecting, the way it is when the eyes tell everything about a person. His, in particular, revealed a genuine spirit of kindness.

"My hobby is making things with wood. I build temples all day with sandstone, so this gives me a chance to express my creativity in another way. She is a dove I watched years ago, who nested near my house. I carved her as a tribute. When her babies hatched and began to run around, she allowed me to get close enough to observe their delicate little figures."

I gasped at the intricate bird. Leandro's sensitivity stunned and overwhelmed me. We both had an admiration for the doves, and he had shared something created from his heart. I was beginning to feel a connection to Leandro but couldn't put my finger on it.

"This gift is meaningful. I will weave her into this," I said, pointing at the shell necklace I wore daily. "She will have a prominent place in the center."

Leandro's face broke out in a broad grin, happy that his gift had found the perfect recipient. Even though I wanted to tell him of the white dove in my garden back home, I didn't dare.

Leandro's work was precise but not slow. The building seemed to arise out of nowhere and was halfway completed. What would happen to this building once Ignatius took over, if he did? Would this still be my personal workshop to formulate the medicinals needed for the community? Only time would tell but I was going forward, business as usual. Leandro's hand had healed, the ointment I made for him easing the pain and reducing the bruising. He didn't ask much from me and continued on in a humble manner. More and more, Leandro's company brought me a certain sense of comfort. I felt he was out for my best interests and wanted nothing in return. Could I add him to my list of trusted allies?

I wondered if Ries had kept our little affair a secret, as we discussed, or if he bragged about his conquests. Life here could be an open book, so as much as I used to value my privacy, I knew it probably was not possible here. Leandro was a nice man and treated everyone with respect, not just me. There was no love interest between us, just a growing friendship. My circle of friends was expanding, each one offering a unique element to my life. Except Ignatius, my nemesis and challenge. Speaking of, I wondered if Iris had come up with a plan or strategy to stop him from his power rampage. I decided to make a visit to her, this time taking something for the gods so as not to raise suspicion. I gathered dried garlic heads that I kept hanging in Jory's shed and made my way up the hill.

This day Iris was back in Castor and Pollux. I could tell by the strand of laurel she had placed near the door. Sometimes she did this to indicate she was there, either with someone or speaking with the gods on behalf of someone. I approached quietly in hopes of not encountering Alexander again. Fortunately, Iris was in the front, placing objects on the altar and murmuring words I could not understand. I waited a few minutes and she turned around, sensing my presence. We walked toward each other and gave our usual hugs. Iris stole a glance at the door, as if to make sure no one else was watching or listening.

"I spoke to Alexander," she whispered. Shivers went down my spine in anticipation of the news. In a hushed voice she said, "He said he knew nothing of this plan and was happy with you and Jory managing Kolymbethra. He seemed upset that Ignatius would go behind his back. I told him you preferred to keep this private."

The cat was out of the bag. Alexander could either side with me or be convinced by Ignatius that the added income would make Girgento even stronger, a good argument. I would have to wait and see. I thanked Iris for her discretion and gave her the garlic I brought as offerings.

"Do you need more of my tincture to help you sleep or have the nightmares vanished?" I asked.

"The woman isn't chasing me anymore, thank goodness. The herbals are easing my mind. I still have plenty, but thank you."

I thought that maybe Alena was the crazy woman chasing her in her dreams but didn't dare broach the subject today. I'd had enough gossip to carry me through the week.

Sparta was waiting for me when I returned to my gardens, sensing my need for a hug. I wrapped my arms around his body, which was the size of a large wolf. His silky, long white fur comforted me in a way no man could. We had found each other, and our feelings were mutual, the one soul I could trust unconditionally. We made our rounds of the sprouting herbs and vegetables and picked a few ripe pomegranates to eat with dinner. When Sparta was around, we ate together, me sharing whatever I cooked with him. Most of the time, I suspected he hunted small rodents and ate remnants of pork or goat bones and scraps. He never begged and was always grateful for anything I could spare. Even though he was large, he tended to slink between bushes and vanish almost into thin air. Sometimes I didn't see him for days, but he always came back to me like a feral cat.

We snuggled together after dinner and were just getting comfortable when Sparta let out a deep growl to alert me of someone near my house. I heard it too, the crunch of footsteps just outside. Jory often walked around at night, but Sparta wouldn't growl at him, so even though I usually felt perfectly safe here in my gardens, a sense of trepidation came over me.

"Jory," I called out. No answer.

I wanted to open the door, but my fright held me back and I decided to stay put. The footsteps receded and we both settled down. Normally I would have summoned up my courage and faced whoever was intruding upon my space, but with all the uncertainty surrounding my life right now, I was glad I didn't. I could have let Sparta out to confront the person but knew he'd do anything to protect me and didn't want him to get hurt. We both finally fell into a restless sleep, eagerly anticipating the light of a sunrise.

Sparta's nose hit the ground the minute I opened my door in the morning, detecting the scent of the stranger last night. I grabbed a shawl, the days beginning to cool off, and followed him down the pathway. The door to our workshop was ajar. I peeked inside, even though I knew whoever had been there was long gone. An open cabinet showed the bottles inside had been disturbed and moved around. Jory and I were the only ones who knew what was in each bottle. We had our system, so was the person who had been here searching for something else? Then I noticed my large vase of concentrated valerian was missing. Valerian, the herb for sleep, took longer than other tinctures to make because it was derived from a root. To replace this would take time, especially because I diluted this concentrate for single and mixed medicinals. I carefully inspected the rest of my inventory and found only one other item absent—the small cloth bag of bee stingers Philo had left in my company. I couldn't figure out why he gave them to me; maybe because he didn't want them to get into the wrong hands. But now they had. And who would even know I had them in my possession? The mystery deepened.

I woke Jory to tell him of my discovery and the missing items. He said he hadn't heard anything last night and couldn't think of anyone who would want valerian. I kept the theft of the bee stingers to myself. Whoever took these two items knew what they were doing. The combination of valerian, a sleep inducer, and the bee's stinger could cause a person to go into a deep sleep before being poisoned. The perfect murder weapon. The tainted tincture could be added to wine with the designated victim suspecting nothing. I had given valerian to many of my clients, mostly as a combination with other herbs. I guessed this society had the same pressures as my old one, anxieties about work, family, money. But the thought never crossed my mind that someone would use my medicinals for harm rather than good.

Jory advised that we should report this theft to Alexander, and I agreed. He relied upon us to keep Girgento safe and healthy and had a vested stake in our business. Jory and I would both approach Alexander as a team to try to solve the mystery. In the meantime, we vowed to each other not to say a word, lest the gossip be released and the thief forewarned. I needed to protect myself. My trusting nature made it difficult to pin this violation on anyone we knew. Ignatius was the only one I was at odds with, and I hadn't even met him. What would he care or know about my tinctures, especially the stingers? But instead of dwelling on this incident, I made a decision to ride it out and let nature take its course. It did no good to speculate. I would take better care to put any stingers I acquired in the future into the cave with the other stored items like olive oil. They could be easily hidden behind rocks. I didn't understand why it was necessary to save the stingers until Philo confided in me how they had saved his life at one time. The stingers worked in ways I hoped I'd never have to use. I should have guarded them more carefully, but it didn't occur to me that anyone else knew of his secret. Stealing was a crime but not heavily punished unless it involved harm of another. I would wait and see on this.

22

SPARTA'S STRUGGLE

I spent the next days down below, buried in my garden, not even showing my face in Girgento. It was November now, and the mystery seeds had grown to a height of about fifteen inches tall and boasted blue and white daisy-like flowers, along with the serrated thin leaves reminiscent of the vervain. Unlike the vervain, their scent was of violets, and they attracted an abundance of bees.

In my old garden back home, I often left flowers to go to seed rather than cut them, so I could have continuous color in my yard, but I knew what I needed to do now. Scott had given me these seeds for a purpose, I surmised, so I would honor him by cutting the flower tops along with their leaves to make a few experimental tinctures and infusions. There weren't that many leaves and flowers so this batch would be small, a trial. Our workshop smelled like dried mint and oregano and basil; an Italian restaurant. I was in my comfort zone here, alone with my thoughts, often with Sparta napping nearby. He hadn't come around today and must have been out hunting for mice or scavenging scraps from the more affluent citizens.

I worked deliberately, using the methods Jory had taught me to measure the petals, then carefully packed the herbs into a small vase, covered it with wine, and tied up the rest to dry for a tea. I could try the new herb both ways. This would be my secret, without even Jory knowing my latest creations. Scott was often on my mind, almost channeling me, and I felt assured he would not let me down.

On day three after the theft, I started wondering where Sparta was. He had not shown up for his every-other-day meal and I began to worry about my dedicated pal. I decided to walk the gardens, starting at one end and continuing to the other, checking behind bushes just in case he was sleeping. Near the pond of fish, I heard a whimpering. Nausea gripped my stomach, anticipating something bad. Sparta lay hunched up near a lavender bush on his side and in obvious pain. I saw no evidence of blood or wounds. Could he have eaten something rotten to make him sick? He had an iron stomach and seemed invincible. I gathered him up in my arms and by some miracle, lifted him up to my shoulders and carried him back to my house. Lucky for him, he had a mom who had the resources to care for him.

I placed him on my bed to be comfortable and inspected his eyes and nose for signs of excess mucous. His stomach was tender to the touch, so I rubbed his temples and ears with lavender to relax him. Sparta trusted me and knew he was in good hands, his limp body succumbing to sleep. I mentally put together the combination of mint, chamomile, licorice, and slippery elm as I hurried to my workshop. These herbs, brewed collectively, could possibly relieve whatever what was disturbing this now frail life. His breathing was sporadic, and I was beginning to worry. When the tea cooled down, I gently poured some of the liquid into his mouth, his tongue unwilling to move it toward his throat. By tenderly massaging his neck, I was finally able to get him to swallow, giving me more relief than him. I covered him with my blanket and lay down next to him, my arms wrapped across his body as I said a prayer for his healing.

I didn't sleep a wink. Sparta's breathing accelerated and recessed like a waxing and waning moon, causing me to hold him tighter. This whole experience reminded me of my dear Lucas who had passed away last year. I would not let Sparta die. Not on my watch.

I must have finally dozed off because I awakened to someone licking my face. Relief poured over me and I gave words of gratitude to whatever god would listen. My Sparta was recovering but I would not let him out to roam for a long while. I had gone into protective mode and was not willing to lose another friend so soon. Questions loomed in my mind. Could Sparta have been poisoned? And how many people knew that we had a friendship? There were no toxicology reports in this life, and death by poison was suspected but never verified. My life had become one big question after another. The life I thought was so idyllic had just taken a big right turn for the worse, and I hadn't even glimpsed how extreme it would get.

Sparta took a few nibbles of cooked barley, along with more of my herbals— some burdock and milk thistle as a detoxifier for whatever hurt him. He actually licked up the bitter liquid almost with the intention of understanding it was helping him. This is what I loved about his complete trust and surrender. His weak body could use some protein, so I would net a fish for him. Anything to help my best friend and protector. Sparta was now my project and priority. Perhaps I would give him a dose of my newest tincture. I had a feeling it had components that would do both of us good.

When I knew Sparta would sleep for a while, I closed my door to keep him inside and left him to travel upstairs into the world of commerce. The Agora Magna always tempted me to enter its world of exotic international goods. It reminded me of a bazaar with its blazing colors of orange, blue, and red fabric table coverings, and flags to draw attention. I could use the escape into another place for a while. I hadn't cooked for myself much in the past few days and followed my nose to the aromas of simmering spices. Large pots with fire underneath contained something that looked like curry with onion, peppers, and pork. Another, more Greek-style stew held olives, capers, eggplant, and tiny octopus, fragrant with marjoram, oregano, and parsley. I asked for a small bowl of each and was offered a piece of nut bread to dip into the medleys. Wanting to enjoy this meal by myself, I sat on a bench under a tree, away from possible visitors. Many people knew me, or of me, and I often was asked for remedies while attempting to take alone time. After all that I'd been through these past days, I was in no mood to be interrupted. With time to finally think, I made a plan.

I finished my lunch, returned the bowl to the merchant, and got lost in the maze of offerings. Dried fruits from Egypt, salt from Trapani, vibrantly dyed fabrics from Greece, and Greek-style cheese. I bought a few special tiny vases for new herbal mixtures and a larger vase to replace the stolen valerian bottle.

In the booth next door, a hefty, olive-skinned woman sat on a stool, her fingers rapidly clicking two knitting needles together as if on automatic pilot. Her narrow, dark eyes looked up at me quizzically as if she were reading my thoughts and then glanced down to focus on the birthmark on my left arm.

She finally spoke. "You have just arrived?"

The woman caught me off guard with this question.

"I have been here a few months, er, I mean a few lunar cycles," I uttered. I had slipped up; hopefully this woman didn't notice my careless comment about months.

"I am Sibylle. You have had many lives."

I took a few steps back, almost losing my balance. How did she know? Her gaze stayed locked on my eyes.

She spoke again, "You have a purpose here."

Knowing I could not fool this Sibylle, who must have been a seer, I took a chance with my response. "I think I know my purpose."

"Your presence will have a great effect upon many lives. Make your choices carefully," she warned.

Sibylle was making me nervous. My birthmark triggered her attention. Maybe it had a significance. What else could she tell me? She could tell I wanted more information but instead looked down at her knitting. Discussion over. Mystified, I pondered her comments. Maybe I should be more careful about who I associated with. Who was she warning me about?

Breaking my thought process, she finally spoke, saying, "This shawl will protect you," as she unhooked a beautiful gray and white heather-colored shawl from the lineup of sweaters hanging above her head. It had the nubby texture I adored, that extra thickness that made the shawl cozy warm. I rubbed the soft goat hair against my cheeks and felt the long, silky fur, much like mohair.

Observing my obvious pleasure, she said, "I weave the shawls from the hair of my Girgentana goats. They are ancient, wise creatures."

The emotion behind her voice told me her goats were her pride and joy. Not only did these goats deliver fur for warmth but were also a source of sustenance, rich and creamy goat milk and cheese. Sibylle was right. The shawl met my needs and besides that, was crafted with the utmost love for her goats. How could I resist? I asked her if I could trade honey for part of the cost of the shawl and she agreed. I would treat myself with the cooling weather approaching and wrapped the warmth around my shoulders to wear it home, back to check on Sparta.

Just one more stop for Kalista's tangy goat cheese, a staple of my diet. Then I made my way past the sizable wood-fired oven, the line of customers waiting their turn to either cook their own bread or purchase it, and headed toward the downward stairs, lost in the aromas of the baking loaves.

"Alexis, are you leaving?"

I spun around to see Ries practically behind me, almost as if he had been following me.

"You frightened me, Ries. Yes, I'm leaving. There's still much to do in the garden this evening."

The dedication to my gardens almost irritated him sometimes. I could always find something to repair, prune, weed, or plant. The process continued and did not go on hold for vacations or time off.

"Would you like to walk along the beach tomorrow? Maybe we can catch an octopus lounging in the rocks? It would make a nice dinner."

The thought of killing an eight-legged monster reminded me of being in a myth, conquering the demon, and it did not appeal to me. I liked eating octopus but preferred not to watch them die.

"A walk would be nice but I'm not so sure about the octopus. How about we just enjoy the sand, crystal clear water, and sound of the waves?"

Ries looked at me and nodded, probably hoping he

could impress me with his fishing skills but those were not the type of things I valued in a man. He didn't have to know that. Ries was good company, kind, and loved to laugh, a quality I did value.

"We will see what the weather holds in the morning. I have a few tasks to do but after that can spare a few hours." I didn't want him to think I was his for the day. I was learning to set boundaries.

"Great, I will meet you at the Concordia early midday," he said.

"See you then," I agreed.

I really liked Ries, but was he trustworthy? Scott's advice again rang in my ear. To use your power, you needed trust. But more important, who to trust?

An idea popped into my head to give him a tincture of just chamomile and tell him it was a powerful herbal that would ignite his creative spirit and help him to design even more spectacular temples. Okay, so I am exaggerating, but something along those lines. The idea made me giggle out loud, so sneaky and mischievous. I'd get to the bottom of whoever tried to harm Sparta, and the thief who stole my stingers.

Sparta's eyes had cleared, and his ears perked up when I came into our house. The undisturbed sleep gave him the rest he needed to begin healing. I breathed a sigh of relief as he stretched his legs and headed toward the door. I fashioned a leash out of one of my braided belts and slipped it around his neck for a little walk. He wouldn't be far from my sight for the next few days. I would leave him in my house again while I walked with Ries tomorrow, but he would not know of Sparta's illness.

Later that evening I discovered a hidden pocket woven into the shawl's left upper shoulder. Sibylle had said the shawl would protect me. She also had a warning for me.

Was this pocket meant to hold some kind of protection? The knots in my stomach these thoughts provoked caused me a restless night. Would Demeter protect me, if it came down to that, or was I on my own?

The clouds were gathering the next day, but I decided to brave the weather for the beach. I draped my new wool shawl across my shoulders and with bare feet, walked through the archway of fruit trees, all the way up to the pond before ascending the back stairs. The Concordia sat on this side of the city and today I preferred the sights of the garden to the crowds. Ries was waiting for me with a basket in his arms.

"Picnic?" I said, not even knowing if they had picnics or knew what the term was. Ries gave me a puzzled look.

I started to explain, "A gathering of foods . . ." when he said, acknowledging the basket, "Yes! I have made fare for our outing. Ready?"

I was impressed by his thoughtfulness, and all ideas of him possibly being a traitor vanished. My heart lifted a little and he grabbed my hand for the duration of our adventure.

23

EMBRACE YOUR POWER

Three weeks had passed since I tinctured the plants from my phantom seeds, and now the dried leaves and flowers I had hung to dry were ready to infuse into a tea. I heated some water one morning and dropped in a few dried herbs to let them steep for ten or so minutes. The aroma was just as lovely as the flower itself, with scents of violet and sugar. A few sips of pure bliss and I knew this tea would be in demand, as long as it had no ill side effects. I finished the tea, leaving the leaves in the bottom to refresh my cup later in the day.

Last week I shook out the seeds from the dried flower tops and stored them away in a safe place. I now had more seeds than I started with since I hadn't used all the seeds in the first planting. I was getting ahead, just in case. It wasn't like I felt euphoric, but I did feel optimistic about my role in this beautiful oasis of Kolymbethra. Ignatius had not come back to the garden to talk to Jory so perhaps he had changed his mind about taking charge with his own men. Life had settled back into a good pace. Alena, at three months pregnant, had not bothered Iris in a long while. My love life with Ries was enjoyable and rather comfortable. I appreciated his intellect and he kept me entertained, but for some reason I didn't trust him entirely.

Our new workspace nearly finished, Leandro was now making shutters for the two windows, rather than the one I had requested. Some days I didn't even think of my old life, it seemed so long ago. Days here were longer with more time to contemplate, without the rush of meeting deadlines or driving in traffic. The gods and goddesses set the pace. I drank another cup of tea and relaxed into this thought. Feeling rather sentimental, I decided to name our workshops and name my house as well. I'd use shells and small stones to write out the words and have Leandro hang them over our doors. Maybe Jory would like his house named too. I decided to call my new workspace Hesper, meaning Evening Star; the shared workspace, Armonia, harmony; and my home, Eirene, peace. Scott had named his workshop, but I didn't dare copy him and name mine "Magic happens here."

"Why not start now," I said out loud, the only being to hear me, my Sparta.

I had amassed a large shell collection from my outings to the beach with Ries. Shells that I had never seen before, delicate and winged, probably from a kind of clam or mollusk. I had always had a fetish for shells, collecting them on vacations until it was no longer environmentally responsible. Wherever I lived, bowls of shells decorated my tables, and here was no different. I felt almost the same way about stones, finding fossilized rocks in Italy as well as the mountains near my home in New York.

For this project, the rocks that adorned my signs came from the caves that stored and kept cool our excesses of olive oil and foods. I sorted the shells and rocks and made a template to see how the new signs would look. Satisfied, I made glue with limestone and water, the same materials used to build our massive temples. I scavenged leftover pieces of wood, to use as my base, from the shutters Leandro had built, and used a rock to smooth out the rough edges. With everything ready in place, I easily assembled my signs, adding creative touches of feathers for wings and a few sprigs of dried flowers. They were beautiful! Usually, this sort of project would take me days of pondering and deciding, back and forth, before still not being satisfied with the final product. But today I had created three distinct signs and could not be prouder of them. Just as I laid the last stone in place, Leandro appeared, to check in and I hoped to help me put the finishing touches on our new Hesper house.

I stood up, allowing him to view my signs, hoping for accolades.

"Alexis! Those signs are fantastic! I could not have done better myself. They inspire me in so many ways."

Me, inspire him? After he gave me the delicately carved dove, with details down to the tiniest feather?

"Thank you, Leandro. That is quite a compliment coming from you. Do you think you can hang them over the doors? I've named each house for the attributes my work brings to them. I had a moment of enlightenment and couldn't stop."

We carried the signs into Armonia house to let them dry completely just as thunder roared and a crack of lightning flashed through the trees.

"Come in for some warm tea," I urged.

Sparta rubbed up against Leandro's leg, asking for a pet. This was something he had never done with anyone but me. When I thought about it, he never growled at Leandro either like he did every time Ries showed up.

Leandro followed me, along with Sparta, into my new Eirene house. I crushed up some of the leaves I now called "Dimitri" and heated some water. I was curious to see what he thought of the new possible addition to my herbal collection. Sparta lay at Leandro's feet, another message that he was a good guy and could be trusted. I relied upon Sparta's judgment when mine was in question.

"I have a surprise for you. A new tea I've recently made. I'd like to know what you think," I said.

I poured the hot water over the dried herbs and watched Leandro's head tilt up, his nose sniffing the fragrant aroma that drifted throughout my tiny home.

"If this tastes as good as it smells, I will love it," he said.

We both sipped in silence, listening to the muffled sounds of snoring coming from a sleeping Sparta. A bolt of lightning struck close to the house, causing me to jump up, almost spilling my tea. Leandro caught my arm and steadied it as I nervously sat back down. I hadn't experienced thunderstorms since leaving Albany and they still unsettled me, just like they did back then.

Noting my nervousness, Leandro calmly said, "Have you always been frightened of the cloud weather?"

The words "cloud weather" certainly made sense but I had never heard this term before.

I replied," Yes, even as a child. I guess I never fully embraced this part of Mother Nature's wrath."

"When this weather arrives, I go outside and watch the gods shout at each other, sometimes wielding a lightning stick. I am fascinated by it," Leandro added.

Leandro's description made it seem like entertainment and I liked how he took a lighter view on the subject.

"This tea is seductive, Alexis," he said to change the topic.

I'd never thought of it that way, but yes, it was. It had just the right amount of sweetness, a little tang from what must be lemon verbena, and a violet scent from an unknown flower. I mentally visualized adding some mint to it as a digestive. The combinations were swirling around in my head. This might be a base for healing tinctures that had bitter components. I wished I had a pad of paper to jot down the flashing ideas. Maybe the lightning triggered the inspiration. Or was it the tea? Or was it Leandro?

The rainstorm passed, and Leandro thanked me for the company. I asked him to stay for dinner, but he politely refused. His company was addictive and anyway, he would be by tomorrow to hang my signs and to install the window coverings. Before he left, he asked me a question so profound my knees buckled underneath me.

"Do you have an intention for this new tea of yours?"

Scott always reminded me to have an intention for my tinctures, my seeds, my life. Now this man in front of me was urging me to do the same. Was this coincidental or was Scott once again channeling me? Or was Leandro just asking what I intended to do with the tea?

I finally spoke. "It is just experimental at this stage, but now that it has passed the first test with you, I will decide how it will be used, if not just for pleasure sipping."

With that, he gave Sparta a pat, me a smile, and was out the door, on to his next project.

Almost as soon as Leandro left, a knock came on the door and Ries stood there, his face scrunched up in a scowl. He must have seen Leandro leave just before he got here.

"Hi Alexis. Is Leandro still working on your new shop space?" he asked sarcastically.

I could see the jealousy in his eyes, a trait that didn't sit well with me. "Yes, he came by to install the window shutters, but we got caught in the thunderstorm so waited it out here," I said without emotion.

"I just wanted to check on you since I haven't seen you in a week," he said.

He seemed sincere. He always seemed sincere and managed to worm his way back into my heart every time I began to question his motives.

"Are you busy making medicinals? How do you manage to work the gardens as well as the healing tonics? Jory can't be much help. Maybe some of the slaves can help. I can ask Ignatius."

This stream of sentences felt like cold ice running down my back. Could he be in on Ignatius's plan? At first, I didn't know how to reply to this news.

"The gardens are fine, Ries. No need to involve the slaves," I said curtly.

"It could be for the better, Alexis. Trust me."

That word, trust, again.

As if to recoup his standing with me, he carefully formulated his words. "Many citizens are grateful you are here with your magic tonics. You are truly helping people. The Council notices."

Ries was once again questioning my gardening skills and at the same time acknowledging my good work. On our walks, we never talked shop. It was all about nature, food, even the gardens, but never medicinals. I resisted telling him about my new Dimitri tea. It needed to be tested out more and I hadn't even tried the tincture yet. Also, I still didn't know who was behind the poisoning and hadn't told Leandro or Jory. It was my secret to keep.

"Is this the reason for your visit or is there something specific I can help you with? Do you need a remedy?" I asked.

Perhaps he was just beating around the bush because

he needed something that might embarrass him. A digestive, headache solution, herbs for insomnia?

He answered, "The Carthaginian slaves get sick frequently and there aren't enough men to work on the temples. I am physically lifting sandstone blocks rather than managing now. I could use something for endurance and my men need help with stomach illness. Can you help?"

I wasn't sure if this request was an excuse to relay a message, or a legitimate plea for assistance.

"I'll need to know what the sick men's symptoms are in order to make the proper healing tinctures. Can you take a survey and get back to me? For you I might have the perfect herbal, but it won't be ready for a week. Can you wait that long?"

Ries was visibly relieved and gave me a huge hug as a thank you. I think he wanted me to ask him to stay for dinner, but I had a date with Sparta tonight. A long walk to make sure nothing was damaged in the storm and a bowl of soup for both of us. Ries would have to practice patience.

Even though Philo's beehives were now safely in our keep, the question of the bee stingers weighed heavily on my mind. I made the trek to his house for an impromptu visit. I would go under the guise of taking him a few jars of honey and some dried figs. Philo sat on a stool in front of his house carving something out of wood.

"Hello, Philo!" I exclaimed. "It is a fine day."

"You are welcome here anytime, Alexis."

I handed him the basket I'd prepared for him and he invited me inside.

After the usual chitchat, I summoned the courage to say, "Can you tell me more about the bee stingers? Why would someone else want them?"

I had just given myself away but trusted Philo.

His tilted his head downward, shaking it from side to side. "Who got ahold of the stingers?"

"I don't know. They were stolen out of my workshop along with a large bottle of valerian."

Philo grew quiet. "I think I know who took them. There is only one other person I know of who would want them."

I stared at him, waiting for him to continue.

"Alexis, I believe I can trust you when I say this person is dangerous. You must be on your guard."

"Who is it?" I pressured him.

"He is a man of power. His brother died of poisoning and this man blamed me. You see, this bad man wanted to expand his wheat fields and buy my land. I refused and we became enemies. However, his brother, Nico, and I were friends. I always gave Nico my honey. One day, Nico became very sick. He recovered physically but not mentally and ended up living in a cave outside of my village in solitude. Eventually he died of madness. This man thought my honey had poisoned him and he ransacked my house. He found the stingers that I removed from the hives and decided that their poison was the culprit."

"How would he know this?" I asked.

"It's a myth that goes back centuries. A story was told about a woman who used a bee's stinger, soaked in honey and herbs, to kill her lover so her husband wouldn't find out about her affair. It has never been proven but nevertheless, I remove all stingers from the hive to keep any suspicions at bay."

"Have you ever tried it? I mean using the stinger for harm?" I asked bluntly.

Philo paused before answering my question. "There are things I've done that I'm not proud of. It's better that you don't know."

"So, can you tell me who this man is? How did he know I had the stingers?"

"He was probably looking for something else and ran across them by accident."

Instead of feeling reassured, I felt the opposite. Someone was out there who intended to use the stingers as a weapon, and possibly frame me.

"Was this man Ignatius?" I queried.

"Yes. Ignatius is a powerful man who will stop at nothing to get his way. His fierce and aggressive behavior has kept the Carthaginians from taking over Girgento. To Alexander, he is valuable, but I have always been suspicious of him and his ill temper. Keep your distance, don't be afraid to use your power, and never reveal your weakness."

24

NICO'S CAVE

These days, Jory was more in charge of the vegetable gardens, and I, the herbals and bees. The fruit trees were mostly dormant, waiting for spring to warm their buds and give birth to flowers, then fruit. I bottled honey once a month; my customers had a steady demand and I used it to temper bitter tinctures, especially for young children and older adults. I knew from my old life that raw honey contained many beneficial components including an antibacterial so took a spoonful myself every day to stay healthy.

The Dimitri tincture had matured for three weeks and was ready for a trial. Of course, I was always the first person to test them out. I placed ten drops under my tongue, pleasantly surprised at the taste. The tincture did not taste as bitter as most did, but like the tea, had a sweetness and strong, concentrated flavor of lemon and violet. What magic would this bring to my new community?

After a week of taking the tincture, I noticeably felt stronger, more creative, and happier. Why would Scott give me a mood enhancer? Could this be a version of his Forza I took back home? The Forza had more herbal overtones but had the same effects as the Dimitri. An idea suddenly occurred to me. There was a missing ingredient in the Forza that I couldn't remember. Maybe this was it! I would prepare another formula using the Forza ingredients and add in the Dimitri. Scott had given me a puzzle to solve, and I hoped this was the solution. I wasn't sure how I was supposed to use this new tincture. It wasn't just for fun and games. Or was it for a game of survival? What did Scott know that I didn't? The mystery of my presence here deepened, with clues showing up and asking to be discovered. My body tensed with the increasing pressure, something that was occurring more than I'd like.

I packed Ries's herbals in a basket and planned to drop them off at his worksite. Inside the Concordia, I found him and Iris discussing exactly where the altar would be installed.

They were deep in conversation, and I turned around to leave when Iris said, "Alexis! Come talk with us."

I loved how Iris included me in her conversations with others, always making me feel welcome.

"Hello you two. I have your tinctures, Ries. Your men will be feeling better in no time," I said.

"How about for me?" he questioned.

I was proud of this new formula recently created and was anxious to see how he responded to it.

"Yes, Ries, special for you." I smiled.

"What is so special about it, Alexis?" chimed Iris.

"I will bring you a bottle too. It's a combination I have been working on for a while and think it's quite magical," I said.

"Magical?" said Iris. "I love magic and think anything

you prepare will be transformative." That word "transformative" said it all. What they didn't know!

"Thanks for your confidence, Iris," I fired back with a laugh.

"Alexis, are you free this evening for a walk?" Iris asked. "I want to talk to you about an upcoming ceremony where I'll need some special foods."

I had a feeling this wasn't really what she wanted to discuss but replied yes.

"Meet me at the sanctuary of Demeter at sunset."

I nodded my head in agreement before parting ways, but not before Ries grabbed my elbow, pulling me to his side.

"I'm grateful for your help, Alexis." He paused. "Have you considered the offer?"

Not knowing how to respond, I said quietly, "I can watch out for myself."

It just came out and I didn't know why I said it. Maybe he would interpret this as a signal to stop badgering me. My trust in him began to fade, but he still had that charm and ability to sway me with his sweet talk. I wondered if I was reading him all wrong. Maybe he just didn't want me to work as hard as I did and recognized the control freak in me. I had showed him a level of commitment to help his men, and hoped it would someday be reciprocated.

Iris stood huddled behind one of the temple columns, a white shawl wrapped around her willowy body. Her eyes darted back and forth as if making sure she wasn't noticed. I approached cautiously. A cool breeze from the south brought with it a salty dampness in the air.

"I've received a message today," Iris revealed.

"Demeter led me to darkness, a cave perhaps, with pine cones scattered on the floor. Could this be in reference to the missing wheat?"

Iris didn't know that I had secretly visited the ceremonial cave of Thesmorphoria to add some of my seeds to the sacrifices already placed there by Alena before the annual ceremony was to take place. I remembered seeing pine cones and remains of piglets, signs of fertility, in mounds by the sacrificial altar.

"How much time do we have before the dark moon occurs?" I asked.

"About ten sunrises. Do you think the urgency of making something happen before the moon darkens is related to the missing wheat?" Iris said.

"I definitely think they are related. Let's start by checking the caves to the south. It would be easier for whoever stole the wheat to move it to a location close to the fields."

We strode in tandem along the garden's perimeter to remain unnoticed, aiming to reach the cave furthest from its entrance. From out of the bushes emerged Sparta, eager to act as our bodyguard. After about ten minutes at a quick pace, we arrived at the cave. Thankfully it was a full moon, or our torches would have given us away. I peered up into the chamber, and with the visibility low, decided to hoist myself up to get a better look.

"Iris, keep watch," I whispered.

My hands moved in front of me, searching for something large, like a bag of wheat, and then along the dirt floor for pine cones. Sparta's sharp warning bark caught me off guard and caused me to almost fall off the ledge. I stilled my body and listened. Leaves crackled.

"Iris?"

No answer. Sparta's low growl and then long thuds told

me he was running or chasing something or someone. I eased myself down, out of the cave, calling for Iris, when I almost tripped over her body.

"Iris, are you okay?"

"I'm all right. Someone pushed me down and then ran off. I think they were trying to scare me. Sparta ran after them."

"Oh no! Sparta, Sparta," I cried.

Within minutes Sparta was at my side, panting but not hurt. Relieved, I said to Iris, "Someone must have been following us."

"Who knows that we are looking for the missing wheat?" I asked. "I haven't told anyone. Jory is the only person other than you."

"Whoever it is must be desperate to frighten us but not harm us," said Iris.

"Do you want to continue our search or leave it until another time?" I asked.

"Our enemy is gone for now. We can keep looking on our way back into the garden."

Iris and I investigated three more caves with no success before deciding to call it a night. Sparta invited himself into my house, intent on protecting me. As I crawled into bed, hugging my furry friend's body tighter than usual, I pondered the evening's activities. An adversary lurked nearby, but how did I draw their suspicion? That night, I pleaded with Demeter to send me a message. She was the only one who knew the truth.

The next morning, I prepared my usual herbal tea and sat outside to plan my day. Demeter had abandoned me last night. Maybe she was hoping I'd figure all this out myself. Yesterday's events made it difficult for me to concentrate, so I focused my energy on my latest creation.

Word spread quickly and the Dimitri tea became a

community favorite. The experiment with the Forza combination I called Panos, tried so far only on myself, would also prove to be beneficial. Unbeknownst to anyone else, I had been feeding our veggies, herbs, and fruit trees with this Dimitri herbal. Crops were strong and healthy and abundant. Fruit trees were doubling their blooms and the artichokes had increased in size by a third. The Dimitri was producing record-breaking crops, leaving Ignatius silenced. He knew he could never compete or even recreate what Jory and I were doing. Jory was innocent in all of this. I never wanted him to have to answer for me so kept these "fertilizers" to myself. At least I thought it was to myself. Whoever was spying on me had certainly done a good job.

Iris appeared at the entrance to our workshop, her sagging eyelids giving away her restless sleep.

Yawning, she said, "Demeter, Persephone, Zeus—all had words with me last night. They are pleased with the progress on the temples and see Girgento as a city essential to the continuation of Greek life. Certain things must be dealt with in order for growth to occur. Persephone asked me to help Demeter so she could continue her transition to the upper world, once a year. Zeus demanded that all wrongdoing be righted, and Demeter pleaded with me to find the wheat and return it to prevent devastation. They all pointed to you as the answer."

This was a lot of information to digest so I stood there, speechless, trying to process it all.

"Tell me, Iris, do the gods and goddesses speak with you like this all the time?"

"No, it is quite unusual. I always ask for the general

well-being of our community and often have specific requests from the Elder Council. They have never involved someone from the outside for help. Why have they chosen you, I wonder?"

My face flushed with heat, just about ready to confess to Iris that I was not one of them—not Greek and not a real gardeness. As much as I wanted to tell her the truth, and with her status as a priestess, she might understand, I decided to play along, at least until we solved the mystery of the wheat.

"I have an idea, and if my intuition is working, we might just find our answer. Why don't you pretend to make an offering in the sacred cave used in the Thesmophoria ceremony? That way, you can get into the dwelling without being suspect and it will give you a chance to look around in the daylight. I remember seeing pine cones there. Maybe take some pomegranates?"

"Do you really think they would hide wheat in such an obvious place?"

"It's just a hunch. We need to at least be able to cross it off our list."

Iris agreed and said she'd need to visit the Temple of Zeus first, and then would make her way to the holy cave.

"Please let me know right away if you find something, and try to be discreet."

"Meet me in the sanctuary when the sun is full in the sky."

"I'll be there," I said in anticipation of the mystery solved.

I entered the sanctuary of Demeter but did not find Iris.

Something more urgent must have come up. Just as I was leaving, Alexander entered and looked bewildered. He was obviously looking for Iris too.

To my surprise, he asked, "Have you seen Alena?"

"No, I was looking for Iris."

"She said she had a meeting with Iris today. It's about the health of the child she is carrying."

"If I see her, I will let her know. Maybe they have gone somewhere together," I suggested.

With that, he hurried out the door, his face pale and eyes angry. Alena held secrets and Alexander was becoming suspicious. There had always been something about Alena I couldn't put my finger on. All I knew was that I didn't trust her, even though trust was the virtue I had been advised to embrace by Scott.

Jory mostly buried himself in his work and today was no exception. I found him tending to the cabbages, picking off bugs that had been eating the leaves.

"Jory, do you have any idea where the missing wheat is?" I queried.

"Alexis, do not involve. Will be bad. Ignatius hurts."

"I know he is threatening, but something must be done for the good of the polis," I insisted. "Demeter wants me involved."

"Demeter? You must follow her. She brings us food."

So, Jory's attitude would change if Demeter was at the apex of this situation. "Demeter is trying to tell me where the wheat is so it can be planted for the next season. There is a traitor here in Girgento and I must find out who it is."

"Many traitors."

The polis was large enough for multiple people

sparring for power. It happened in all successful communities.

"Go to Philo. He can help," Jory stated.

To get another person involved didn't seem right, but if this is what Jory wanted, I would not doubt him.

"Thank you, Jory. I'm on my way."

Today I wished I had a horse to get me up the hill to Burgio quickly. I moved my legs in long strides, the long dress I always wore hampering my speed. It took about an hour, but I finally spied Philo foraging for greens in the distance.

Sweat dripped from my brow as I caught my breath to say, "Hello, Philo. I have something urgent to discuss with you."

I sat down next to him, looking over my shoulder to make sure we were not being watched. Even though we were far from Girgento, I could not be too careful.

"You spoke of an evil man who blamed you for his brother's death, and it was Ignatius. Would he want to steal the polis's wheat for personal gain?"

I spilled it all out, including my sessions with Demeter, with the faith that Philo could be trusted and perhaps be the missing link to solving this puzzle.

"I do know of many people who want power over the health of the city. I suspect Ignatius is at the top of the list. What he did to Jory revealed an example to all of his evil spirit. I have learned from the bees and their stingers. They warn you first by buzzing nearby and if you don't leave them alone, they attack with a sting. You must see the similarities. You were warned when they broke into your workshop."

"Does that mean this person or people want to kill me now? Why am I a threat?"

"They see a power in you that you don't see. They are

afraid of you. Afraid you will ruin their plans."

"How can I defeat them before they defeat me?"

"Follow your intuition and the advice of the gods and goddesses. Demeter knows you will be the one to save Girgento."

Dizzy and feeling faint, I put my fingertips on my forehead in an attempt to clear my mind. Demeter sent me here to be her henchperson, not to be the gardeness of Kolymbethra. I was in disguise so as not to be suspected. These visions of Demeter started back in San Francisco to prepare me for this journey. It was now all on me. I was certain the people I trusted, Philo, Iris, and Jory, were here to help me. But how to go forward and could I succeed?

"The wheat must be discovered before the moon goes dark. We only have a few days . . ."

"I heard a story about wheat from Egypt stored in a safe place, in case of crop failure. This information came from Nico, but we all thought he was crazy in the head and was making it up."

"Maybe he wasn't crazy and the emergency supply is in his cave. Do you know if anyone ever visits there?"

"No, it is too remote, and many are scared to enter, that they too will become crazy."

"Will you go with me now?"

"What will you do with it if you find it? You will need horses to help you haul it out and then your enemies will be after it. For now, it is a secret only between you and me. You will find the right path to take."

Philo was telling me he would not be part of the scheme and I understood why. This was my mission to fulfill, and I would have to make a careful plan and not rush to conclusions. This was only the backup wheat, if it was in fact there, but my true goal as instructed by Demeter was to find the Girgento wheat. So many problems to solve and I had no idea where to begin.

"I appreciate your advice, Philo. You have been helpful." Before I left, I asked him for directions to Nico's cave, and with that, I meandered down the hill, not especially eager to return to Girgento and what might await me there. The walk would give me time to think.

Iris had to be notified in case something happened to me. I felt a sense of urgency to find her and checked every temple for her presence. Finally, in the Temple of Heracles, I found her curled up asleep on the floor in one of the side alcoves. I gently shook her from her slumber.

"Iris, wake up. I have news!"

"I'm so tired. I don't know what's wrong with me."

"I met with Philo. I have so much to tell you. Try to wake up."

I told her the story in a quiet voice, trying to remember every detail from my visit with Philo as Iris attempted to pay attention despite her yawns.

"Alena came unannounced today and warned me about you. Said you have ulterior motives. You must be wary of her."

"Where were you at our assigned time to meet today? Did you go to the sacred temple? I went to the sanctuary and Alexander was there looking for Alena. He said she had a meeting with you about their soon-to-be baby."

"Not true! She came specifically to warn me not to trust you. She is lying to her husband. It is Alena that cannot be trusted. I felt I was being watched so did not go to the temple."

"Could Alena be conspiring with Ignatius? Both of them own large wheat fields. Both have a grudge against me. Maybe they wanted the wheat all to themselves for profit, and to enlarge the military."

"Yes, I had thought of that," Iris quipped.

"If the wheat is in Nico's cave, we must distribute it as soon as possible to the smaller farmers so they won't be shut out. I will bet the powerful one's motive is to take over the small farmer's land."

"They could even be in an alliance with the Carthaginians. This might be why Demeter is so concerned," Iris chimed in.

"Can you leave the temples now and come with me to Nico's cave?" I asked. "Let's go separately. I'll meet you before sunset at Philo's. We can go together from there."

I hurried back to my gardens, not eager for the hike up the hill, twice in one day, but anxious to get to the wheat before our adversaries did. Jory sat outside his house with something in his hand.

"Here," was all he said as he placed a small purple stone in my palm, wrapping my fingers around it. "Keep you safe."

Intuitive Jory. I didn't have to ask about it, just nodded and smiled a thank you as I tucked it into the secret pocket of my shawl.

My pace accelerated past olive groves and tall grasses, the views below of the aquamarine Mediterranean Sea so spectacular it distracted my mission. Every part of Girgento province stimulated my senses in a way Northern California never had. The purity of the land, unpolluted air, and abundance of wild food. Nature at its finest.

Iris and I really didn't have a plan except to see if the grain was actually in the cave. What we would do if we found it would be another conversation.

Iris was waiting for me at Philo's. We assessed our surroundings and when we were certain to be alone, headed east past the old beehives, and then north where the trees grew taller and denser. Philo had not been specific about the exact location, but I knew we could figure it out by his descriptions of landmarks.

"After you pass through the cypress groves, follow the path along the creek, and turn left at the three-meter rock that looks like an old man's face. Look for the cave that is overgrown with rosemary."

The cave was partly obscured but we were able to identify it. With apprehension, we both peeked inside, stepping over, then breathing in the deep woody scent of rosemary. The place was abandoned, and pieces of fabric and animal carcasses were scattered across the dirt floor. Just past the debris, the cave opened up and on either side were large bags marked with black ink. A closer look showed the markings to be hieroglyphs. It was the Egyptian wheat!

"We found it!" cried Iris and embraced me with a hug.

Not knowing quite what to do, we sat down in the dampness to craft a plan. It would be challenging and require the cooperation of a few small farmers, but we felt confident we could make it work. Demeter would be pleased.

Arm in arm, we walked the path to Philo's home, then split up for the remainder of our journey to Girgento. I reached into my shawl for the stone given to me by Jory and worked its soft polish through my fingers. A strength came over me at that moment that I cannot explain. All I knew was that this was my opportunity to make a difference, and nothing would get in my way. Nothing.

My mind pushed tomorrow's tasks to the wayside, and I slept well that night, Sparta by my side, a full moon shining through my shutters. If everything went according to our plan, the Egyptian wheat would soon be in the hands of deserving farmers. Our next issue would be more difficult—where to find the stolen wheat and how to confront its thieves.

The next morning, I told Jory about Nico's cave and our discovery. He seemed pleased but only said, "Be careful."

I apologized for not being in the gardens the past several days to help him, but he didn't seem upset in the least. He knew what needed to be done for the safety and well-being of Girgento's citizens.

I asked him the names of farmers who would be willing to help us and not afraid of possible military interference, and he was quick to tell me about Macedon, Dorus, and Khristos. All three had horses with wagons and had courage to defend themselves.

Macedon looked almost Herculean in his height and stature. He agreed almost immediately and began to hook up his horses. I had to stop him and tell him he and a few others would follow me up the hill the next morning.

Dorus was not easily swayed. Jory had said he had a fragile nature, so I had to explain to him several times that some people did not have his best interests at heart. I had made herbals that helped his wife after childbirth. She finally convinced him I had good intentions and encouraged him to help me.

Iris knew Khristos because his daughter was destined to be an oracle. He had faith this was the right thing to do.

We all met the following day at sunrise to begin our trek. At this point, I felt confident in our task and didn't care who saw us. It took us about twice the time to get there because of the horses and wagons. The men worked together to gather the bags of wheat and hoist them onto the wooden wagon planks. In all, they recovered twenty bags, each weighing thirty kilos, enough for twenty small farms to survive for another year with a little left over to save. Not all farmers could be subsidized, and this was why it would be imperative to find the missing grain.

The men laughed and joked as they steered their horses down into town. We all agreed not to tell the other farmers about the missing wheat in case a few disgruntled men decided to make trouble. This wheat was a gift, to be used to diversify their crops in case of disease or drought. A kind of reserve to have on hand. As we traveled from farm to farm, most were amenable to the gift, knew me from my medicinals, and trusted me. Some were hesitant and refused. One bag would be reserved and stored in a secret location for emergency use only. Iris, Jory, and I would be the only ones to share this confidence. At the end of the day, all the wheat was distributed, and Iris and I felt extremely accomplished.

"First mission, successful!" Iris practically shouted.

"Today is the Magna Agora. We should celebrate," I announced.

"I'm hungry. There's a woman who makes delicious lentil stew with fennel and capers. She's near the end."

Weary but famished, we walked the length of the market to find Helena's booth of red lentil dishes. Garlic, pepper, and fennel aromas rose from her steaming pots, and with the cooler weather I could already feel the spice of the soup warming my body. We each gave Helena a few coins and found a spot under a tree to sit and eat as we recounted our handiwork. Would there be repercussions, and would the higher leaders find us guilty of some crime? It seemed impossible. All we did was distribute the wheat. It did not belong to anyone, as far as we knew. Still, better to be aware of people asking questions, possible traitors. Ries again entered my mind as one of them. It couldn't be, but money does change people. I would find out the truth eventually.

Iris and I parted ways, smug in our victory. As I rounded the corner to start down the stairs to the garden, a figure appeared in front of me with a hood pulled up over her head. I recognized her pregnant belly.

"Do not interfere with Girgento society. You are not from here and do not understand our ways. Consider this your last warning." And with that, she was off.

Alena and Ignatius had to be co-conspirators. But why leave out Alexander and lie to him? Things were getting dangerous and suddenly our triumph diminished. Jory would be told everything so he could be on his guard as well. Iris and I had outsmarted them once. Could we do it again?

25

CONSPIRACY AND BETRAYAL

Dark clouds loomed between glimpses of early morning sunlight and signaled possible rain, which might work in our favor for exploring caves. If we did locate the wheat in Thesmophilia's cave, I had a plan worked out to move it to a safe place. It was ingenious if I might say so myself.

Today I would let Iris tend to her oracle duties and I would search the cave alone. Only one person walking the trail would not arouse suspicion. The cave was a fifteen-minute walk and I kept to one side, hugging the trees to avoid notice. At the point where the path curved and led up to the cave, a figure emerged, and in haste, walked the opposite direction in long strides. He didn't notice me, but I noticed him. It was Ries. Had he just been inside the cave? And what was he doing here? My instinct told me to follow him, but I resisted and, now knowing it was safe, descended the few steps into Thesmophoria's cave. The dirt floors were clean, as if someone had used a broom on them. Pine cones had been pushed to the side and all signs of sacrifices were gone. The cave was empty. Disappointed, I took the trail Ries had and headed to the city.

Ries was not at his usual site of Concordia. Leandro, in

the drizzle, worked diligently on the columns, not realizing I was watching him.

"Leandro," I called. "Have you seen Ries this morning?"

Whirling around, Leandro caught my eye and stopped what he was doing to walk toward me. "Hello, Alexis." He smiled. "Ries? Haven't seen him today. Can I help you with something?"

"No thanks. I just had a question for him. Come by for a cup of tea sometime."

Leandro nodded his head in agreement, flashed a grin, and returned to his work. Next stop—the Academia. I was contemplating whether or not to confront Alexander and tell him what I knew. It was all a risk at this time and if Alena was there, could prove fatal.

As I approached the building, two people huddled together under an eve, deep in conversation: Alena and Ries. Were they collaborators? I felt sure he was telling her that the wheat had safely been moved. I still could not understand what was in it for him. Maybe she was blackmailing or bribing him. I put nothing past her. Quickly, I took a turn and departed behind the other side of the building to walk east alongside the back entrance of Kolymbethra. I would ask Jory for advice again. Even though he was a man of few words, each one of them counted.

Jory perched on his stool inside our workshop with a cup of hot tea in his hands. I rarely saw him like this, but the rain now poured down in sheets, preventing any real work to be done outside. I wiped down my arms and smoothed out my wet hair before taking a seat next to him. At least we were alone here and could talk freely.

"The cave of Thesmophoria is empty," I told him. "I thought we could get to it first, but they must have moved it recently." I left out the part about seeing Ries there.

"Alena and Ignatius hold wheat hostage. If we don't find it, Alexander will lose control."

"This is why Demeter's message is so urgent. It could mean the collapse of our polis!"

My voice rose an octave as I said, "Demeter, we want to help but need your guidance." It was a plea to the powers, but I wasn't convinced she was listening. She had remained silent the past week and was leaving it all in our hands to figure it out.

"Demeter protects wheat. Look in unexpected places," Jory stated as if he'd been channeled by the goddess herself.

It must be in someplace obvious, right in front of our nose, I thought. The aqueduct? The Academia? The Concordia? Ries was in charge of the Concordia and it was not finished, so Iris would not have used the temple to speak to the gods. It was the perfect cover. Ries could keep watch while the builders worked, unaware of the treasure they were hiding. Iris would know best how to approach the temple to take a look.

I shared my idea with Jory, who smiled and nodded his head. "Find it, Alexis," were his parting words as I exited the workshop in the pouring rain to look for Iris.

Iris spent more time in the sanctuary than the others, in hopes of connecting even further with Demeter. I heard her prayers as I entered.

"Demeter, goddess of the harvest, help us protect our people from harm," she whispered.

I watched her for a minute as she laid a wreath of wheat stalks on the altar.

"Iris," I called.

She turned around with a gleam in her eye, like she had just had a brilliant idea. "Demeter had a message for me today," she said, her voice rising to an excited pitch. "She said my power is protected."

"What do you mean, Iris?" I asked.

"Demeter will keep me safe." Her tone filled with confidence.

"That is good news, Iris, because I have a thought to share with you."

Iris reached for her necklace and went from stone to stone, fingering each one as if it were a rosary as she listened intently to my theory about Ries harboring the wheat in the alcoves of the Concordia.

"It is possible. How can I help?" Iris replied.

"Could you go to Concordia and ask about altar placement? It would be a good excuse to go and look inside," I suggested.

She released her grip on the necklace and grabbed my hand as a replacement. "I will go today and be convincing. They know we work together so I will bring gifts in good faith and trust in my role as an oracle. The dark moon is in three days' time."

I shuddered at this thought. What would happen if we failed? I changed the subject. "Come to the gardens after you visit the temple. With the luck of the gods, you will find the wheat or a clue to its whereabouts."

Iris felt snug in her new role of detective. Another plan would need to be formulated if the wheat was in the Concordia. Moving it would be impossible. But, exposing it to Alexander and proving Ignatius's disloyalty would take the responsibility off of me. I calculated my next move with care. No longer frightened by Alena and Ignatius, and empowered by my new ally Demeter, I would soon be able to deliver the gifts as requested so long ago.

My gardens were in need of pruning and care, even though the winter's cooler weather required less maintenance than the summer's. I had been absent for days and it was time to get back to work. Jory and I clipped and trimmed as if nothing had happened and Sparta, my protector, seemed to cling to me more than ever. I desperately wanted my life to revert to my role as just an herbalist and gardener. Not having to watch my back. Life before Ignatius decided he wanted to be the tyrant. I tried to push the past events out of my mind for this day. Violet lavender and deep-blue sage flowers scented the air like a huge sachet, and I took advantage of this to tincture some oil. This act would bring calm to my life, if not just for the moment. The white dove landed across from me as I was plucking the aromatics from their stalks.

"Mama," I asked, "what is your secret to survival? You have enemies but always avert them to return to the gardens."

The dove pecked away at the dirt and did not look up, trusting in her safety. I wished I could feel as confident as she, but still had a nagging feeling that the evil forces were more powerful than I was. Iris's visit to Concordia would reveal whether or not our hunches were correct. I trusted her and knew she would discover the truth. I did fear for her security, but she was an oracle and had brought good fortune to Girgento. Was that enough?

The sky closed in on evening, and no sign of Iris. I was beginning to worry and debated going upstairs to find her. I decided to sit tight and be patient. We had three more nights, according to Iris's messages, and then what? In silence, Sparta and I ate our dinner of lentils, red peppers, olives, and preserved artichokes. I did enjoy cooking with the freshest of ingredients, in the simplest way, compared to the cupboard full of items that barely were used back home.

A knock came on my door.

"Yes?" I queried.

"It is me, Iris."

I quickly opened the door and closed it behind her just as fast.

Between panting breaths, she said, "I am not one hundred percent certain it is there, but I did find a room with a closed door, closely guarded by a military man."

"It must be! But how to find out for sure?"

"Alexander must be notified tomorrow. I can approach him and tell him that the military has no permanent place in our temples and that I suspect something is being hidden in the room."

"But what if Ries tells Ignatius and they decide to overthrow Alexander then and there?" I asked.

"I do not think it will happen that easily. Remember, the wheat is being held hostage. Ignatius will negotiate with Alexander first, most likely for a larger share of the profits, and then want to take over the gardens for even more power. Ignatius did threaten Jory, but your crops were abundant, and he could not justify the takeover at that time. It's complicated."

"But it's a risk we must take to uncover their plot. We trust in Demeter, right? She won't lead us astray," I said in the hopes I sounded confident.

"Alexis, you need to stay away from this confrontation. Let me handle it. Besides, the lunar eclipse is approaching, and Alexander knows this can be a time of disruption. I am sure he will not want anything extra to deal with that could create more societal turbulence."

"All right, but I will be nearby to observe. When will you meet with Alexander?"

"We already have a time, before the sun is at its highest, to discuss future ceremonials. I will ask him to follow me after our meeting and show him the room. Ries will have no choice but to let us enter."

"You have earned your intuitive status, Iris. Your plan is perfect," I said.

Iris left like a mouse, creeping down the trail, not a sound to be heard.

Sleep was impossible. I tossed and turned, knowing that tomorrow would bring redemption or loss. I finally got up and brewed myself a cup of chamomile to calm my nerves and to lure me into a twilight sleep. Demeter loomed over me, her gaze unwavering, just like the statue back in San Francisco. She handed me a stalk of wheat, bowed, and backed away from me to disappear up to the heavens.

I awoke to a wet tongue licking my eyes. Sparta, my true and trusted friend. I wrapped a long piece of cream-white linen around my body and fastened it with small clips, and tied my long locks up in a bun, then covered it with a scarf. It would be important to blend in today and not be noticed. After a quick tour of the grounds, and a quick splash of Dimitri onto my garden plants, I made a visit to the sanctuary with a gift of clary sage and some pinecones I collected on the way. Demeter needed to know I took her seriously and would do my best to deliver the gifts. I asked her for Iris's, Jory's, and my safety, the day being uncertain. It was time.

The Agora Magna booths stood in neat and tidy rows along the plateau, and crowds began to appear to shop for wares and necessities, or just to browse what was new and different. Street musicians provided entertainment; the notes of the aulos, with melodies of the clarinet, accompanied the singing. I mingled in with the masses, looking for a secluded place to observe the activities soon to take place at the Concordia.

Iris emerged from the Academia, followed by Alexander, who towered over her. They marched toward the Concordia, swallowed up in people, and it became difficult for me to keep track of them. A man perched on a podium tried to engage me in his philosophical rhetoric, but without a glance I kept moving toward the temple. I finally located them deep in conversation with Ries, who was pointing in the direction of Zeus. I couldn't imagine what they were discussing. The three of them finally moved inside the Concordia, much to my relief. I waited, impatiently, beads of sweat forming under my armpits. Suddenly, Alena appeared and pushed her way through the crowd, and ran into the temple, tripping on a step. Serves her right, I thought.

The minutes ticked away, and I wished I had a watch to see how much time had elapsed. I was about ready to forge ahead and join the group when all four of them reappeared, going their separate ways. A strange, nauseating feeling washed over me, and I felt unsettled with this outcome.

"Arrest her!" a voice called out. I looked around, not seeing a perpetrator, and turned to make my way back to my gardens.

"She's getting away!" the voice cried again, this time much louder. "Get the sorceress!"

Alena was on the philosopher's podium, her gaze fixed on me while she waved a finger in my direction. I gathered my long robe up into my arms and began running to the west entrance of Kolymbethra. Jory would know what to do, but could I get there before someone else captured me first? Alena was smart. She redirected the wheat theft to me for blame. And she was calling me a sorceress to create fear. When this assignment started, I knew it would not be easy and the risks were enormous. Without me in the picture, Alena could manipulate and lie to her heart's content. Poor Alexander. He didn't realize Alena's deception but was sure to find out sooner or later.

I could see two military men in the corner of my eye, searching for me, but I eluded them, darting in and out of the crowds. Right before I was about to descend the steps to the garden, a hand reached out, grabbed me, and shoved me behind a large rock.

"I am so sorry, Alexis," whispered Ries. "I never meant to hurt you. I never thought they would come after you. Alena misled me and said the wheat was under threat from the Carthaginians. I didn't think she was using me. I will protect you."

Confused and not knowing whether to believe his story or not, I acquiesced.

"I need to talk to Jory. I'm sure he can help."

"You need to hide, Alexis. Ignatius has a temper," Ries said. "Trust me."

That word trust again. Who could I trust? At this point, only Jory, Iris, and Demeter.

"I will be okay, Ries. Please let me go," I said as I released his grip on me.

He scrunched his face in a frown. "Let me at least walk you home to safety . . . for now."

I agreed, and in silence we traveled the pathway to my house where Sparta waited by the door. I bent down to hug him, feeling his warm energy calm my shaky body.

"Be careful, Alexis. Your freedom is only temporary," warned Ries.

I treaded lightly to be as quiet as possible and checked the caves behind our homes for Jory. He was putting things into a small bag when I interrupted his task.

"Jory, Alena accused me of the theft." I spoke in a low tone.

"I prepare for you, in case," he muttered.

"But I'm innocent," I stammered.

"The cycle will end soon, with the dark moon. Don't be afraid."

For some reason, I always trusted Jory but wasn't sure what he meant by the cycle ending soon. Maybe Alexander would arrest Ignatius and I just needed to wait it out. Iris would be on my side, and everyone trusted her. I was trying desperately to reassure myself.

Jory handed me the small purse and told me where to hide it. I had no idea what was in it, but I felt certain it had some kind of herbal tincture to aid me, should that time come. No one had appeared in our gardens to arrest me, so maybe there was a change of circumstances?

I could not be that optimistic. I decided to do a little preparation myself.

26

KIDNAPPED

Despite the events of the day, the cool evening prompted me to grab my wool shawl and drape it around my shoulders as Sparta and I checked on my herb garden. A soft cooing alerted me that the white dove was nearby, perched on a pomegranate branch, like a guardian of my treasures. I usually fertilized my herbs and vegetables bi-weekly, late in the day, when no one was around, still preferring no one know of my secret Panos, the combination of the Forza and Dimitri tinctures. It was nearing the time to start more seedlings and harvest the herbs that were ready to pick. My collection of seeds was growing, and they were hidden in a safe place, along with the bee stingers. Now that the bees were on my watch, I had decided to follow in Philo's footsteps and collect some stingers, in the hopes I never had to use them.

Behind me, I heard a rustle and the crunch of footsteps on dried leaves. Sparta let out a low growl. It could be an enemy, or it could be a friend checking on me. Iris? Ries?

"Who's there?" I called.

No response.

It all happened so quickly. A putrid smelling hand forcefully covered my mouth to silence my screams, and then thick fists tied my hands behind my back to restrain me. I swung around to an unfamiliar face.

"Take me to the hiding place of the Egyptian grain. Also, your crop seeds." This command startled me. I didn't know where the wheat was now, and what did they want with my seeds? Jory was right. They wanted control of it all. Would I be arrested even if they didn't find anything? He released his hands so I could respond.

"Ask your boss where the grain is. And what do you want with my seeds?" I said in a snarky voice.

The stocky man shoved me forward and out onto the pathway. "Take me there, now!" was all he said.

Slowly, I walked toward the cave that kept our spares of seeds, olive oil, and dried ingredients, and contemplated my next move. I could offer him olive oil, wine, but what would he want with my seeds?

He thrust me inside and ordered, "Gather them up, quickly. Is the grain here?"

I shook my head no and reached in between some rocks that served as drawers, removed a packet of seeds, and handed them to him. When he looked down to inspect them, I slipped an envelope of stingers into the pocket of my shawl along with another small package of seeds and the small pouch Jory had prepared for me.

Not satisfied, he pushed me out of the cave while another man threw me down and tied a piece of cloth tightly over my eyes to disguise whoever was abusing me.

"Get up!" he shouted.

I rolled to one side, the sharp pang in my knees making it difficult to rise. Where was Jory? He must be aware of all this noise.

I heard a deep warning growl and my attacker let out a scream.

"The dog bit me on the leg!" he bellowed.

My hero, Sparta.

"Where is he? He vanished," the other man said.

I prayed for a speedy escape to his hiding places where he could become invisible for a few days.

"You are a witch and have made the wheat disappear. For this you will be banished and severely punished," one of the offenders uttered in my ear.

I heard a voice cry, "Take her to the boat," before I was knocked out cold.

I woke up in what felt like a large coffin with the sound of sloshing water hitting the hulls. I was the only person down here in the cramped quarters that looked like a mini storage room. My ties had all been released so I was free to move about, even though I was sure they had secured the door, which was affirmed after I tried the handle. I sat on the cold, hard wood floor to review the evening before, and could not understand why these men wanted my seeds and what they planned to do with them—or with me for that matter. My head and knees hurt, and I was woozy from the motion of the boat. The lull of the ocean made me want to sleep this whole nightmare away. Just as I was drifting off, the door swung open, and a man held out a bowl of thick porridge. The thought of food caused my stomach to lurch, and I spewed out my last meal at his feet. He dropped the bowl and backed out, closing the door behind him. The wretched smell invoked dry heaves until my exhausted body curled into a ball and fell into another uncomfortable sleep.

Days passed, or so it seemed. I could only tell time by the slight lightness or deep darkness of my cramped room. A few boxes lined the slanting side of the hold. Thinking there might be something to eat in there, I opened one up to inspect its contents. Luckily, I found some hard bread and dried figs. Their emergency food, I guessed, but it was good enough for me. I needed my strength if I was to survive whatever was before me. My throat was so parched it felt like I had swallowed sandpaper. No water was to be found so I called out through the door, "Water, please." A few minutes later my request was granted, and a large vase was handed to me by a heavily bearded and light-skinned man. I drank slowly, savoring each drop, not knowing when this opportunity would come again.

Shouting from above woke me from a nap. The boat slowed, I assumed from the lowering of sails and the men readying to dock the ship. A figure appeared at the door with some rope and once again tied my hands behind my back but did not cover my mouth or eyes. This person led me to a ladder to another deck, and then another ladder to the outside world. I faced a bustling harbor, alive with activity and what looked like an ant colony of people shuffling here and there. I asked the man who brought me to the outside world where we were.

"Carthage," came the reply.

The city-state of Carthage was the closest block of land to Sicily, next to the Italian peninsula, and home to the Carthaginians, bitter enemies of the Greek Girgenti. I had been kidnapped. Stumbling down the pier, now by myself, I was greeted by a tall man with a helmet who ushered me ashore.

"You are the gardenmaster in Girgento?" he questioned.

"Yes, and who are you and why am I here? I demand to know!" I shouted at him.

"Silence! You will be shown why you are here. My servant is waiting for you up ahead with a horse to take you to Monastir. You will receive instructions there." Surprisingly, these men spoke Greek, probably because of their close contact with all the neighboring Mediterranean countries.

The helmeted man motioned me to his short and stocky servant, who signaled me toward him. Escape was impossible at this point, with too many people around and no place to go. I'd need a boat to go back and that wasn't currently at my disposal. Begrudgingly, I followed orders, and swiftly, the man grabbed my arm and swung me up behind him onto his palomino-colored horse. No introductions, no conversation. We rode up into the hills and into a valley, away from the city. When we dismounted about two kilometers later, a ghost town of a garden lay in front of me. The trees looked alive so there must have been a water source of some sort, but they were badly in need of trimming. Neglected, overgrown vegetable gardens littered the ground with little organization. Was this why they had brought me here? To resurrect their garden? This was insane.

"Your life is here now, to make our gardens famous and help our people with medicinals," the man said.

How did they know of me? Was there a spy in Girgento who was allies with the Carthaginians? Was Ignatius behind this? I felt like I had gone from one bad dream to another, this one being even worse.

"There is food and water in the shed over there"—he pointed at the dilapidated lean-to—"and tools for your work. I am Haman. Now you will work."

Haman hopped on his horse and rode into the sunset, leaving me alone in this desolate space, void of even chirping birds. The shed contained a few vases of water, a bag of barley and one of wheat, a few dried figs and dates, and an old, weathered shovel. No gardening gloves or trowels or baskets for weeds. As basic as it got. I supposed this was also where I would sleep, not seeing anything else in the near distance. I checked my shawl pockets and yes, the seeds, stingers, and pouch I had snuck in from the cave were still there. I would need to find a safe hiding spot for them, hidden but in plain sight, as Jory had advised me of the missing wheat.

The garden area was about half the size of Kolymbethra, without the pond of fish. I wept for myself and also the plants hanging on for life, so disregarded and left to die. For now, and seeing no way out, I would do my best to salvage what was here, but it would be months before any sort of progress was visible. I sat next to one of the vegetable beds, picking out weeds to uncover their identities. Cucumber, pepper, onions ready to pluck out of the earth. The first thing I needed to do was to hide my seeds—the herbals that made my tinctures—and the stingers before someone else came to visit.

Why not just hide them here, in the vegetable bed? I could put them in a small water vase and bury them deep in the dirt. No one would ever suspect. Next, I inspected Jory's donation. The pouch he had prepared for me contained two bottles: the Forza and the Dimitri! How did he know about the Dimitri tincture? I thought I had kept the secret well, but I guess I hadn't. Thank you, Jory, I said to the sky.

I looked around to make sure I wasn't being watched, then started digging, but not before taking a few drops of the precious Forza liquid. The garden beds were the perfect cover-up.

The night approached, and after pulling non-vegetable matter out of the gardens and creating a pile to compost, I decided to raid my skimpy garden for something to eat. This place made my Eirene home seem like a palace. At least I had a bed, all the food I needed, and a mostly peaceful lifestyle with access to the community. I missed my Sparta and I'm sure he missed me too. Here, I was hidden away, like a secret. Would they have an unveiling when I was finished? Would I be allowed to go home?

The sun's rays beamed through the cracks in the wood, waking me at sunrise. I might as well get an early start. The sooner I cleaned up this mess, the sooner I could go home; or so I thought. My pile of weeds was growing, and I dug them into some nearby dirt to start composting them. You could now tell which vegetables were in one of the garden beds, but this was only the beginning of many, many more to clean out. I made the vegetables my priority, and then would work on the trees. I had no tools for pruning and would ask Haman for some the next time I saw him. My shawl served as a hat to shade my face, the sun hotter here than on the south coast of Sicily.

Days passed before Haman returned. He inspected my work and nodded at the progress. I asked him for more tools, and he said he'd ask his boss.

"Will I be able to go home when I have returned your garden to life?" I asked.

"That is not for me to answer," he said grimly.

Haman was just my supply man, bringing me food and the additional vases I requested. This time he surprised me with a small vessel of wine. I always thanked him, wanting to remain on his good side should I need him in the future.

I was beginning to get lonely with only the trees and plants to talk to. The birds were returning, and soon bees found their way to pollinate the now blossoming fruit trees. I had been here close to a month by my calculations and soon some of the winter vegetables I had resurrected would be ready to harvest. I figured Haman would take them back up the hill and into the city for purchase. I had no seeds to plant, except the special seeds I brought with me, so could not replant the garden until I had obtained seeds from the current crop. Starting from scratch was no easy task and I hoped they, whoever they were, were patient. If you didn't understand the lunar cycles and when to plant, it could be disastrous with low yields and stunted growth produce. The thought occurred to me to plant a few of my Forza seeds in with the veggies. No one even came near me these days so they wouldn't even be noticed. I would need the flowers as a backup in case I wasn't released.

Why hadn't anyone come to find me? Did they even miss me? Jory would know right away that I was gone, but would he figure out I was snatched right out of the garden? There must be someone who would figure it out. If not soon, then it would be up to me to formulate a plan to escape. This solitude was creating anxiety, and my already trim body grew thinner. The moon was waxing, the perfect time to plant, and tonight I would ask the gods to give my seeds strength and courage to battle what seemed to be a war of wills.

The next morning it wasn't Haman who came into the valley to check on the progress, but another man in fancier clothes. The men from Carthage dressed like the Greeks but their personalities were much more serious from the little I had observed.

"The spring gardens must be planted. Why haven't you started?" the man demanded.

The calendar of stones I kept told me it was February, and with the warm weather here in Carthage, spring would come early.

"Hello, my name is Alexis, and I would prefer it if we were on a friendlier basis, considering the drastic improvements I have made to your gardens," I said sternly with a hint of sarcasm.

"You will do as I say and not tell me how I should act. You belong to us now and must follow my orders," said the ill-tempered man.

My heart sank with this news. I belonged to them? But why? I wanted answers and would have to find someone to give them to me.

"Please, tell me why I'm here. I don't understand," I begged.

The man's heavy hand slapped my face viciously, knocking me to the ground. I got the message. It would be up to me to survive and find a way out. Where was Iris or Alexander? They had power and clout. They should have been here by now to save me. Then I remembered what Scott had said on his voice message right before I traveled back in time. "Your power has no limits. But to tap into it, you must trust and accept your path." My impatient nature asked how I could trust when I was being held prisoner in this desolate place with no one to talk to and very little to eat? I collapsed in a heap, my desperate situation triggering uncontrollable sobs. I felt helpless. Crying wouldn't solve my problems, but it felt good and right at the time. I needed to release my frustration and come to grips with my situation.

If Haman could get me some lavender flowers, I might be able to recreate the Panos tincture. I could use the rescued herbs from the garden, along with the herbs I had foraged, to create my formulation. I'd need some more wine but if I gave Haman some peppers, maybe he'd grant me some favors too. I prayed that it be Haman, not the unnamed man, who visited me previously.

I was relieved to see Haman's golden horse ease down the valley. He usually brought me a vessel of water, although I could access it from a well near the aqueduct. I think Haman enjoyed his visits with me. I was kind to him and treated him with respect, something he most likely did not get from his boss.

"Hello, Haman," I greeted him.

"Hello, how are you today?" he replied, never wanting to use my first name and not knowing my last.

"Would you be able to bring me some lavender flowers and more wine? I want to make some healing remedies for your citizens but don't have everything I need," I asked. "Also, do you have a source for honey?"

Honey was always a great carrier for the tinctures, making them easier to ingest. "I will try, miss. It might take me a while and I would need to be careful," he said sheepishly.

"Whatever you can bring me would be greatly appreciated," I said as I made eye contact.

I actually got a smile out of him before he mounted his horse to return to civilization. Something was clicking in my brain, but it was too soon to be hopeful. I was ready to heed Scott's advice, even if it was from afar, and trust my power.

Four days later Haman was back with more than my requested items. He quickly unloaded a vessel of wine, lavender flowers, and a large vase of honey. Inside the package of lavender, which was wrapped in a cloth, were the seeds from my cave the kidnapper had taken in Girgento. "Dolion wants you to plant these," was all Haman said. So, the mean-spirited man had a name. And Haman was off again, into the evening sky.

In the coming weeks I scavenged the gardens for every herb I could find. Many of them grew wild in the nearby field. Foraging was a natural part of life here, not a planned activity with a guide. I was easily able to find wild mint, oregano, garlic, coriander, and fennel. The tinctures or tonics would be slightly different because of the soil nutrients, but I could prepare a few, integrating the flower tops from the seeds I had planted. Of course, I would test this on myself first and manipulate the strength as necessary. How I wished I had valerian. The roots might be deep in the hillsides as well. That would be tomorrow's task. The man who pulled me from Kolymbethra thought he was getting my seeds of power, but really I had grabbed chamomile. He wouldn't know the difference if his life depended on it, I giggled to myself.

With little equipment to work with, I started pulling herbs together, shoved them into the small vessels Haman had brought me, and covered them with wine. I could speed up the process by making reductions in a more concentrated manner. The days were becoming warmer, and the garden revival, after three months of hard work, showed my progress. I packed up baskets of vegetables I had revived for Haman to take to Dolion along with a few small vases of the tincture. I assumed he wanted it, or why else would he have demanded the seeds? The potion was more of a placebo than anything else, although it did contain properties for vitality and health. I reserved the true Forza tincture for myself, knowing I'd need it for the upcoming escape I planned.

I'd sourced valerian from the hillsides and tinctured the smelly herb into a bottle. Buried under the dirt in one of the garden beds, it would keep the valerian warm to accelerate its potency.

The sickly garden I inherited progressed into vigorous beds of lettuce, fennel, artichokes, celery, and leeks. Onions, garlic, cucumbers, and forms of squash grew on a hillside where they could spread out. May had arrived and the warm weather with it. My fair skin suffered sunburn, then tan, and my hair had lightened considerably. These gardens offered less shade than Kolymbethra, and unlike my valley gardens, Monastir lay exposed in the open with few trees surrounding her. I dreaded the upcoming hot summer months. I'd had enough of this place, and after gaining Haman and his superior's trust, knew the time was near to make my escape.

Haman returned earlier than usual that week requesting more of the tincture I called Vida. I gladly refilled his vase and told him a honey mixture was forthcoming, special just for Dolion. Haman left some food and supplies for me then departed without saying a word. As I unpacked the cloth-wrapped package, I noticed something I had not requested. Tucked into the sack of barley grains was a shiny, sharp knife, the size of a steak knife but with a wider blade. Haman was here to help me. Perhaps he felt sorry for me. Maybe he had a wife or a daughter and could see my struggles from their angle. I didn't want to get him into trouble so would manage my escape by myself, this new addition of a weapon making it possible.

Dolion had not stepped foot in the garden since he slapped me, leaving the responsibility to oversee me to Haman. I prepared a special honey infusion, adding in a surprise. I had never used the bee stinger but now seemed the perfect opportunity. It scared me to think of harming anyone since I was a healer by nature, but in this world, you did what you had to when it came to survival. The stinger had soaked in the honey for four weeks and, according to Philo, would cause major sickness and possible death. I would bottle the valerian and sweeten it with the stinger-infused honey. This would buy me time to board a cargo boat back to Sicily without arousing suspicion. Haman would take the tincture to Dolion later in the week as a special gift from me, and I'd leave immediately after. I had been here about five months, and home in Girgento never looked so good.

Haman rode up on his horse two days later and I handed him what I hoped would poison Dolion, or at least make him incapacitated for a while. He seemed to know something was up but didn't let on. I'd leave as soon as he was no longer visible over the hill. The night before, I dug up my tinctures, the seeds, and stingers and wrapped them in a cloth to hide in my shawl pocket. The knife was another issue. I undid a piece of wool from the wrap and by tying a series of knots, fashioned a protective cover for it. The bag of barley would make a small knapsack in which I would hide the knife. I took a long sip of the Forza, along with a deep breath, asked the gods and goddesses to return me home safely, and repeated my mantra. "Trust your power."

27

NARROW ESCAPE

The rocks slowed my progress, so I crisscrossed the sloped and rugged terrain, making myself as small as possible to avoid detection. It would have been a straight shot, down the hill and up the other side to the harbor, but I didn't dare risk it. I hadn't really decided on a plan for the boat ride back. Boats came and went all day long, Carthage being a major departure and arrival point for goods from around the world. The only problem would be finding the boat that went to Girgento or at least to Gela, another port close by. I tightly braided my long hair and covered my head with my shawl to disguise whoever might recognize me. I had been taken away so swiftly, it was doubtful I was known, but I couldn't take any chances.

The heat was oppressive. Despite the blazing sun, I hurried along, knowing time was of the essence. My faster pace caught up with me and I slipped on a patch of dry dirt, twisting my ankle. "Ow!" My voice echoed. Had I just given myself away?

I crouched down to massage my ankle and looked around for signs of human activity. The only noise was from the drone of muted voices down the hill. This was a close call. As I exhaled a breath of relief, I began to doubt my plan. So much for my progress, especially with a hurt ankle. I scanned the landscape for a long stick to use so I wouldn't have to put so much weight on my injured leg. I had to keep going. About twenty meters in front of me lay what looked like an old olive branch. That would do just fine. With my new support in hand, I limped toward my goal, and felt more determined than ever to escape this depressing place. After about three more hours of my slow hobble, the harbor was in sight. I tossed aside the stick so I wouldn't look vulnerable and summoned all my courage to put weight on my foot. I mapped out where I would go; to the most crowded part, to look for a ship going east.

It was easy to blend in with the port so busy, like a giant cruise ship had just unloaded. Before I could react, a young boy grabbed for my pack that was slung over my shoulder. I spun around, now holding the pack with both hands, to face the thief. As we struggled for control of my life's necessities, a third person, a woman, entered the picture.

"Cyrus! Let it go!" she yelled.

Grateful for this interception, I was also now on display for the surrounding masses. I nodded my head in thanks to the stranger, then shrunk back into the crowd.

"Wait!" a voice cried. Instinct told me to ignore this call but for some reason, I turned around. It was Haman, the man who had brought me supplies and the knife. "Are you leaving? Dolion is sick and needs more remedies."

I reached into my pack and handed him the bottle of chamomile I had prepared just in case I needed a placebo. I could not risk parting with my other tinctures.

"Please don't tell Dolion you saw me here," I pleaded with a shaky voice.

Haman gave me a hard stare. He seemed different. Maybe Dolion was making life difficult for him.

"I need to go home. The garden is restored and ready for someone to take over. Please," I said.

Haman ran toward the city buildings and I was sure my cover was blown. I would need to make haste and find a ship. The first boat I approached was headed to Greece. The next, to Syria. The third, to Gela! I didn't have any money to pay my way so I approached the man at the foot of the ramp. "Do you need any assistance in the galley? I have culinary skills and could assist the cook to pay for my passage."

He turned around and shouted to a person who I guessed was his boss. The boss nodded his head in approval and my request had been granted. Now I had the ultimate disguise to be out of sight in the galley. Within the hour, I was stirring a thirty-gallon pot of barley for the crew.

"Cut more onions," the head cook, Spyro, barked, and I followed his every instruction, not wanting to draw attention to myself. I had one job here and that was to get home, whatever it took.

As I remember, it took roughly four days to get to Carthage, so I braced myself for the ride, hoping I wouldn't get as seasick as I had on the first journey. My Forza was down to the last drops so I rationed it, believing with all my might it would get me through this hellish experience. The seas were calm for what must have been late spring, and we cooked for the crew day and night.

On the third day, Spyro asked me something about artichokes and how I preserved them. Feeling confident and chatty, I offered my advice. "Back in Girgento, I braised them in olive oil with oregano and mint."

Oops. I had mentioned Girgento. I'd been so careful and this was the first time I'd slipped up. Spyro looked at me, tilted his head as if he were thinking, then said,

"Girgento? I thought you were one of us, from Carthage."

To reassure him, I lied. "I am from Carthage. My uncle lives in Girgento and I visited him once when he was sick. He adored artichokes."

Spyro gave me a skeptical look, then returned to his cutting board to chop more fennel. The conversation had ended and I had an uneasy feeling that I wasn't out of the woods quite yet.

Sensing we were close to Sicily, I began thinking of my next plan. When we landed in Gela, I'd have to find a way to get to Girgento. Maybe I could borrow a horse and follow the coastline west; it would be easy with no one looking for me. The day's work of cooking and cleaning finally caught up to me, my adrenaline fading, and I fell into a deep sleep.

As predicted, the boat landed in Gela during my slumber. The cook shook me out of my sleep.

"Let's get going. We need to provision for the journey back to Carthage. You shop for leeks, bread, and eggs, I'll get the rest."

He was awfully trusting considering our conversation the day before. I got myself organized and quickly packed up my things. Spyro handed me some coins and three baskets.

"Be back here as soon as you're finished. We return midday."

For some reason, he had thought I was going back with him, but I had meant for the job to pay for only one way. This was no time to discuss my position, so I went along with his plan.

While waiting for the crew to leave the ship, I noticed Spyro whisper something to the captain while looking at me. They both nodded their heads in agreement, then went their separate ways, the cook following behind me. Had they been talking about me? The thought made me nervous. The agora would be the perfect place to disappear and find transport to Girgento.

We both disembarked and walked down the long ramp, our arms full of baskets to carry supplies back to the ship. I composed myself and tried to win back my confidence. My plan had worked so far, and I felt a spring emerge in my step as I strode through the market with my head held high.

After a few purchases, I began to scope out the agora to see who I might persuade to help me. A young woman holding her horse by the reins stood in front of the vendor selling local produce. I watched as she strapped bags of goods onto the horse, finished with her shopping for the day. It was time to be brave.

"Could I borrow your horse for the day, please?"

It seemed like such an odd request. She looked at me with surprise.

"I promise to bring her back to you tomorrow if you tell me where you live," I pleaded. "I am a healer. It's a matter of life and death." I hoped the part about the "healer" would encourage her to release her horse to me.

I could have grabbed the animal, hopped on, and ridden away, but that would draw attention, so I chose the way of negotiation, hoping it would work.

"I can bring you olive oil and honey for your kindness," I said as a final, urgent request.

The woman suspiciously handed me the reins. I gave her the baskets intended for the ship's supplies, and then mounted her sable horse.

"What is her name?" I called down to her.

"Jade," she softly said. "Take good care of her."

"Jade, take me home please," I said to my new friend and gave her a gentle kick in the loins.

The agora was thick with merchants and buyers, making my exit slow. I navigated as best I could, looking for an open space. We would travel down the beach and head west, the best and fastest way I knew to get back.

A shout roared out from the crowd. "Stop that woman. She is a traitor!"

I knew they were talking about me. Someone from the boat must have recognized me. Or Spyro had been watching and saw me leave. Glancing back, I saw two men on horseback, fighting the masses with me as their target. I would have to go into the hills, the beach being too visible. Jade and I were now at a full gallop, she instinctively knowing the way, and navigating the rocks and streams with ease. I looked behind again and they were gone. How could I have evaded them this quickly? Fearing an ambush, I slowed Jade down to a trot to survey the landscape. Not a sound to be heard except for a few singing birds. Cautiously we advanced through the bush, still with no signs of the men.

We rode a few more hours before Jade's panting indicated she needed water. Streams were abundant in Sicily, so finding a watering hole was no problem. Jade drank for several minutes, and I decided to tie her up and give her a rest. The sounds of nature lulled me into a soft sleep, but only momentarily.

A deep kick in my side alerted me that my escape attempt had failed.

"Ooh!" I moaned, unable to move and wincing in pain. I turned my head to look up at a red-faced man who sneered, "Shut up!"

His strong arms threw me facedown into the dirt as he placed a knee on my shoulders and grabbed my wrists to tie behind my back, without saying a word. I tried to scream but the searing pain in my ribs prevented me from taking a deep breath. The man mounted his black horse, then reached down and grabbed me by the arm to swing me up behind him. My unsteady balance made it difficult to stay on the horse, so I tightened the grip with my thighs. After a couple of miles, I began to regain my breath and knew what I had to do. My knife was close by but not accessible. To remove the ropes, I'd need to cause friction and rub them back and forth to loosen their hold. Because I'd worked specifically with my hands for the past year, I was adept at manipulating my fingers. Now that skill would be tried and it had to be fast, before we reached Gela.

The ropes cut into my hands as I continued to work them free. Finally, I was able to slip one wrist out. With one hand free, I reached for my knapsack and dug deep into the barley for the knife Haman had given me. It took a few minutes to unravel its protective sheath. I didn't question myself. I grabbed the stranger's shoulder, took a deep breath to summon my courage, and dug the knife in as deeply as possible, directly into my assailant's lungs, before pulling it out again. The man gasped, blood now gushing from the wound and staining my hands. With whatever energy he had left, he spun around, grabbed my throat, and began to choke me. Fighting once again for my life, I punched him hard in the eye. He shrieked out in pain, letting go of my neck and clutching his hands to his face. It took every ounce of effort to push him off the horse, and he tumbled to the ground in a heap, blood saturating his garment.

"Oh my God, what have I done?" I cried.

I had never even thought of harming another human being, but survival at this stage in my life was critical. I did what I had to do but was not proud of it. Time was of the essence, and I grabbed the reins, eager to get to

Girgento before they found him.

The horse followed my lead and we headed back to the beach for a swifter ride without the barriers of rocks and trees. We rode for several hours without anyone in sight. I slowed the black horse to a trot and let him wade in the water to cool off his sweaty body. Was it a mirage or were there people up ahead? I recollected my first sightings of Girgento, the way the hill sloped, then the steep limestone cliffs, and finally, a mesa with a vibrant city. Only this time, it seemed more subdued. There weren't the many bodies usually littering the clifftop and it was quieter. I approached a group of fishermen and asked if Alexander was still the tyrant. He was, they said, but the city had changed. There had been a fire, and someone had been killed. Girgento was recovering. I gasped in astonishment and gave the horse a sharp kick to accelerate our final stretch.

28

GIRGENTO'S PLIGHT

I left the horse near the Concordia and walked through the valley of temples. Builders pounded away but not as actively as before. Evening was setting in, my journey an all-day affair. Most people had gone home for the day. My first stop would be to see Iris and ask her about the events that had taken place since my absence. I'd been missing for five months and didn't know where to look for her. She found me instead.

"Alexis!" she cried from the Temple of Heracles, fifty yards away.

I ran into her arms like a lost dog who had just found its owner.

"Where have you been? You just disappeared," she said.

Not able to hold back my emotions anymore and my bravery exhausted, I sobbed. "I was kidnapped and taken to Carthage. They made me revive their gardens. I poisoned a man and left another to die before I escaped."

It was too much information all at once, my story more than what could be described in a few sentences.

"How is my garden?" was the first thing on my mind.

"Oh Alexis, that is a long story as well. Shall I go with

you?"

I assumed she meant to the gardens. "Yes, please come with me. Someone on the beach told me there was a fire."

Iris held her breath, not wanting to give away anything right now. "Be prepared," was all she said as she fondled her necklace, a sign her anxiety was flaring up.

In silence, we followed the pathway and descended into the gardens, like I'd done a thousand times before. In front of me stood the charred remains of my herb gardens and Jory's large vegetable gardens.

"No, no! Our gardens . . . When did this happen?" I cried, feeling a panic attack coming on and bending over to catch my breath. As usual in an uncomfortable confrontation, my birthmark began to itch. The attack left me weak but did not manifest like it usually did. Iris held my hand and helped me upright. She finally spoke.

"Are you all right? Let me start at the beginning. The fire began in the late evening, the same time as you left. It was hard to put out the flames in the dark. Everyone helped, retrieving the water from the aqueducts, but it was too late. Fortunately, the trees were spared," she explained.

"Jory, where is Jory?" I asked.

Iris drew me into her and hugged me tight. "Jory was the first to notice the fire and wanted to get all your medicinal supplies out of your workshop. He piled them up in baskets and took them outside for protection, then returned to try to save his vegetables, at all costs, including his life."

Unable to handle this unexpected news, I broke down and my body shook uncontrollably. My quiet, trusting mentor was gone and I hadn't been here to save him. Jory confided in me, helped us solve the mystery, and saved my life with his package of tinctures for Carthage. It just couldn't be so. My sobs turned to anger.

Outraged, I was now ready to take on the arsonist. "Does anyone know who did this?"

I was sure it was Ignatius and his gang, trying to create a distraction from my kidnap.

"Alexander is furious, especially because you left without a word and he has yet to replace you."

"I didn't leave, I was taken against my will!" I interrupted.

Iris continued. "At first, many thought you had set the gardens on fire, then gone back to Greece. There are still a few who believe this."

Stunned, I took in this information with a saddened heart. People were so quick to judge. I had helped so many, given my soul to Kolymbethra, and now I'd have to justify my existence with a story of kidnapping, which probably would seem far-fetched.

"What happened with the wheat? Did you find it in the Concordia?" I asked. "I watched the whole thing and then Alena accused me of being the thief and a sorceress."

"Yes, the wheat was hidden in the Concordia. Ries confessed to Alexander that it was a plot by Ignatius and Alena to overthrow him. Not wanting to go down alone, Ignatius told Alexander of his affair with Alena and how it was her idea to manipulate him into submission. Humiliated and angry, Alexander found Ignatius guilty of treason. He received the harshest punishment: he was bound and gagged, and sewed into an empty wheat sack, then thrown into the ocean to die. His execution was just."

Punishment was severe, especially for traitorous activities. If Ries had not admitted he knew about the duo's crimes, it might have been me in the sack. I shivered at the thought.

"Ries's life was spared for admitting the truth, and he was sent back to Sparta," Iris added.

"And Alena? What about her baby?"

"Alena's baby will arrive soon. She is sequestered in hiding and not allowed outside until the birth. The baby will be sent to Athens to be raised by Alexander's brothers, in training for future leadership. Even though Alexander loves Alena, the Council determined her fate. After the birth, she will be stoned in front of the polis as an example of her betrayal."

"I can't believe all that has transpired since I left. What happened to the wheat?"

"It is now safely back in the granary with a guard," said Iris. "Demeter is pleased."

I wondered if Demeter even cared about me. How I risked my life to save the grain and her precious community from starvation. It was over now. I would need to find my way, either here in my adopted home or think about a way to go forward and return to my life in San Francisco. Life just would not be the same without Jory by my side. Then I remembered Jory's secret cellar. Was the extra grain still there?

"Iris, I have something to show you."

Iris followed me to Jory's home. I opened his door, expecting to see him sitting at his work bench, the one with the carved horse hooves as table legs. Looking around to make sure no one was watching, I closed the door and pushed away the floor rug. The pull lifted easily to expose the room below. Iris inhaled and let out a gasp.

"Go ahead of me and I'll follow you down," I said.

A heavy scent of must filled the air, the cellar closed up for months. Iris observed our herbal ingredients and storage of extra food and supplies. Kora's necklace still hung in place on the wall, a reminder to Jory of his deceased wife. In one corner lay the large bag of grain we had hidden.

"Please do not tell anyone about this room," I pleaded. "Jory dug it himself for Kora to use when she created the herbals. It now hides the extra wheat, should the farmers need it. I wanted you to know about it in case something happens to me."

"You are safe now, with the three who were undermining you gone," Iris stated.

"I am not so sure. Remember I told you I might have killed a man who tried to return me to the ship back to Carthage? He and his men will continue to look for me."

"Alexander will protect you. I'll explain it all to him. Stay in your power, Alexis."

Where was my power, the power that I used to come all the way home from Carthage? I felt weak in the knees and needed to sit down. I would tell my story and stand by it. All nonbelievers would come around sooner rather than later. Everyone needed to eat, and my produce was by far the tastiest in the southern region. It wouldn't take long.

"Thanks, Iris. I trust you will make things right with him," I said with a lingering doubt, not about Iris, but about the vengeful men.

I had gained strength in Carthage by trusting in myself and had succeeded in returning to Girgento, something that would have left me terrified back home. I could deal with the threat now.

Iris left me to tend to her makers, and I remained in my desolate, sad garden, once again responsible for its revival. The first thing I did was to see if any of my herbs had survived the months of neglect in the garden. To no surprise, most of them had been raided, leaving a few stragglers to fend for themselves. Yes, this was another start-from-scratch project. I ran to the cave to see if the seeds in safekeeping had been discovered. A few bottles of olive oil sat on the dirt shelf, along with some wine, probably fermented beyond consumption. I reached in between the two rocks that sequestered the seeds from Scott and let out a sigh of relief when my fingers pulled them out from dormancy. At least I'd have something to work with as I put my gardens back together.

As much as I wanted to get back to my life here, my energy was depleted, and I just wanted to sleep this whole adventure off. I was safe back in my home and all that was missing was Sparta. He was a survivor, a trait I thought of while in isolation in Carthage.

Just then came a bumping at the door. I had no fear. I'd been through hell and back and could tackle whatever was thrown at me. I swung open the door to find my long-lost friend, wagging his tail and asking to be invited in.

"Sparta!" I cried, "I missed you so much! Tell me everything."

Of course he couldn't, but I wished otherwise. His wiggling body told me how much he had missed me, and I returned the sentiment, cooing softly to him and stroking his soft fur. Just knowing Sparta was still here lifted my spirits and gave me hope for a returned normalcy to life. We slept curled up in each other's arms like lovers, and I never wanted us to be apart again.

At dawn, I rose to inspect the damage and evaluate my options once more. My money had been stolen, along with the ravaged medicinals, so I thought of going to Alexander to ask for a loan to get started again. For now, Iris was the only one who knew I was back. Would making an appearance in the upper world make me a ghost? I had no choice.

The reactions I received with my reappearance were mixed. Some looked at me and turned away, while others embraced me and welcomed me back, asking for their favorite herbals. I searched the crowd for a familiar face when Leandro ran into my arms and lifted me off the ground. "Where have you been?" he shouted.

"It's a long story, Leandro. I was taken against my will to Carthage," I said, wanting to hug him close.

"Oh my, this is a story. Are you all right?" He noticed the cuts on my wrists caused by the ropes during my escape.

"I'm okay, but I am devastated about Jory," I said.

"Me too. A little quirky, but insightful, kind, and with a love of nature." Leandro always knew the right thing to say.

"I would like to confide in you but now is not the time. Can you come to my home this evening?" I asked.

"Of course. I'll bring some food. You must be starving." He held both my hands and stood back as he scanned my body. "You look thin," he commented.

I would tell Leandro everything, including my dreams of Demeter and the missing wheat. All at once I could trust him completely. Sparta had been a good judge of character from the beginning.

29

FULL MOON'S MAGIC

These were my gardens now, not to be shared with my mentor and friend, Jory. But were they really still mine? From the looks of it, someone had attempted to rebuild a part of it.

Singed edges on the entrance to our workshop revealed how close the fire had come to burning it down. A determined Jory had tried to rescue my herbals. If Ignatius's army had planned to take over Kolymbethra, they certainly were too lazy to do anything to repair the damage, and with their leader now exiled under the sea, must have given up. I'd need support from Alexander, in the form of another experienced helper. To manage Kolymbethra was too much for one person, although Jory did it until I arrived. Jory had taught me survival and then revival of the plants. I would take his lessons to heart and get our gardens in prime shape again. This thought was interrupted by a voice calling my name.

"Hi Alexis." Leandro stood in my doorway and immediately noticed the anguish in my face. "Under the circumstances, I'd say let's celebrate your return, but you must be in shock from all the changes here—and losing your friend, Jory."

My eyes welled at the mention of Jory's name. Leandro set down his armload of food and wine, drew me close, and hugged me like he never wanted to let go.

"I've missed you," he whispered.

I looked up at him and smiled for the first time in months.

"How about if I make you dinner and you can tell me your story?" he asked.

Even Sparta was happy to see him and nudged between us, requesting a pat from his favorite visitor. My trusty white dog was a good judge of character and jumped up to give him a kiss.

Leandro had always been there for me, so why hadn't I noticed it before? He embodied Scott's characteristics of kindness, love of nature, and creativity. This realization caused my heart to beat a little faster.

"I'm hungry. Can I get started?" said Leandro, trying not to notice the sudden change in my attitude as I gazed into his eyes with tenderness. My anxiety had melted away and I was fully in the present with someone who had become maybe more than just a friend.

Onto the table went a smoked fish, dates, some local goat cheese, a small loaf of bread, asparagus shoots, and olives. It was like a country French picnic. I handed him two cups, and from the vessel he brought, poured us both wine, diluted with some water as was customary.

"It is not the same without Jory. I still cannot believe he is gone. I loved him for being true to himself and always looking out for us. He can't be replaced. I'm not sure I can handle the gardens without him," I said.

"I admired Jory's humble attitude. He told me a few times about your keen skills in the garden. You two had a special friendship. A few of us carried his stone coffin to the burial ground. I engraved an epitaph on a piece of limestone and laid it over his grave. I can take you there later, if you would like."

"How nice, Leandro. I would like to pay my respects. So much has happened since I left, and I have so much to tell you. Where do I start?"

As we ate what seemed the best meal of my life, I recounted the evening of the kidnapping, boat ride to Carthage, slavery conditions in the gardens, poisoning or sickening of Dolion, and my final escape to Girgento on horseback, including the stabbing of the man who tried to capture me near Gela. How could all this be real? I thought to myself. I never thought I was capable of taking charge of my life in such a dramatic fashion, but I had survived to tell the tale. Leandro just stared at me, speechless, not able to believe my words.

"You know, they will come looking for you," he said solemnly.

In my heart I knew this was true.

"I don't know who to trust anymore. You and Iris are the only ones to know my story. I'll need protection. I have a feeling Ignatius was behind this. His plan failed, and he is dead. I don't know who took over from him and if he knew of the plan."

"We must tell Alexander, Alexis. He has the ultimate power to protect you. I think it is worth the risk."

Risk? "Do you mean he might have known about this? If he did, why didn't he send his men to save me?"

"I don't think anyone knew where you were taken, or even if you were taken. You just vanished and it was evening, so no one really knew you were gone until after the fire."

"But I am back now, and committed to this garden, this way of life. I never wanted to leave . . ." I said, my voice cracking.

"I believe you, Alexis," Leandro said, throwing an arm around my shoulder, "but there are always people who thrive on control and Girgento is no different than anywhere else."

This statement hit home. Leandro sounded just like Scott. Even without the comforts of home, Girgento and the gardens had become the piece of paradise I was looking for. Minimalistic but rich in clean, natural resources, intelligent and philosophical people, pride in workmanship, and deep gratitude for all that was at their fingertips, provided by nature. It seemed so idyllic, but now that vision started to shatter.

"I understand," was all I could say.

Leandro filled me in on the last several months: Empedocles's latest ideas, the temple progress, and his own personal woodworking projects. We drank wine and talked long into the night until we both began nodding off. He rose to go, grabbed my shoulders gently, then kissed my forehead. I froze. It was a friendly gesture, but this is how Scott always ended our times together. It wasn't like I got kissed on the forehead that often either. The coincidence was too much. We said our goodnights and parted ways. Was this a signal to return to San Francisco or let things fall out here? The next few days would give me the answer.

Sparta and I were both startled out of sleep several times. The wind roared throughout the night, and I dreamed of Jory. The gardens would never be the same without him. I would never be the same. All we had worked for now destroyed, including my pride. Someone was sure to discover the dead or injured man near Gela. Would they make the connection that it was me, or had I gotten away with it? I lay in bed, procrastinating the inevitable of facing the day alone without having formed a strategy.

I decided to let ideas come to me as I picked through the ashes, looking for seeds to replace what was lost. I noticed tiny sprouts, from a squash seed, pushing through the black dirt. This garden was sturdy and loved and would always be there for its people throughout the ages. The ingredients could not be destroyed—good soil, water from the aqueduct, the perfect climate, and seeds dropped from the garden birds. It would weather the storm and soon almost recreate itself. The thought comforted me and helped me to put my life into perspective. There would always be challenges but life goes on, regardless.

The next day Cato, one of Alexander's men, walked down into the garden and strode right up to me. "Alexander would like a meeting with you today. Please come to his headquarters when the sun is high."

I knew what this was about. I hoped Iris had met with him and told him of my innocence.

"I will be there," I promised.

I was nervous but knew I needed to tell him the truth about what had happened. Alexander had always been kind to me, and I did not for one minute think he would turn me over to the Carthaginians, or anyone else for that matter. I would go and speak my peace and hope for protection; or at least reassurance that my job was still a vital part of Girgento.

I knocked on the door of the Senate House and was greeted by one of Alexander's guards.

"I am here to see Alexander," I stated. "I am Alexis."

The guard acknowledged me and opened a door leading to a hallway. I followed him to another door, where he knocked and announced my arrival. I had only met with Alexander under casual circumstances, not with this formality. Alexander was sitting behind a large wooden desk, embellished with carvings of horses, and motioned me to sit across from him. Visions of my last meeting with Stephen.

"Alexis, I'm glad you are back but have many questions for you," he said.

I had questions too but held my tongue.

"I can explain everything," I said in a calm manner.

With that, I told him my story, leaving out the part about me poisoning Dolion and stabbing the man who tried to take me back to the ship. Alexander watched me intently, analyzing every word.

"Sources said you are to blame for a man they found murdered near Gela. Is that true?"

How would "sources" know? I figured that Iris had not confronted Alexander yet and this was the first opportunity for me to plea my innocence.

"I was protecting myself. They were trying to kidnap me again and take me back to Carthage," I said, my voice cracking. "Did Ignatius arrange for my kidnap so his military could take over the gardens?" I asked, hoping for a truthful answer. "He knew I distributed wheat to the small farmers and maybe wanted revenge."

Alexander remained quiet for a minute, almost designing his reply in his head before he spoke the words.

"I know Ignatius had ulterior motives, but I had no idea he was planning to sell you to the Carthaginians or that he wanted to take over the gardens."

"I was kidnapped and forced to work as a slave in Carthage all this time. There must be some evidence to prove I am telling the truth," I pleaded. "You know he stole the community wheat from the granary, and what kind of person he was."

Unsure what to believe, or of the Carthaginian's involvement, he just shook his head and wrinkled his forehead in confusion. Finally convinced, he said adamantly, "The Carthaginians have long wanted Girgento for their own. Ignatius must have been involved in a conspiracy with them. Even more reason for his tortuous death."

"The fire!" I added with a cry. "He set Kolymbethra on fire, as a distraction. He ruined your food source and killed Jory in the process."

This was too much for me to take but I put on a brave face, not wanting to appear weak. "Can you offer me protection?"

"I will find out who was behind this. They will probably want you to return as their slave. I will alert the military to be on the lookout for those who do not belong to Girgento. We will meet tomorrow after my investigation."

I stumbled out of his office and ran all the way back to my house, the late afternoon sun casting ghostlike shadows from the temple columns in front of me. To curb my anxiety, I made barley bread from what little flour I had, while Sparta watched and politely offered his paw for scraps. I reviewed what items remained in my tiny house. The exquisitely painted vessel Ries, the traitor, had given me still sat on the shelf, along with the box from Leandro containing the carved wooden dove that I now wore around my neck. Scattered about were a few small empty vases that used to contain my famous tinctures, a bag of barley, a few leftover dates that Leandro brought the other night. It wasn't much but it had been my home for the past year or so and it was comfortable. I wanted Alexander to punish my kidnappers and protect me so I could continue living this dream. Or did I? I was never great with confrontation but had learned how to fight my way back and I would fight again. Just as I was lost in my thoughts, I heard the thunder of horse hooves, and my heart froze.

"Alexis, come out. You are under arrest!" called a man whose voice I didn't recognize.

I waited a few minutes before answering, "Give me a minute, please."

At least I would be polite before they saw my contradictory spirit. I quickly gathered up a few things and exited the door, Sparta following behind.

"Why am I being arrested? And by who?" I asked.

"You are guilty of murder," he shouted.

There were five other men with him, his protectors, I guessed, so the odds weren't looking good for me.

"It was self-defense," I claimed. "You cannot arrest me without Alexander's consent."

"Leave Alexander out of this," he said. "Men, arrest her!" he commanded his troops.

I was not giving up that easily and started running as fast as I could toward the stairs that would take me up to the city. It would be harder for them to arrest me with people around. I shouted and screamed, hoping someone would hear and come to my rescue, but was left to my own solutions. One man caught up to me and grabbed my arm. I turned around and kicked him in the groin, causing him to bend over in pain. I swiftly reached into my shawl and pulled out the knife Haman had given me.

"I am not afraid to use this!" I shouted, waving it in front of my next attacker's face, slicing off a piece of his nose. He backed off, realizing I meant business. Someone came behind me and knocked me to the ground. I still had the knife in my hand but was brandishing it in thin air.

I heard Leandro cry, "Alexis!"

My hero, Leandro, would save me. He kicked the man who had pushed me down, grabbed me by the waist, and threw me over his shoulders. He ran at a gallop, trying to outpace the other men on horseback. At first, we were ahead of them, then they gradually caught up to us, shouting for us to stop and surrender. We ignored all their threats, and I could hear Leandro's heavy breathing, indicating he was running out of steam.

"Let me down, Leandro. We can both run," I shouted over the noise of the horses' hooves.

He obeyed and as I ran, one of the men's horses reared up and came down hard on Leandro. I heard his screams and looked back.

"Go to the sanctuary of Demeter, Alexis!" he shouted over the noise.

I wanted to go back but kept running, listening to his screams of what was now torture from the henchmen. He had stalled them for me. The temple was up ahead, and I said a silent prayer for Leandro as I ran for my life.

The hoof beats felt like they were right behind me as I ducked into the temple, wishing Iris were there. From a side room she appeared and ran in front of me just as two of the men approached the entrance.

"You are safe here," whispered Iris.

"Come out and surrender," one of the men shouted.

Iris appeared at the temple entrance and delivered her authority to the men. "You must leave this holy place. The gods have spoken and will bring harm to you if you do not listen to them. Alexis is shielded by the goddesses for her good work. Leave now."

In silence, the men turned around and mounted their horses. I was protected, for the present moment.

"Is this true, Iris?" I questioned.

"Yes. Demeter has spoken to me and is pleased you

have worked so hard to save the wheat. Stay here until we hear from Alexander."

I was unsure how she knew about my upcoming meeting with Alexander, but she was, after all, an oracle with extraordinary powers.

"Leandro!" I exclaimed. "He was injured by the men's horses. We must find him."

"I will bring him here. Do not leave," she instructed, just as Sparta's nuzzle peeked into the temple. "Sparta will keep you company."

Relieved that Sparta was allowed to join us and the deities, I called to him and assured him it was all right to enter. He pounced into my lap, slapping wet kisses on my face as I stroked his ears and hugged him tight. A dog would always be a part of my life.

"Help me, Alexis." It was Iris holding up Leandro, who was having a difficult time walking. Blood dripped from his jaw, but he still managed a smile when he saw me. I ran into his mud-cloaked arms, relieved he was alive after the screams I heard.

"I have some creams for your injuries but will need to go to my house to get them," I said, eager to help.

"I will go," said Iris. "Tell me what you want and where to find them. You both need to stay here to be safe for the time being until we can tell Alexander what has happened."

"Go to the Armonia house and see what is left. I'll need arnica, chamomile, valerian, and vervain," I urged as she raced out of the temple.

I turned my attention to my hero. "How are you feeling, Leandro? You need to lie down."

I tried to wipe some of the blood off with a piece of my dress. Bruises were forming all over his battered body. The injuries looked serious but not life-threatening.

"I'll be good," he said stoically. "I was coming to tell you good news about your garden when I saw the men chasing you. The gods and goddesses have protected you."

"What's your news?" I asked.

"Macedon's daughter and Dorus's son have been clearing the garden in your absence. I think they could be mentored to help you with Kolymbethra," Leandro suggested, knowing of my concern for the gardens.

"I will need assistance with Jory gone. Do the men approve of their children doing garden work instead of helping with the grain harvest?" I asked.

"Yes. They are grateful to you for saving a possible disaster. This would be their repayment."

"I don't need repayment, just a couple of strong bodies." I laughed. "When we leave here, we will meet with them and make the arrangements. They can stay in Jory's home if they would like."

At that moment, a group of men gathered at the entrance to the sanctuary, but they were not the Carthaginians. They were the farmers we had distributed wheat to. One of them stepped forward, into the temple.

"Alexis, we are here to protect you. You won't be harmed by the Carthaginians again. We caught the men who tried to hurt you and told them of their fate should they attempt a return. You are safe to go to your gardens."

Leandro and I looked at each other and even with his painful body, hugged.

"Thank you, my friends. I will watch over you too and help with medicinals for you and your families. I want to continue to be a part of this polis," I said in gratitude.

Leandro and I left the temple, moving slowly due to his injuries, our escorts leading us back to the gardens. Iris had lit a lamp and was still there, going through my cupboards for the healing aids for Leandro. We told her what happened, and she insisted we still needed to talk to Alexander the next day. Iris returned to her temple telling me to continue to be aware. Leandro stayed in my house so I could tend to his wounds.

"Please lie down and rest. Your body sustained quite a trauma," I offered.

While Leandro dozed, I prepared Sparta's dinner and made myself a cup of Dimitri, lost in my thoughts. Could the farmers really protect me? I didn't want to be paranoid the rest of my life but had that gut-wrenching feeling that this wasn't over yet. Relying on Alexander didn't seem to help diminish my unease. He had better things to do, like run a society.

Sparta gently jumped onto the bed and nestled in right next to Leandro. I took his cue and lay down alongside Sparta, who enjoyed being in the middle. Soon all three of us drifted into a deep sleep.

"Wake up, Alexis." It was Leandro pushing on my shoulder. "I had a dream, and you were in it. Demeter was telling you it was time to go home and that your mission here had been fulfilled."

Groggy but awake, I listened to Leandro, stupefied. I had had the same vision.

"Leandro, there is something you need to know about me . . ."

"What does this mean, Alexis?" he asked.

"I've had conversations and visions with Demeter for many lunar cycles. It was she who sent me here from Siracusa to help the gardens."

I thought about telling him the truth about me being from the future but wasn't sure if he'd understand. "She's saying I have a half a lunar cycle here before I am to leave for the next community that needs me."

Leandro's eyes welled up. I was growing fond of him

too. I loved my life here in Girgento, and with a possible budding relationship with Leandro, didn't really want to leave. But I knew I had to follow my destiny, and Demeter had never let me down.

"I will gather Troy and Diana from their farms so you can start teaching them," Leandro said in a stoic voice.

Leandro left in a hurry so I wouldn't see the tears that sprang from his eyes. Sparta and I climbed the stairs up to the city to find Iris who must be told this news. The oracle who had become my best friend and advocate was kneeling at the altar in the Temple of Heracles. She heard my footsteps and turned her head around, then rose to greet me.

"I know," she said. "I had the same vision as you last night. The goddess Demeter is pleased and has work for you to do in another world."

"Another world?" I gasped.

"You will seek the truth and use your power to help other communities." Iris didn't even seem the least bit curious about Demeter's statement. She was intuitive and realized that she was here to advise the society with guidance from the gods.

"I have one half-lunar cycle to finish my work here, Iris, and will have help from the farmer's children, Troy and Diana," I said.

"Yes, they are destined to be the new caretakers of the gardens. Teach them well."

"What about Alexander?" I asked.

"We will both speak to him today."

The choice about me staying or going had been made. For the next two weeks, my job was to give the two young adults as much knowledge as I could. Kolymbethra was meant to remain a part of Girgento forever and its continuation was now left up to me. As a team, we cleaned up the veggie gardens and made repairs on the houses. I taught them as much as I could about herbals and medicines, and they listened attentively. I showed them how to make the Forza and Dimitri, the herbal formulas that restored the gardens the year before, but asked them to keep it a guarded secret. I would let them find Jory's hidden cellar for themselves. It was like teaching an accelerated class, cramming as much information as I could into their eager minds. The bees would need special care. The new gardeners would need honey for their medicinals too. But asking these children to take on another responsibility would be overwhelming. Perhaps Philo could help out and chose the new beekeeper?

The days were winding down and my time in Girgento was coming to a close. How could I leave this paradise? What would await me back home? Or was there somewhere else Demeter was sending me?

Iris and I explained everything to Alexander, and he agreed to let the farmers protect me until I left. My emotions ran high my last few days in Girgento. I really loved this place, its people, the simple yet sophisticated lifestyle. Could I truly trade it in for my old life back in Oakland? My time here had been a welcome respite from the everyday stressors, especially my old boss Stephen. Ignatius had replaced Stephen as my nemesis, but here I had allies in Iris, Leandro, and Alexander. Together we had battled evil so that good could prevail. My new friends had power, but more than that, they were people who I trusted and who trusted me. That word again. Trust. Fear creeped in thinking about going home, if that is where I would be sent. How would I battle the evil Stephen with only Scott to trust, even if he wanted to get involved? It was then I realized that it wasn't just the power and confidence of my friends, but mine as well. I had been an integral part in the recovery of the wheat, and I was the one chosen to lead this battle. I took a deep breath and suddenly knew I would be okay.

I wanted my friends to know how much I appreciated their kindness and support this past year so invited Iris and Leandro to join Sparta and me for dinner. A happy time together and something for me to remember long after I was gone. I'd make one last visit to the Agora Magna to gather ingredients for the special meal. How I loved this market! It was an expression of art in every variety. Musicians entertained the crowd as sellers vied for the customers, often shouting or even singing about their products to get attention. Red and black hand-painted vases were displayed alongside gold jewelry embellished with stones and shells. The freshness and purity of the food offerings, the large wood-fired oven scenting the air with warm bread, the shopkeepers who loved to tell their stories to you. Yes, we had farmers' markets in Oakland, but not like this. Today I stopped by the fishmonger's stall to buy freshly harvested sardines and anchovies. I would cook the fish with onion, fennel, dried grapes, olive oil, and a pinch of saffron. This would be tossed with cooked barley and topped with dried breadcrumbs for some crunch and perhaps a sprinkling of chopped pistachios. I would recreate my famous fig cakes, and the wine would flow.

A dove cooed in the distance as the three of us sat outside in the warm summer evening, enjoying our meal. Sparta lay beside me, hoping for the leftovers, sardines being his favorite food. Leandro talked of the future and warned that the Carthaginians would never give up the idea of acquiring Girgento for their own. Iris mused about the gods and how they foretold many future scenarios, most of which she was sworn to secrecy. It was difficult for her to hold onto this knowledge and perform the necessary rituals to manifest them. But she was, after all, an oracle and she accepted her destiny with grace. I hoped Leandro and Iris would become good friends and continue to rely on each other for help. I loved them both and said a silent prayer for their safety and well-being. How could I leave? The three of us hugged, this last meal together signifying a new beginning for all of us.

On my last day, I was summoned to the Concordia by Alexander. He stood on a pedestal, a crowd of people surrounding him and awaiting his announcement.

He spoke. "Alexis restored our gardens and healed our polis with her medicines. She has been a valuable resource to us and will be missed by all. The gods have called upon her to leave us to help another community in need. I wanted you all to know of her destiny, and for each of us to wish her well."

I stood there, stunned at this speech by the tyrant, the one who almost turned me in for murdering a man. Iris must have told him of Demeter's message. The crowd suddenly surrounded me, giving gifts of flowers and beads, and telling me how much they appreciated my work. In the distance I spotted Philo, who waved his hand goodbye. I had never received so much attention in my life. Teary-eyed, I wanted to ask Demeter to let me remain, at least another year, but I knew what she would say. I stayed until everyone had said their goodbyes, then turned to Iris and Leandro, who had known about this surprise.

"I don't want to leave," I whimpered.

"It's time. We will lead you to the cave," said Iris in a comforting voice.

Sparta appeared and rubbed his furry body against mine. How could I leave him? We followed the path I had taken after I arrived what seemed so long ago, until we saw the cave that was used for the Thesmophoria ceremony.

"Be well," I said to both Iris and Leandro, hugging them so tightly they had to peel me off of them. "I love you both forever."

"The gods and goddesses will take good care of you. Hold onto your power, and never forget us," Iris said.

Leandro choked up and mouthed, "I love you, Alexis."

I looked at him, nodded, and held up the necklace I wore with his carved dove intwined into the string. "I will never forget you."

I knelt and gave Sparta a big hug while he covered my face with kisses. Bravely, I climbed up the side of the cave, inhaling its dampness for the last time, and looked out over a rising full moon, my arms raised in gratitude. It was time. I said a prayer to Demeter, closed my eyes, and again felt the swirling of energy wrapping tightly around my body. The cool air lifted me up and I was flying as Demeter guided me through the skies. I heard Sparta bark, then all went black.

PART THREE

30

THE CARVED DOVE RETURNS

July 2017

When I opened my eyes, I was sitting on the big rock that had transported me through time, exactly where I was when I left this place, in my own garden in Oakland. Was I dreaming again? Where was Leandro? Iris? Sparta? I felt disoriented, took a deep breath, and closed my eyes. The night was still and quiet with only a cicada humming her song. I inhaled the lavender and sage, seduced by their scents, and was almost lulled into a slumber. To orient to my surroundings, I forced my eyes open to a view of my blooming herb garden, lit by moonlight, reminding me of where I'd been. It looked exactly as I left it. How long had I been gone?

I finally stood up and walked toward my house, observing every detail, remembering my tiny home in Girgento. Inside, bottles of tinctures I had been making were sitting on my kitchen countertop. There was a vase of freshly picked garden flowers next to my cell phone on the dining room table. I clicked the "home" button on my phone and saw the icon that meant there was a voicemail for me. With trepidation, I hit the speaker and listened.

"Welcome home, Alexis!" was all it said.

It was from Scott. I sank to my knees, unable to speak or move. What had just happened? What day and year was it? Picking up my phone again, the date read Saturday, July 22, 2017. The calendar reported I'd only been gone one week, but in Girgento's time, I'd been gone about a year.

Fatigue took over and I removed my Greek-style kaftan, took a warm shower with lavender-scented soap, and looked in my closet full of clothes for a nightgown. It all seemed so decadent compared to my last dwelling. I crawled into my very comfortable bed and snuggled with Lucas's favorite old stuffed animal, a chipmunk, and fell into a deep, deep sleep.

Another strange dream about Demeter woke me up but I didn't open my eyes. I reached over to pet Sparta's soft fur but was met by a pillow instead. How I wished Sparta could have returned with me. My eyes welled up with the thought of the big beast, always there to watch over me, the dinners we shared together, and his eager ears that listened to me when I needed a friend. I would miss him most. Reality setting in, I lay in bed recounting the day before and wondering what was happening in Kolymbethra today. Or was there even a today so long ago? I reached for the necklace with the dove Leandro had carved for me, and that I wore daily, to find it missing. This would have been proof to myself that I had actually traveled to Girgento. Wait—I had left here with seeds in my pocket that I discovered once I arrived in Girgento. I quickly grabbed my kaftan and dug into the pockets. One object remained, tucked deep into the seam. The tiny carved dove from my necklace.

⸙⸙⸙

"Would you like a visitor today?" I asked as Scott answered the phone. It was a Sunday and I assumed Scott would be home, working in his garden.

"I've been waiting for your return," was all he said.

It felt so strange to drive a car, and all the people on the road! I felt claustrophobic and longed for the community that walked most everywhere or rode horses. As I pulled into Scott's driveway, a wave of relief poured over me. I knocked on the door but there was no answer. The side gate was unlocked so I made my way down the pathway, the same as Kolymbethra's pathways, until I saw him tending to his herb garden.

"Scott, you will never believe what happened to me!"

"Yes, I will."

With that he grabbed me close and instead of kissing my forehead, went straight for my lips.

We kissed for what must have been ten minutes before I pushed away and said, "How did you know …?" He just grinned.

"Let's go to the patio and talk about it," he said, leading me to two Adirondack chairs set between the trees.

"You won't believe what I am about to tell you," I said uneasily.

As I recounted my Girgento adventure, Scott listened attentively, nodding his head as if he already knew what happened.

"Scott, you act as if you know Girgento. Are you some kind of wizard? Did your special tincture send me back in time?" I asked, feeling a little queasy.

"Sometimes we are called to perform duties at a level higher than we've ever dreamed of that challenge us to our core. It looks like you were the chosen one."

There were too many coincidences. His resemblance to Leandro, his garden a replica of Kolymbethra, the words they both spoke to me of truth and power.

I remained speechless until Scott broke the silence.

"It's time for you to come back to the museum," Scott stated. "Stephen is still there but you are needed, especially with your advanced knowledge of Agrigento."

"But Stephen doesn't want me there. Won't he have to approve?" I said, reverting to my old lack-of-confidence self. I was procrastinating and dreading the confrontation. Another hurdle to tackle besides putting up with Stephen.

"Where is your newfound bravery, Alexis? Go and challenge him. You have nothing to lose."

Changing the subject, I asked, "Is there any news on the missing Demeter?"

"No. But I think together we can find out the truth. Are you game?"

"Anything to clear my name. Do you have any ideas?"

"As a matter of fact, yes. Why don't you stay for dinner tonight? I'll cook."

I flashed back to my welcome home dinner with Leandro. How sweet he'd been to care for me after my harrowing escape. Now Scott was modeling the same behavior.

"My friend Mike brought me some fresh albacore. How does that sound?"

"Fantastic! Did I tell you about the large pond of fish in Girgento?" For some reason, I was still in the 440 BC time zone and wanted to remember every bit of it.

"Please write down all that you remember. It will help us create an expanded exhibit that lends an authentic feel. You could do a narration on the day in the life of a gardener and herbalist in Girgento."

"It would be a fitting tribute to all the people I loved and learned from, and to showcase their talents and spirit as a community," I added.

"On Monday we can mock it up and I'll get started right away."

"Won't we need approval from Stephen?"

"Yes, but I'll make it my idea and convince him an exhibit of this size will attract national attention. Besides, he will eat up all the publicity it generates."

As much as I missed Girgento, it felt comfortable to be back home with Scott. Scott, who understood me and believed me. His connection to Girgento mystified me but he really didn't care to go into detail about it. Maybe things are best left as they are.

I spent the early morning in my garden, tending to my herbals and watching the doves, not yet ready to enter the real world. I mentally prepared myself to go back to work and face my boss, who probably still did not trust me. Girgento taught me that I had value and worth, and with the right people by your side, you could conquer the everyday challenges that were delivered to you. I'd had my triumphs and disasters but managed to make the best of each situation. My confidence returned and I was now ready to face Monday morning.

My moka pot bubbled to tell me my coffee had finished brewing. It had been ages since I'd drunk coffee and the buzz accelerated my anxiety, but it tasted so good. I gathered my laptop, water, and lunch for the day, just as I'd always done, and headed out the door. The frenzied drivers on the freeway into the city put me on edge. It was like I was caught up in the crowd at the agora again, only more dangerous. I used my key to unlock the back door of the museum and looked around for a familiar face. It was early and I was one of the first to work, except for the one voice who called out to me.

"Good morning, Alexis. Has this past week shed any light on where Demeter might be?"

It was Stephen's voice, and he was still badgering me about Demeter. All I wanted to do was to return to my job.

"Good morning, Stephen. I'm happy to get back to work and to put this captivating exhibit together," I said, ignoring his question about Demeter.

With this comment, Stephen retreated, back to his cave of an office. After dropping my bags off in my workspace, I headed to the basement to see how much progress had been made. The arrival of more shipments filled the room. Frances must have been working overtime to process all the new artifacts coming in. In the sacred room with all coveted ancient relics, I viewed vessels, and hydras, painted in black and red, exactly like the ones I had witnessed in Girgento. Coins featuring the river crab, an emblem of the city, lay on a special cotton fabric so they could be labeled.

After inspecting the new artifacts, I reached for the inventory list that confirmed Frances and I had checked in the sculpture of Demeter. Where could she be? I flashbacked to the day I unpacked her, her gaze the same as in my dreams. That same list named a crate, number twenty-one, that contained jewelry. After moving several boxes off the floor to see behind them, I spotted the number. Squeezing myself into a corner, I pried open the crate and lifted out all the padding material to reveal several smaller boxes. The first one contained a pair of elaborate gold earrings decorated with olive leaves— something Alena would have worn. The next, a man's bronze necklace with a lion head in the middle, the sort Leandro wore. The third had an outside layer of shredded wood fiber and inside, the object was padded with lavender buds. How curious. Gently, I pushed aside the lavender and lifted out a necklace I recognized immediately. This was Kora's necklace, the one Jory kept hanging in his secret cellar! I bent over to touch the delicate shells and stones, then hugged the piece to my chest, my shoulders shaking under my sobs. I really was there, and this was Jory's message to me to continue the work, at all costs. I vowed then and there to never let him down and hold onto the power he so strongly believed I had.

"Alexis, what's wrong?" asked Frances, coming to my side.

I spun around to see my co-curator, someone I hadn't seen in a year but to her had only been two weeks. Holding back my feelings would be difficult.

"Frances! This particular piece of art touched an emotional part of my soul," I explained. "It's so good to be back here with you and all of this," I said with a wave of my hand.

Every piece of art I unpacked brought back a memory. I wanted to tell Frances but decided against it. It was too far-fetched to believe. Stephen had not called me into his office, and I assumed he had no grounds to prohibit me from coming back to work. I was here now to get this exhibit off the ground and that was all that mattered. We were due to open in four weeks, so no time to waste in the preparations.

31

CLUES TO DISCOVERY

The next two days proved uneventful Stephen-wise, so I continued as if nothing had happened between us. He was cordial enough, but I knew he was up to something. On day three, Scott came downstairs and said he needed me to consult with him on the finishing touches for the Concordia and on the sanctuary of Demeter that we decided to add after my adventure. I followed him upstairs to his office and sat down as he closed the door.

"I had a meeting with Stephen this morning to get budget approval for the enhanced exhibit features and to look around his office for any clues to the missing Demeter. His phone rang and he took the call outside in private. I took the opportunity to look over his desk, and this is what I found!"

Scott pulled out his cell phone and showed me a photo of a piece of paper that read:

7 p.m.

Dmt

3592 S. Pacific Drive

I stared at the photo in disbelief. "Do you think Dmt stands for Demeter?" I asked. "Let's check it out. We can look up the address and see who lives there."

Scott typed in the address and found a Victorian-style house in the Pacific Heights neighborhood. "The owner has lived there for thirty years, so is well-established. We could find out their name from the County Assessor-Recorder."

The sleuthing continued until the name S. Travinsky came up as the current owner.

"Let's find out who this person is. It may be a dead end, a friend or relative. I'll try to keep my hopes up that it leads somewhere," I said.

Continuing the search, Scott said, "Here's an article on her." He read me the link: "'S. Travinsky is a wealthy art collector and donor to the museum. She travels worldwide in search of unusual items to add to her collection. Her passion is Greek mythology.'"

"Stephen must have met her at one of our events and remembered her. Do you think he is selling or has already sold Demeter to her? This is a huge crime."

We found out all this within an hour with the aid of a computer. I didn't have this luxury back in Girgento when Ignatius and then the Carthaginians were stalking me.

"How do we deal with this? We can't prove anything yet so can't get the police involved," Scott said.

"I say we take matters into our own hands. If Stephen is selling museum pieces, he must be stopped. I know the police should be involved but let's catch him in the act first." I'd been through too many challenges to count, and this would be no different.

"Here's my idea," Scott said. "We go to her house, knock on the door, and ask her if Stephen has contacted her regarding the sale of an ancient Greek statue. Maybe she thinks it was a legal sale. If she denies it, we bluff and tell her we will go to the police because we have evidence. If she says she has it, we tell her we will not reveal she was the buyer if she cooperates with us to implicate Stephen. What do you think?"

"It's worth a try. How's tonight sound?"

"The sooner the better. Let's get you cleared of this mess so we can move on with the exhibit."

Scott and I left the museum and drove up the hill to the Pacific Heights area of beautiful old homes with views of the Golden Gate Bridge, and a large park surrounding its perimeter. We easily located her home and parked nearby.

"Why don't you explain to Ms. Travinsky that the artifact in question is owned by the Museo Archeologico in Agrigento?" Scott asked, wanting me to take the lead.

With confidence, we grabbed the large door ring and knocked. I could feel eyes watching me and figured she had an intricate alarm system to guard all the valuables inside.

"How can I help you?" came a British accent over an intercom.

"Hello, my name is Alexis, and my friend is Scott. We've come as representatives from the San Francisco Art Museum to talk with you about a certain artifact you may have in your possession," I stated.

"I have many collectibles, all obtained legally," she said coolly.

"Would you mind if we talk to you person-to-person?" I requested.

The door opened a crack, and we showed her our identifying name tags we were required to wear at work. Peering out, a small, frail woman eyed us suspiciously. I guessed she was in her late seventies; attractive with coiffed silver hair, steel blue eyes, and a diamond as big as my pinky fingernail draped around her neck. She seemed so innocent, and I wanted to believe she wouldn't buy anything illegally.

"Please," I requested again, "can we come in to talk?"

Ms. Travinsky cautiously opened the door and allowed us into her entryway. I strained to see beyond, into her living room, but had not been invited yet.

"Come sit," she said.

"The item we are searching for is a statue of Demeter's head. It belongs to the Museo Archeologico in Agrigento and is on loan to our museum for display only for a short while. It is missing. We are desperate to find it and hope you can help us locate it. We found your address on our head curator, Stephen's, desk."

We all remained silent for several minutes. I glanced around the room, decorated in heavy antiques, Grecian vases, and paintings of Italian masters, looking for any sign of Demeter.

"I did have her, for a short while," she began to explain. "You see, I've always had a fondness for the goddess Demeter. When Stephen approached me and told me had found a source for a statue of her, I responded immediately. I did not know it belonged to another museum."

"Where is Demeter now?" I asked in anticipation of an easy answer.

"I don't know. After Stephen delivered her to me and I paid him handsomely, I had a change of heart. Something didn't sit right. I've purchased a lot of antiquities and the paperwork did not seem authentic. I called him and asked him to pick her up and return my money."

"When was this?" I asked.

"About a week ago. He told me he was busy and couldn't come until yesterday."

"So, he has possession of Demeter?" I asked.

"I assume he does," Ms. Travinsky said.

"Do you still have the paperwork he gave you?" I

asked. "And a copy of the check you wrote to him?"

"Yes, I can make copies for you. I assure you I had no idea it was stolen merchandise. Will I be charged with anything?" she inquired.

"That's not up to us. We just want her back to go on display for the upcoming exhibit. She plays a prominent role in the story we plan to tell," I said. "As far as I'm concerned, you are innocent. You have been very helpful. We hope to see you at the opening."

Scott and I left with paperwork in hand but no statue. Stephen must be hiding it, but where? Jory had told me to look for the wheat in plain sight. We would do the same back at the museum. It would be too risky for him to keep Demeter at his house.

Exhausted after the day's discovery, we stopped in North Beach for a light plate of ravioli stuffed with ricotta and lemon before heading back to the museum and our own cars. As I drove home, I imagined where Demeter could be hidden. Stephen was most likely looking for another buyer. We would have to work quickly before this occurred.

The next morning, I arrived at the museum early, eager to hunt for the missing goddess. I started out in the basement, looking through the opened crates to see if she could be hidden with other artifacts. No luck. What about the exhibit rooms? I made my way through Scott's construction, searching every nook and cranny with no success. Another idea crossed my mind, but I would need Scott first and he hadn't come to work yet. I'd wait impatiently.

"Scott," I said as I peeked into his office, "I think we should check Stephen's office."

"And how do you plan to do that with him there?" he asked.

"You will distract him. Ask him to look over the temples to see if they meet his specifications. Make him feel important," I urged.

I retreated to the basement and to the task of grouping artifacts together for their display. One room would feature the foods grown in Agrigento, vessels, cooking implements, foraged herbs, and an explanation about the fishpond. Another room with the Doric column temples would feature a hands-on feel of limestone, with rocks the guests could use to attempt to carve out the intricate designs in the sample stones. The guests would learn by watching a short video of the methods used and understand the difficulties the artisans faced.

While I was gone, Scott had put together an archway you walked through to enter Kolymbethra. I guess he'd decided the exhibit wouldn't be complete without the sustaining gardens and aqueduct system. For this display, we would borrow trees and plants from a local nursery to line the pathway, and build a mock house, like Jory's, where the gardener lived and worked. I provided the expert knowledge, via a narrated story, about the gardens, exact fruit trees and vegetables grown, and how the aqueduct fed the natural landscape. Our goal was authenticity.

A smaller room would tell the myth of Demeter and Persephone, the statue of Demeter—when we found her— prominently displayed. I wrote a short narrative about the festival of Thesmophoria, and how wheat played an intricate and important role in Girgento, its value recognized throughout the Mediterranean.

As planned before my departure, the agora would be a virtual experience with the guests wearing goggles to get a real idea of what it was like to be among the crowd. Alexander would be there, Empedocles, Ries, Leandro, and Iris, their recorded voices describing the roles they played in the polis. Scents of peppered stew and freshly baked bread would waft in the air. Background music provided by street musicians with aulos, a double-reed clarinet, tympana, or drums, and castanet-like krotalas would lend a lively atmosphere. For a history buff, our exhibit would bring to life every aspect of life in ancient Sicily. And I was proud to be able to help make it so.

My cell phone beeped with a message from Scott that he was with Stephen in the exhibit area. The coast was clear.

I tucked my phone into my pocket and pranced up the stairs to Stephen's office. The old room with gray walls contained a closet, weathered desk, and oak bookshelves. Nothing under the desk or behind the books. The closet remained my last hope. A jacket, a camera, a blue backpack, and other miscellaneous items competed with boxes of paperwork for space. It would take time to rifle through this mess. I inspected the boxes first—they were large enough to hold Demeter. No luck. Even though it seemed too small to hold the artifact, I reached across the boxes for the backpack, thinking I could lift it easily. As I grabbed the straps, it stayed in place, despite my tugs. I bent down, and without picking it up, unzipped the nylon case. Demeter gazed up at me, unprotected by wood shavings or padding.

"You beast! How could you leave her like this?" I said, not realizing the height of my voice.

I snapped a photo, zipped her up, and closed the closet door. My heart pounded as my body tensed with anger. As soon as I got around the corner, I entered the bathroom for privacy and sent Scott the evidence of guilt. My gut told me to rescue her immediately, but I could not be seen with Demeter or risk getting myself implicated.

"Meet me in the break room at one. Let's go out to lunch," was his response.

I met Scott as planned and we walked to a nearby outdoor café for dumplings and green tea. "We must catch Stephen in the act. Take a video of him with the backpack in his possession. I think he'll move her quickly to get her away from the museum," Scott said.

"There's a board meeting tomorrow. It would be fitting to expose him there," I said, still angry.

"Let's wait for him to leave today and see if he takes Demeter with him. If he does, we've got proof he is the thief, along with the paperwork evidence from Ms. Travinsky."

"And if he doesn't take her?" I asked.

"We tell the police where to look. They bring the statue up to the meeting with their findings and we show the photos and paperwork necessary to convict him right there on the spot."

"Assuming he shows up tomorrow, I think we've got him." The feeling of revenge bubbled up inside of me and it had never tasted so good.

At closing time, Scott and I took our places in a corridor out of sight of Stephen, in anticipation of his departure from the museum. Like clockwork, he closed and locked his door, looked around, and hefted the blue backpack onto his shoulders. Both of us took videos of him leaving the museum and putting the backpacked Demeter in his trunk. He drove off and we high-fived, knowing this evidence was enough.

32

DEMETER COMES HOME

That evening I cooked myself a pot of barley stew, poured a glass of red wine diluted with water, and sat at my counter, trying to remember that first meal I'd had with Jory. He'd have been so proud and would have mumbled a few words of praise. I missed the little, wrinkled man with the crooked fingers. Before bed, I took a dropperful of Forza, for old times' sake, and sunk into my silky sheets. Just before dawn, Demeter appeared in a dream. She was flying and kept coming closer and closer to me. When we were eye to eye, she touched my face, like I had touched her statue. Her energy, full of kindness and gratitude, made me weep and I awoke to a flood of tears. Demeter was thanking me for my efforts to release her from Stephen's grip. As soon as the exhibit was over, she would be shipped back to the museum in Agrigento where she belonged.

It would be an early morning. The board meeting started at 8 a.m. The board had asked Scott to present his progress on the almost finished hardscape fixtures for Agrigento. This was the perfect entry to expose Stephen. We had placed the photos and paperwork evidence on a flash drive to insert into the projector for all the members

296

to see after Scott's presentation.

The members gathered and took their seats. Stephen sat in the middle of the long table, sitting upright and fidgeting with his pen, clicking it on and off in an irritating manner. His eyes were downcast, focused on the minutes in front of him. Stephen's dark side was about to be exposed and I didn't feel sorry for him in the least. Normally, I was not a vengeful person, but at this moment, felt a surge of adrenaline, knowing justice would be done and my name cleared. This news would surely hit the papers, and his career as a managing curator would be over. How many other art pieces had disappeared under his watch? I was certain there would be an investigation.

"I've asked Alexis, the curator who traveled to Sicily to make this exhibit possible, to sit in on our meeting in case anyone has any questions," Scott said.

Scott left out the part about my little time travel journey and how I was able to gather first-hand information while dodging bad guys and learning about bee stingers. I took a seat beside him.

Scott's video presentation evoked oohs and ahhs from the members, impressed by his inventive and authentic recreations. My eyes glazed over as I watched the temples, workers, and people I'd known come to life. My spirit was there, but my physical body, here. Clapping hands jolted me out of my daydream.

"Thank you, Scott," said Max Birdman, the board's CEO. "Opening day is in three weeks. It looks like you are almost ready."

"I have one more item to present," said Scott, "if I may? And then we can move on to questions for Alexis."

"Go ahead, please," said Max.

"One of the features of our Agrigento exhibit is the importance of grain to the society. As we all know from

Greek mythology, Demeter was a goddess for fertility and harvest."

I watched as Stephen stiffened in his seat and then began to squirm.

Scott continued. "The head statue of Demeter, circa 450 BC, has gone missing from our museum."

The group gasped almost in unison.

Stephen rose from his seat, his face pale avoiding eye contact, and headed toward the door.

"Excuse me, please," he said.

"If you could just take your seat for a few more minutes?" Scott asked. "I'll continue. The statue belongs to the Museo Archeologico in Agrigento, and it is imperative that she be returned. Alexis and I have discovered the thief and have evidence to prove his guilt."

The board members began talking among themselves in quiet whispers.

"If I can have your attention," Scott asked as he inserted the thumb drive into the projector. "Demeter was taken from the museum and sold to a collector under the pretense that it was an obtained piece of art, not stolen. Once the buyer realized her mistake, she returned the statue to the thief, who hid it here at the museum. Here is the receipt for payment and certificate of authenticity, which was forged." The screen showed the paperwork and signatures of Stephen and S. Travinsky.

Scott then flashed the photo of the statue in the backpack in Stephen's office, followed by the video of Stephen putting the backpack and Demeter into his trunk.

"We assume Stephen was looking for another buyer for the artifact."

All eyes turned to Stephen, who became flustered and uttered, "I've been framed! This is all a mistake. I don't know this woman. She is lying! I want an attorney."

With this outburst, he jumped up and ran toward the door. One of his board colleagues, Mr. Figly, stood up to block his way.

"Easy, Stephen. You'll get to tell your story in court. If this is true, you have betrayed every one of us who has financially supported the museum for years."

Two police appeared at the door with the backpack and headed toward Stephen. "We found this in your trunk and have enough evidence to arrest you. Please come with us."

Stephen struggled at first, then said, "Please, no handcuffs. I don't want the other staff members to see me like this."

One of the police handed me the backpack and I set it down on the table by Scott. I unzipped the pack and carefully removed the ancient head of Demeter. As I held it up for the members to view, I felt a sense of satisfaction, that everything I did to help Demeter in Girgento was coming full circle and now she would be safe for the time she spent here. She had returned and would not go missing again, not under my watch. We had formed a special bond that would never be broken, and she would always inspire me to hold onto my power and not give up.

33

CELEBRATION

"How about we pop some bubbly tonight?" suggested Scott after the board members scattered.

"My name is cleared! Time to celebrate a new beginning. My house this time. Is your garden producing tomatoes for soup? It's been ages since I've eaten a tomato. Can you bring your briny olives?" I piped in.

"I'll bring a bag of produce and we can sort it out—maybe cook something together. How does a bottle of Italian prosecco sound?"

"Sounds like I'm back home!"

For dinner we cooked fresh tomato soup with oregano, dressed cucumbers and peppers with a drizzle of Italian olive oil and cilantro, tossed pasta with a mint pesto, and nibbled on a dessert of fresh dates and pistachios. We sipped prosecco throughout the meal and toasted each other and our accomplishments. I told Scott about Philo and how I had learned to be a beekeeper and even made a poison out of the stingers. I could hardly stop talking.

"Shhhh, my Alexis," he whispered as he kissed my forehead, then my cheeks, then my lips. This night it was Scott who didn't return to his own bed.

Khalil, Stephen's assistant, became the interim head curator and agreed heartily to my wishes to incorporate more technology than initially planned. Many of the displays included interactive features with accompanying narration on side panels written by me to describe life in 440 BC Agrigento. He often commented that I must be up all night doing research. Little did he know.

The day finally arrived and the Agrigento exhibit would open tonight. To make it authentic, I decided to play the part and dress in an olive-green polished cotton fabric, that wrapped around my body like Charissa had taught me, using clips to create and hold the folds of material in place. I braided my hair on top of my head and dressed it with a wreath of herbs and olive leaves. Around my neck I wore a macrame necklace I had fashioned out of small shells and sea glass, with Leandro's tiny carved dove placed in the middle. Gold sandals finished the outfit—an ode to Empedocles. I felt like I was ready to enter a temple and find Iris there, speaking with the gods.

The exhibit had been a team effort, but since I was mostly responsible for bringing the artifacts to San Francisco and creating the interactive displays that gave life to the show, I was asked to give the opening remarks.

"The Agrigento you see here today flourished from 502–406 BC, as one of the most prosperous communities in the Mediterranean. We have done our best to capture the essence of the activities that happened every day in this city, and take pleasure in its recreated Kolymbethra gardens. I want to thank the people of Agrigento, past and present, for making this exhibit possible."

The people I really wanted to thank lived long ago and

had changed my life for the better. This was the best way I knew to acknowledge them and to deliver to them the gifts of appreciation.

The month flew by with newspapers and magazines asking for interviews and raving about the carefully planned details that made Agrigento an interactive exhibit. The success was overwhelming, and the intimate experience helped make it happen so brilliantly. Soon, we would be packing up all the artifacts and returning them to their home in Sicily. I would be pleased to see Demeter back where she belonged, perhaps to ask someone else a favor in the future.

One of our big donors threw a party for the museum staff at a rooftop restaurant with a view of the city. Scott and I noshed on the exquisite Sicilian cuisine the caterers had prepared.

"Care for some caponata?" Scott said with a grin as he guided a slice of baguette topped with the spicy relish toward my mouth.

"Delicious!" I exclaimed taking a sip of champagne between bites. My flirtatious side kicked in and I asked in a soft whisper, "How about a date with a gardeness to delve into one of my new Sicilian cookbooks?" The answer was a kiss on the forehead.

It was all so spectacular, but I missed my starry nights and snores of Sparta. I would have to come to a compromise of sorts with my lifestyle; maybe volunteer to help someone with their beekeeping or practice the herbal skills I had learned from Jory. It had been scary at times, but I wouldn't trade the experience for anything. I trusted myself and my newfound power.

I checked my mailbox as I entered my front door that night, grabbing a handful of ads and readying to toss them in the recycle bin, when one envelope caught my eye. Its return address was from the Smithsonian Institution. Puzzled, I pulled apart the lip of the envelope and retrieved the letter.

> *Dear Alexis,*
>
> *One of our curators was lucky enough to visit your interactive exhibit on Agrigento last month. He described how your elaborate narrations and authentic gardens made an impression on him and took him back in time more than any other exhibit he has seen.*
>
> *We are currently putting together an exhibit about the Ottoman empire and wish to utilize some of your unique concepts. Would you consider joining our team, here at the Smithsonian, as a lead curator in the National Museum of Natural History?*
>
> *Of course, we would pay for your relocation expenses and three months' rent in Washington, DC. Please consider this offer and reply at your earliest convenience.*
>
> *I look forward to hearing from you.*
> *Sincerely,*
> *Marcos Dimitri, Director*
> *Smithsonian National Museum*
> *of Natural History*

Stunned, I poured myself a glass of Sicilian Rosso and sat down in my warm patio to reread the letter. I was just making a name for myself here in San Francisco and beginning a relationship with Scott. Was Demeter sending me away again, on another mission? I stuffed the letter back in its envelope and left it on my kitchen counter. First things first. I opened my computer to the Adopt-a-Pet page. Sparta, where are you?

RECIPES

RECIPES FROM
ALEXIS'S KITCHEN & GARDENS

I've created a few recipes Alexis made at her home in Oakland and then in Girgento. Most of them use Sicilian ingredients, although I've modernized them a bit. For instance, I include sugar in the fig and fennel bars where the Girgentis used honey and concentrated grape must as a sweetener. Lemons didn't appear in Sicily until the ninth century with the influence of the Moors. I love the tang of a lemon as it heightens and brightens the flavor, so I added lemon in the braised artichokes and in the pasta with sardines. In 440 BC, vinegar or fresh grape must would have been the acidic ingredient.

If you enjoy cooking and travel as much as I do, stay tuned for my next book—an anthology of travel stories accompanied by my favorite recipes, old and new. You can follow my progress on my website maryknight.net to see photos, watch videos, and even learn some gardening tips. Please share your favorite Italian places, foods, and wines with me!

Coming soon . . . the sequel to *The Sicilian Sorceress*!

Carrot Soup with Almond-Mint Topping

This soup has a depth of subtle flavor from the cardamom, and the mint topping really adds that extra zing that marries nicely with the creamy carrot. Makes 4 servings.

For the carrot soup:
    3 tablespoons (45 ml) extra virgin olive oil
    2 medium leeks, white parts only, thinly sliced
    ¼ teaspoon (1 g) salt
    ¼ teaspoon (1 g) ground cardamom
    2 lb. (900 g) carrots, scrubbed and sliced into ¼-inch rounds
    1 quart (1 liter) chicken or veggie broth

For the almond-mint topping:
    1 cup (250 g) Greek yogurt
    ¼ cup (15 g) chopped mint
    ½ teaspoon (2.5 g) ras el hanout (Moroccan spice) or more to taste
    ½ cup (50 g) almonds, chopped and toasted

Heat the olive oil over a medium heat. Add the leeks and sauté on medium until soft but not brown, about 10 minutes. Add the salt, cardamom, and carrots and stir to mix.

Add the broth, cover, and let the carrots cook on a low heat for about 20–30 minutes. Test a carrot to make sure it squishes between your fingers—then you'll know it will puree easily.
Remove from the heat.

Using an immersion blender, puree the carrot mixture until creamy. You can also use a food processor or blender. Taste for seasoning. You want a carrot-forward flavor.

Mix the yogurt, mint, and ras el hanout together. Ladle the soup into bowls. Add a dollop of the yogurt mix, a splash of olive oil, and sprinkle the almonds on top.

Girgento Braised Artichokes

This dish takes a little time to prep the artichokes but is well worth the effort and keeps nicely for weeks in the refrigerator. Add them to an antipasto platter, toss them with warm pasta, or include them in a fresh salad with Niçoise olives and grape tomatoes. Makes 2 pint (half liter) jars or 4 servings.

>   1 lemon, juiced
>   2 medium artichokes, or 6–8 baby artichokes, prepped
>   ½ cup (120 ml) extra virgin olive oil
>   ½ cup (120 ml) dry white wine
>   1 tablespoon (15 g) minced garlic
>   2 tablespoons (30 g) chopped fresh mint
>   2 tablespoons (30 g) chopped fresh oregano or marjoram
>   ¼ cup (15 g) chopped parsley
>   ½ teaspoon (2 g) peperoncino
>   ½ teaspoon (2 g) salt

To prep artichokes:
Fill a medium-sized bowl with water and add the lemon juice. As you finish prepping each artichoke, drop it into the water to keep from discoloring.

Peel away about three-fourths of the leaves until the pale interior color is revealed. Trim the stem, and with care, use a knife or vegetable peeler to remove all the dark green until you again see the pale green. The dark green tends to be bitter and fibrous. Trim around the base of the artichoke. Cut off about 2–3 inches of the dark green tops. If you are using baby artichokes, cut off about half an inch of the top. You want to be able to eat the entire artichoke when it's finished, so don't be shy!

Cut each artichoke in half vertically, and using a spoon or melon baller, gently remove the thistle, also known as the choke. Rub the interior with the used lemon half to prevent discoloration. Cut each half in half, vertically, and half again so you have eight slices of artichoke.

Combine the rest of the ingredients in a two to three-quart (liter) heavy pot such as cast iron. Remove the artichokes from the lemon water and add to the pot. Cover and cook over a low simmer for about 30–40 minutes or until just tender. Serve warm or cold.

If you are keeping them for another time, store them in the olive oil marinade. Use the marinade for dressings, grilled veggies, with pasta or rice.

Caponata, Adele's Way

Caponata is a popular Sicilian dish and has many variations. Here is my dear friend and Roberto's mom, Adele's, recipe as taught to me in her kitchen in Catania. Serves six.

> 1 eggplant (aubergine) cut into 1-inch chunks (eggplant will shrink significantly as it cools)
> 1 red pepper, sliced thinly into strips and then strips cut in half
> 2 cups (450 g) red or yellow grape tomatoes (cherry plum tomatoes), halved or quartered if large
> 1 medium onion, sliced thinly into rings
> 1 tablespoon (15 g) capers in brine, rinsed to release their saltiness
> ½ cup (65 g) Kalamata olives, halved
> 2 tablespoons (30 g) white raisins
> ¼ cup (120 ml) olive oil
> 3 tablespoons (45 ml) red wine vinegar
> 1 tablespoon (15 g) sugar

¼ teaspoon (1 g) white pepper
2 tablespoons (30 g) toasted pine nuts or almonds

Preheat the oven to 350°F (180°C).
Combine the eggplant, red pepper, tomatoes, and onion, and arrange on a sheet pan.

Mix the capers, olives, raisins, olive oil, vinegar, sugar, and pepper. Pour over the vegetables and toss to coat.

Bake for about 45 minutes, stirring every 15 minutes, until veggies are soft but still retain their shape. They should not be mushy! Add salt to taste.

The capers and olives add saltiness to the caponata, so I wait to add more salt until the end. Stir in the nuts. Serve warm or cold.

Roberto's Pasta Con le Sarde

Roberto taught me to make this many years ago. Don't fret about the sardines! They have a milder taste than tuna and give this pasta a delicate and unique taste. Serves 4-6.

2 cups chopped fennel fronds and stalks, not the bulb. Look for a fuzzy bulb!
2 tablespoons (30 ml) extra virgin olive oil
1 large onion, chopped
3 anchovy fillets canned in oil
16 oz. (450 g) dried penne, rigatoni, or bucatini pasta. It's best to use a pasta that can hold the delicious sauce!
2 tins, each 4.2 oz. (120 g) wild sardines canned in olive oil —use the highest quality you can find
1 cup (250 g) raisins soaked in warm water to soften, then

drained. I use golden raisins.
½ cup (125 g) toasted pine nuts
A generous pinch of saffron—don't be stingy!
½ cup (125 g) breadcrumbs, browned in olive oil
Extra virgin olive oil and lemon juice to taste

Preheat the oven to 325°F (165°C).

Bring a large pot of water to a boil. Add a teaspoon of salt and the fennel frond. Continue with the rest of the recipe as the fronds soften over medium heat. This will take about 25 minutes.

Sauté the onion and the anchovies in the olive oil. As the onion cooks and softens, add spoonfuls of the fennel water to the mixture to keep it moist.

When the fennel fronds are tender, strain them out and add them to the onion mixture. Do not discard the water. It will be used to boil the pasta. If too much water has evaporated after cooking the fennel, add a few more cups and bring back to a boil. Add the pasta to the fennel water and cook until al dente, so still firm to the bite. This will take about 10 minutes. The pasta will continue to cook as it bakes with the rest of the ingredients.

Meanwhile, stir the sardines, raisins, pine nuts, and saffron into the onion mixture. Use a wooden spoon to gently mash the sardines.

When the pasta is cooked, reserve about a cup of the water. Drain, then gently stir the pasta into the sardine sauce. Add as much reserved water as needed to moisten it. I use the entire cup.

Pour into a 9-inch (23 cm) casserole dish and sprinkle the breadcrumbs on top. Bake until just heated through, about 15 minutes. Drizzle some olive oil on top and a splash of lemon if you'd like.

You can also enjoy this straight out of the pan without baking. Just toss in the breadcrumbs and, in true Italian style, mangia bene!

Note: You might notice that there is no added salt, except in the pasta water. The salt in this recipe comes from the anchovies and the sardines. Feel free to add more for your taste. Lemons had not been introduced to Sicily during Alexis's time. I find a squeeze of lemon juice brightens the flavor of the dish.

Fig, Fennel, and Goat Cheese Bars

I created this recipe with some of the ingredients Alexis would have used, like almonds, goat cheese, yogurt, and figs. The creamy goat cheese filling tames the sweetness of the figs, and the almonds in the crust give it crunch. If figs are out of season, feel free to use jarred fig jam. Fennel was a popular ingredient in ancient times and provides a unique twist. I love this dessert because each layer has its own character, and they marry together beautifully. Makes 16 servings/bars.

For the crust:
    ½ cup (125 g) raw almonds
    10 (140 g) full-size graham crackers (4 digestive biscuits)
    2 tablespoons (30 g) sugar
    2 ounces (60 g) melted butter

For the cheese filling:
    11 ounces (315 g) goat cheese
    ¼ cup (70 g) Greek yogurt
    ¼ cup (50 g) sugar
    ¼ teaspoon (1 g) salt
    2 large eggs
    ½ (2.5 ml) teaspoon Fiori di Sicilia extract (optional)*
    *Fiori di Sicilia is an aromatic citrus extract that lends a
    mild citrus fragrance to baked goods.

For the fig jam:

        1 lb. fresh figs (225 g) or one 8.5 ounce (240 g) jar of fig jam. I like Dalmatia Fig Orange Spread.

        ½ teaspoon (2 g) fennel seeds

        ½ cup (125 ml) water

        ¼ cup (50 g) sugar

        Zest of one orange or one lemon, your preference

        ½ cup (100 g) chopped and toasted almonds for topping

Preheat oven to 350° F (180°C)

Line an 8-inch (20 cm) square pan with parchment paper. This makes it easier to remove the bars from the pan.

In a food processor, grind together the raw almonds, graham crackers, and sugar. Pour in the melted butter and process until the butter is mixed in. Empty into the prepared pan and evenly pat down the crumb mixture. Bake for 10 minutes. Cool on a rack.

Place the goat cheese, yogurt, sugar, and salt in a food processor. Process until smooth and creamy, scraping down the sides between pulses. Add the eggs one by one, mixing well after each addition.

Add the optional Fiori di Sicilia and process once more. Pour into the cooled crust and bake for 25 minutes. Remove from the oven and cool on a rack. When cool, refrigerate.

In a saucepan, combine the figs, fennel seeds, water, sugar, and zest. Bring to a low simmer and cook until all water is evaporated and the figs have a jammy consistency, about 20 minutes. Let it cool.

Pour the fig jam on top of the goat cheese filling and spread evenly. (You might not use all the jam). Sprinkle chopped and toasted almonds on top. Refrigerate until ready to serve. Cut into squares.

About the Author

Mary Knight is a writer and lover of history, travel, food, and everything European. *The Sicilian Sorceress* is her debut novel. A Paris-trained chef, and former cooking teacher, her recipes have been featured in several magazines and newspapers. When she's not traveling, Mary lives in San Diego with her dog, Desi, where she can be found tending to her Mediterranean-style garden full of vegetables, herbs, and fruit trees, while dreaming of her next adventure. She loves to hear from readers. Visit her at maryknight.net.

Note to My Readers

Ciao! Thank you for reading *The Sicilian Sorceress*. I hope I have given you a glimpse into the life of the ancient Greek city of Agrigento, on the southern Sicilian coast. Although this book is a work of fiction, the city of Girgento is based on the history of Agrigento, a UNESCO World Heritage site. The archaeological site of Agrigento, with its majestic Doric temples, sits on a plateau with stunning views of the Mediterranean Sea and is now called the Valley of the Temples.

I chose the date of 440 BC because the city was at its peak and flourishing — massive temples under construction, a booming wheat production, a community of intellectuals and philosophers, and a sophisticated culture, rich in the arts. It rivaled Athens but stood in its shadow.

The philosopher Empedocles was a real person, born in Agrigento and philosophizing at the time this book takes place. The "Kolymbethra" is an actual garden, which still lies in an oasis below the temples. According to my research, it was first a man-made lake filled with fish and swans and when it dried up (exact date unknown), became a lush Mediterranean paradise filled with an abundance of fruit and nut trees, and vegetable gardens. An extensive aqueduct system, in place since 480 BC, still runs alongside these gardens, delivering water to the arid soil. For the purpose of this book, the lake and gardens exist simultaneously.

My one and only magical encounter with the Valley of the Temples was enough to prompt me to write this book. She lured me in and whispered her story so I could share it with you. While alone near the Temple of Castor and Pollux, I encountered a large, dirty white, wolf-like dog, slinking through the bushes. He was my inspiration for Sparta, Alexis's protector and companion.

If you enjoyed this book as much as I loved writing it, please leave me a review. Stay tuned for another epic adventure as the story continues with a second book in a series of three.

You can reach me on my website at maryknight.net.

Grazie and a presto!

Acknowledgments

Thank you to my dad, who always had a book in hand. He loved to read so much that he had over a thousand mystery books crowded into his small library. We haunted used bookstores, shared our favorites, and had discussions long before the age of book clubs. He later repaired books for the library, giving them new life for future readers. Dad, I wish you were here to read my novel.

A million thanks to my writing partner, Jolie Tunnell, who navigated me through the historical fiction book process from start to finish. Her encouragement, humor, and persistent push gave me the courage to finish and publish this book. A prolific writer, Jolie has published a series of fun-to-read Loveda Brown mysteries. You can find her at www.jolietunnell.com.

Thank you, Roberto Catalano, my dear friend and tour guide of Sicily, and his friend Chiara Amico, who together introduced me to the wonders of Sicily, especially Agrigento, the inspiration for this book. Roberto—Sicily is all that and more, and you made a believer out of me. Thank you for sharing your beautiful island, outstanding food, and your sweet mama, who taught me so many tasty recipes.

Thank you, Linda Bendorf, writing mentor and teacher, who started my journey to believe in myself and my writing. Among the mountains in Boulder, you guided me gently into the ways of a writer, gave me encouragement, and inspired me to always try harder. I am grateful for our friendship!

Thank you to my sister in spirit, Claudia Kasvin, poet and writer, whose ever-present influence in my life has always been positive. Your guidance and mentorship in my writing adventures are greatly appreciated. Forever sisters!

Thank you, Dee Marley, for my fabulous book cover design and the detailed maps of Girgento you created. Your creative talents never cease to amaze me. Visit Dee's graphic design website at White Rabbit Arts at www.wrarts.com or The Historical Fiction Company at www.thehistoricalfictioncompany.com.

Thank you, Sparky, my beloved companion of ten years, whose warm fuzzy nudges kept me company on the lonely days of writing.

Thank you, Nicky Taylor, for your expert editing skills. Because of you, I have a book to be proud of. Your gentle guidance and wisdom took the fear out of the editing process!

Thank you, Chris, for your unwavering support of this project and your belief in me.

I am grateful to the World History Encyclopedia and their vast library of articles on ancient history. They gave me ideas for the lifestyle of the ancient Greeks and Sicilians and were a constant resource of valuable information. World History. Visit the website at www.worldhistory.org/encyclopedia.

Thank you, FAI (Fondo Ambiento Italiano), for managing the spectacular and extraordinary gardens of Kolymbethra. The feelings that emerged while walking the tree-lined pathways are indescribable, knowing that so many ancient people before me created this space, this paradise.

For more information on Agrigento, please visit Agrigento's museum, Museo Archeologico Regionale Pietro Griffo.

www.maryknight.net